2/22

LUCKENBOOTH

Also by Jenni Fagan

The Panopticon
The Sunlight Pilgrims

LUCKENBOOTH

JENNI FAGAN

PEGASUS BOOKS
NEW YORK LONDON

For Boo,
& Dave Balfour

Edinburgh is a mad god's dream.

Hugh MacDiarmid

Part I

Jessie MacRae (21)

the arrival

MY FATHER'S corpse stares out across the North Atlantic swells. Grey eyes. Eyelashes adorned with beads of rain. Tiny orbs to reflect our entire world. Primrose and squill dance at his feet. His body is rammed into a crevice. The shore is scattered with storm debris. Cargo boxes. Little green bottles with faded labels. Swollen pods of seaweed slip underfoot. It takes me an hour to get from our clifftop to the water's edge. I have a blue glass bottle. It is tincture of iodine. Skull and crossbones on the front. I wash it out. Tell it my secrets. Stopper them. Lay it on the water. When I look back our beach has a long straight line – right down the middle – like the spine of a book.

It is where I dragged my coffin.

I use his oars.

Push the vessel he built for me – into waves. It is not the journey he foresaw me taking in it. My father built one for each of us from old church pews. Knocked them together outside the kitchen window, so my mother would see. She saw the world through those four square panes. Each season. Each sorrow. That night he made her sleep in hers. Then my brother took to his. I varnished mine ten times

3

without any premonition. How buoyant such a thing can be! A light spray fans peaks of waves. I will not look back at him in his crevice. It had to be done like this! Hoick my skirt up. Wade into the sea. Pale bare thighs bloom red in the cold water. I kiss my mother's cross. Set it onto the floor so there's one holy thing between me and oblivion. The sea won't take me. I am the devil's daughter. Nobody wants responsibility for my immortal soul. My address cannot be – The Devil's Daughter, North Sea. I'll never knock at heaven's door. Hell knows I could do far worse than take over. I dip the oars in. Pull away from the island. I watch the dark blue line of the horizon. A seal pops up. Black eyes. Long whiskers. He'd have me sire a seal child if I'd do him the favour of drowning.

On the first night I lay down in my coffin when the winds drop.

Easiest sleep of my life.

When I wake the ocean swells roll bigger and bigger. I sing. Smoke. Thin spires rise up. I breakfast on oatcakes and cheese. Run chapped fingers through the water. The seal brushes them with his whiskers. I eat a raw fish I brought with me. Lob the bones out. It barely touches my hunger. A hairline crack appears in my coffin. Cross myself three times. Wish I had brought more to eat. I see no ships all day. The sun falls with regularity. Her opposition – the moon – rises. It is round and yellow – a single eye to watch my journey.

On the third morning a fog unfurls.

A ship calls out long and low.

The spirits of the sea are matched in sorrow by the living. I rest my elbows on the sides. Scan the horizon. All I can see is a grey abyss that feels like it has come directly out of me. The day passes in misery. At night the skies clear and wind picks up faster and faster until sailing feels like flying. Arms out – travelling through a hundred, million, billion – stars.

I have no compass.

When I draw near land I shout – *where are we?*

Those who don't faint, or cross themselves, or throw something at me – give enough information to get me to my destination. I drift into the Water of Leith at dawn. Four cormorants skim across still water – wings almost touch their own reflection. So graceful! Stash the coffin behind the trawler boats away in a corner of the docks. I tie it up. Leave it bobbing in the harbour. I climb out on rusty wall prongs. Men argue nearby. I strip quickly behind barrels – comb my hair twenty times, tighten my corset, pull on clean stockings, slip my ma's best dress over my head. It is charcoal with a square neck. Low enough to see a heart beat. Tie up long brown hair. My skin is white-blue. My lips are kept fresh with Vaseline. There are neat green buttons on my leather boots. The priest bought them for my mother. She gave them to me. I throw my farm boots over some barrels. Somebody will use them no doubt. My old dress is stuffed in a bag. I pull out the last piece and carefully fix the clasp – her silver cameo.

I'm ready.

Walk quickly along Constitution Street.

The thing is to try and look like a woman.

Not a demon.

I have the eyes of every man on me.

Flawed thing.

All want.

They could find so many reasons to hang me.

I go past the boundary wall. Odd symbols and rubbish and broken tools line it. Some of the children run by me barefoot. They must have soles like leather! Up along Elm Row. Finally – the very fancy new North British Hotel appears. I turn onto North Bridge and wind skelps me in the pus. I can see Edinburgh Castle away to the right: wisps ay steam from Waverley Station below: Arthur's Seat and the crags to the left – a flash of blue further even than waves. It's good to know the sea is nearby. It's important – in any city – to know the escape routes at all times. Da used to bring me here once a year. He'd sell offal, or trade, then leave me to wait in a tavern whilst he went off with a woman. I stop in the middle of the Tron. Behind me there is the Royal Mile, to the left is the Southside and on the right North Bridge. I stand in the middle. Streets crossed below me. Tenements of all heights stand as sentinels on either side. They inspect everyone who passes below. The High Street is cobbled and it slopes up. There's wooden doors and small blown-glass windows or fancier sash panes with wooden shutters. A motor car turns right onto Cockburn Street. The spunk-hawker stacks his tinder. Between the well-dressed and moneyed there are glimpses of the hungry and hunted. A big church has a beggar sat on its steps with his ratty wee dug. A young man smiles. He wants to defile me. An urge to let him. Right here in the street. Who can save me? My father is the devil! Our kind are not holy. I must perfectly hide the sharp tip of my horns. Woodsmoke spirals out of tenement chimneys. The reek permeates everything. Pretty rooftops are tiled like dragon skin. Just as I am about to step forward a black mass flows onto North

Bridge. Along the High Street news signs declare: WORLD MISSIONARY CONFERENCE. One thousand two hundred men of God flock toward me. They stride in tens, twenties, hundreds. I knew God would have a message fir me, but I did not know he would be so direct.

I spit.

Saliva – still tinged pink.

I look at it there on the cobbles, just a tinge of blood – only seen by me.

Everywhere there are black suits and motion.

The men press close as they go around me. Cleric collars. Smooth hair. Clean skin. Moustache or beard. Shiny shoes. They pass like crooked ships on a grey sea. A young minister's eyes slide over my body with thoughts impure as any. I know what lays in his trousers damp and feeble as a mouse. That thing will only stand on end for cruelty. Heat on my temples. I could easily stake him! Shoes click on the cobbles. One by one they disappear into the City Chambers up ahead. The speech crier calls out.

– Evil walks among us!

I step forward.

The spires at St Giles' Cathedral rise up.

Gargoyles crane their necks out bug-eyed to stare.

Edinburgh seduces with her ancient buildings. She pours alcohol or food down the throats of anyone passing, dangles her trinkets, leaves pockets bare. She's a pickpocket. The best kind of thief, one you think of – most fondly.

There is a cage around my heart – made of bone, bone, bone.

I must appear not to see.

Not to know.

7

Rub my foot against my leg. Check the bit of paper again. The drawing has the entrance to No. 10 Luckenbooth Close clearly marked but I am told nobody can ever find it. Ignore the cathedral and the cobbled heart. I walk by the entry to the close three times before I take a few steps back.

Turn down into a shady narrow street.

The sounds of the city quieten.

A man dressed smartly appears and he glares at me. I have to press back against the cold wall to let him pass. He is a reptile. Stones for eyes. Scutes all over his skin – slick, armoured – a tail to flick left-to-right. Over a million years reptiles have perfected their ability to detect and exploit weakness. It is almost admirable. Sometimes they seek easy prey. Other times they enjoy a fight. They sit in courtrooms. Deal out judgement. Turn up to football games. They turn a red leather barber's chair and welcome your child with a lollipop and a wide reptilian smile. They act in theatres. Teach in schools. They hold keys to the police station. They bake your wedding cake. Bow onstage as a curtain falls. They write poems. They take up a good cause. They save things – loudly! They are careful to be seen to be doing things that are nothing at all to do with murder. They are charming. They are liked. It is important to make sure others – owe them. Reptiles lay in bed reading. They get a cold. They take two sugars in their tea. They are concerned for you. They bring a gift. They are often top of the pile. Who would be a top predator and let a nicer person pass? The more talented? The greater thinker? No, no, no! That's not how it works. I am not talking about lizards. This is nothing to do with geckos. I have no issue with chameleons. It has no relevance to turtles. The reptiles I describe – are crocodiles.

God must have mercy on you if you lay down in your bed each night with a crocodile.

If you marry one!

Have its baby and look into tiny baby crocodile eyes!

The crocodile will suckle its victim at night. Each morning they will wake with disdain and a wide-toothed smile. They open their muscular arms only a little. Through evolution they have learnt how to make you want them. Once you step into want they begin to squeeze you tightly. Grin wide crocodile grins as they expel air from your lungs – keeping eye contact all the while. An ancient dance. Spin. Spin. Spin. Descend to the depths. There it is – the deepest ocean floor with a forest of seaweed to filter out the light. Your face will be unbelieving at the end of a death-roll ride! When your body is limp and your expression – incredulous – they will stash you.

Sometimes they will swim back down, sunlight halo behind them.

It won't be to rescue you or apologise – it will be to find your corpse and take another good long leisurely bite. Whilst you'd like to think you were something unique to them what you find as you turn around is millions of other women and children (mostly) all stashed in an identical watery grave.

What I must do is sew my real eyes shut and look out with a pretty blue set painted on.

This is it – No. 10 Luckenbooth Close!

Go down four stairs as a smell of ammonia climbs up my nose.

These tenements are so high!

Laundry creates strange shapes in between me and the sky.

The air is dank down here and much older than on the

street. This place is closer to the castle than I thought it would be. Looking up I can see nine floors, built from huge slabs of stone. The steps are scrubbed clean. I pause with my hand on a freshly painted wooden door like it is a lover's chest.

It's heavy to push open.

The stairwell smells of lemons.

Wall tiles are a dark green, my mother's favourite colour. An ornate balustrade and a huge glass cupola all the way at the top like the church manse library where I hid from my father. Turn onto a landing. 1F1. Raise my hand. Before I can rap lacquered wood – the door swings open. A woman almost as wide as the doorframe – she's clearly angry.

— Yer late!

— I'm sorry.

— Ye dinnae look sorry.

I don't attempt contrition. It's not in my array of convincing facial expressions. I try out impassive. Honest isn't something I carry off. Neither is concerned. My mother always said I did a good line in unreadable and impassive. I arrange my features into something to appropriate those attributes. The woman snorts. Turns around. I follow her into the apartment. High ceilings with ornate cornices, polished wooden floors, long red Persian rugs. There is a smell of tobacco and woodsmoke and brandy.

— They're waiting. I'll show you around quickly before I go. Don't go down to the basement – ever!

— I won't.

— It's locked anyway but you better not.

— I promise.

— Are yer boots clean?

— Aye.

10

– Say, yes – in here and talk slowly – don't use Scottish in front of them.

– I won't.

– He can understand it but he doesnae like it. Mr Udnam is a Minister of Culture, a man of letters!

– I was told.

– If you do one thing wrong – they will hang ye by the morning.

She leans in toward me with manky breath. Grey hairs strain to escape a shiny pink skull – even the woman's follicles don't want to be near her.

– Speak only when you're spoken to.

– Yes.

– Are ye sure those boots are clean? If there's shite on yer boots clean them downstairs. This flat takes up nearly the entire first floor. Below here you've got the entrance way and underneath that you have the basement cellars. You don't want to go into the cellars – you'll no get back out. There's catacombs down there, you know that?

– Aye.

Follow her down a hallway with polished wooden furniture. Lash-less eyes. Dry, cracked, dimpled hands.

– Over here is the lady's room.

A real four-poster bed. Carved tables. Thick curtains. A fancy armchair with winged legs so it can fly away! These rooms are huge! Highest ceilings I've ever seen.

– Is it Jessie?

– Aye.

– He takes his clients in the other room, the consulting room. He does all of his work and socialising in there, he sleeps there as well.

This is nothing like our two-room croft at home. Our place had sheep in there with us when it was freezing, which it was, every winter. She takes me back to the kitchen. There is a wooden butcher's block in the centre of the room. A scrubbed table in the corner. An old range cooker emanates warmth. Herbs hang on a rack. Heavy iron pans sway on hooks. There is a real copper pantry — fitted out to keep every bit of bread or cheese, cool as a shelf in a fancy cheese shop.

— Ye can kip there.

The woman points at a gap under a huge wooden dresser.

— You're near the cooker so the floor is warm. If a rat comes, kill it! You look too delicate to kill anything but you will have to. I saw one last week. Size of a bairn. I used a spade to take its head clean off.

I smile.

— I heard about yer father, barred fae maist ay the islands is he, no? Why'd they no bar him fae this last yin?

— They knew he'd only row back and slit their throats whilst they slept.

There is a silence apart from the grandfather clock tick-tick-tick-ticking in the hall.

— What did he die from?

— I poisoned him.

— Terrible.

The woman tuts. Stacks up china plates. Whatever I say is not what she hears, or often, what anyone does. I'm like the girl in the story who lets toads fall from her mouth but others think they are pearls. I still have the smell of death on me. It will be weeks before it goes.

— What does Mr Udnam's fiancée do?

— Elise is a suffragette, so she thinks. Marched with that

Pankhurst wifey last year. Rich wummin have time fir aw that shite!

The woman inspects the width of my hips.

— Send her in!

We both look down the hall.

A red glow from the fire.

Drapes pulled.

The maid grabs her coat, crosses herself and leaves.

The front door clicks shut.

I smooth down my dress. Pinch my cheeks. Walk slowly to the consulting room. Elise is sat on the desk. Amethysts fir eyes. Her hair is even longer than mine. It is the reddest hair I've ever seen. She wears a green silk dress. Fingernails stained red as if she has dipped them in blood. I fancy she does exactly that each morning. Bare feet. They are tiny. I take the long ornamental pipe she holds out toward me. There is a wicked tilt to her smile. Behind them a huge bay window looks out across the entire city. Views of the sky-line sparkle brighter and brighter as I put the pipe to my mouth and inhale.

Mr Udnam smiles.

I hold the pipe back out, unsure that I can stop myself from dropping it.

He turns to kiss his fiancée's neck and puts his hand out toward me. She leans her head down to hear my heart beat — lays her hand on my throat and strokes it. She takes a long drag and whispers.

— Open yer mouth.

She blows smoke deep into my lungs — heaviness descends through each part of my body taking every bad memory far away.

— How pretty she is, Elise, do you think this one will take?

— Yes, I think she'll do more than fine.

An entire wall of books curves to inspect us. All those characters, plots and locations look toward each other and then me. There is a gap in the top row that looks like a black tooth. An electric hum in the air that is nothing to do with his fancy Tiffany lamp. Mr Udnam pours each of us a drink, green, in a tiny crystal glass. It is sweet and sharp and soothes as much as the smoke from the pipe does.

— You know why your father sold you to us, Jessie?

— Yes, I do.

— The child will be named by my wife.

— Of course.

— We will raise the infant with no knowledge of who you are.

— I understand.

— Do you? You will not approach the child if you see it in the street. You won't speak to us again afterwards. My wife will go into confinement during your containment. When the baby is born Elise will say she gave birth in America. We will never let anyone know the child is not completely ours. You have my word that I will pay you in full and raise the child in the best manner possible.

— Thank you.

— Are you happy to do this?

Elise sounds like she smokes a lot of cigarettes.

— Yes.

— Together? All three of us?

It would be hard not to nod to anything she says — the woman is a walking spell.

— The money was due to go to your father.

14

— God rest his soul.

— As law sees it, he is sadly not alive any more so that can't happen.

— I understand.

Mr Udnam looks at me like he knows exactly what has been in my mouth this week and I get a taste at the back of my mouth like iron and grit and earth and ice so cold it could burn your skin away. He could choose not to pay me. He could send me away easily. I keep my face relaxed. Imagine a tiny house somewhere that has a name I chose for it above the door and no man to keep me.

— So the fee will go to you, is that acceptable?

— Yes.

My heart beats so hard.

It will happen.

One day I will have a place of my own.

Another sip of green liquid soothes me as Elise gently pulls my dress down and traces my shoulders with her fingertips. She kisses the back of my neck. Light kisses. Her lips are soft. I'd like to pretend I don't want this but every bit of my body and mind and soul desires it too. She uses her tongue to flick out and there is a shudder all the way down my spine as she grips my waist and pulls me gently toward her. He undoes her bodice. Her nipples are small. She pulls up her skirt – parts her legs so I can see – blows a smoke ring into my face.

A giant crocodile on the wall bares its teeth.

One hand slips down my front. Another pulls my hair back – exposes my neck – like a swan on the butcher's block.

Flora (33)
the drag ball

THE POLAR bear is at least ten feet tall. She stands on her
hind legs. Salutes! Children at the end of Iona Street jump
up and down. Anxious mothers yank them back. A wee laddie gets a slap over the back of his head. He has bloody knees
and he stares at the polar bear with reverence. The energy
on Leith Walk is palpable. Blue skies! Jazz music spills out
from a tenement window. A woman leans out, watches the
crowd and rolls a cigarette.

Down below her people talk and gesture.

Their words are trumpets.

An old man dances – each step a key on the piano.

His jumper sleeves are mended at the elbows but he glides
with a dance-hall elegance.

Hearts beat like big tom drums.

A barmaid comes out to see it all. There are 460 soldiers
stood either side of Baśka Murmańska.

Handsome, dangerous, war-wearied men.

Baśka has black eyes.

The polar bear weighs 650 pounds and she is an official
daughter of the Polish regiment. The men have a brightness
to them. A luminosity to their eyes. They have seen too

much. Baśka Murmańska has kept more than their spirit alive. She could kill any of them easily. They do not look at her with fear. Outside the bars men smoke and watch, unable to believe what they are seeing. Cloth caps, waistcoats. Smart jackets. Shoes shined so the scuff won't show for a good half hour at least. They are all having a few pints and a nip before kick-off at Easter Road. Opposite them the soldiers mill around chatting to each other beside Baśka Murmańska.

That's exactly how it was.

Flora needs to stop going back to this over and over again but she does not want those memories to fade.

She nods to the barman.

Accepts a second Gin Rickey and twists the stem in her fingertips. Flora can remember every second of that day nine years ago. It was the most important moment of her life. A man she had never met before walked up to her. He was eternity and she was the beginning of time. They had travelled 12.9 billion years to meet each other – at the end of Iona Street. There was some reason for him to say words. Flora said some back. It was all so polite. All the while another conversation was going on below that one. He was in uniform. It was the last day she would ever wear hers. War was almost done. They were ready. To forget. To make love. To walk back to a stranger's flat and go to their bed.

She finishes her second cocktail.

Drinking too fast.

Always.

Nods at the barman again.

His face is watchable and kind. It's not to be underrated in a man. He has a beard. Wild eyebrows frame warm eyes. His lips are too moist. He isn't skinny. Flora can't take that in a conquest. She should not be thinking like this! It's bad. It is. She shouldn't be getting drunk in the afternoon. She should not have had cocaine for breakfast and certainly not with champagne. Flora takes another tiny bump from a phial. Lets it sting her nose. Brighten her eyes. She warns herself. Behave, behave, behave! Do not fuck a stranger ten minutes before attempting a long-awaited possible reconciliation. It's in the big reconciliation handbook! Don't do it.

Her man from the beginning of time had taken her to bed. He made her feel more free than she thought it was possible to feel. He told her she was a chimera. It was the first time she had heard that word. There were other words before that. Freak, hermaphrodite, boy-girl, in-between. He was the first one to tell her she was not two things but one perfect creature made from stardust.

He wanted her in every way.

It turned out in the end that it was him who was two things. What he thought he was. Then who he actually was.

The pain in her is too great.

The barman has a jaded tone that makes him more attractive.

He is not too handsome. Flora is not attracted to conventionally handsome men. They don't fuck so well. She doesn't get that thrill of truly losing control with them. She gets that with flawed men. He laughs at her story and there is a real dirtiness to his laugh. He's the exact kind of (someone else's) husband she ends up in bed with. The risk of this occurring becomes more precarious around drink four. Flora picks up drink three. It tastes so good. She has to find out today. If her ex-lover – who she has not seen now for eleven months – is still – after all this time – the one she wants.

— And this happened when?

The barman pushes a sparkling glass toward Flora.

— Dear God of fuckery please help us all!

— Ay?

— Is this my fourth cocktail?

— Do we need to count?

— Yes, we do.

A smile.

He lights her cigarette.

A table of lawyers in the corner drink in such a serious way. Heads up! All the better to disdain the bar. Not her legs though. Nobody is disdainful toward Flora's legs. She pulls her skirt up another inch. Give them something to make laws about. Arseholes! She turns back to the barman. He is easily ten years younger than she. He tips beer out of catch trays, shines up optics, turns back toward her whilst polishing glasses.

— It happened when the soldiers were evacuated to Edinburgh from Russia, they had been fighting the Bolsheviks, she says.

— And they march up Leith Walk with this polar bear, Baśka Murmańska and you did too?

Look him straight in the eye on reply.

— Aye, all the way along Princes Street everyone was going wild!

— I bet!

The barman turns reluctantly to serve someone else.

Flora swivels on her chair.

Checks out the bar.

There isn't a man in here wouldn't go to bed with her if she let him.

Whether they would stay in it once she undressed, is another matter. If they did most would ignore her in the street later, or they'd cross the road to pretend they didn't see her and if she knew them personally – they'd hope she never mentioned it again. If she tried to bring it up they'd say they didn't want to discuss that. They would want to fuck her but not talk to her. Or be seen with her. They'd want to take her body in all kinds of violent ways in a darkened room but on the street – they would not hold her hand.

Tiring.

– I should've got drunk in Leith, this place makes my teeth appear inferior.

– I ken exactly what you mean, it's so posh it makes me itch, he agrees.

– The thing about Baśka Murmańska – is she was a testament not to war, but to love. What the soldiers couldn't give in the war to those they loved, they could give freely – to this wild creature. Baśka Murmańska saved each and every one of them. Straight up. She did it for love.

– It's a dangerous business, he says.

– War?

– Love.

– Aye, it is that.

– Unsurvivable at times, he watches Flora carefully.

– I'd rather my mind was gone, she whispers.

Round tear-filled eyes glitter in the mirror behind him. The barman has dimples and a quiet, assured manner. If only she could love a man like him, one that was actually decent.

She has to do this.

Just walk a few doors along.

Go down into Luckenbooth Close, then go up to 2F2. Don't climb up the drainpipe. Those days are over. Take the stairs. Go to his landing. Knock lightly. Wait until he opens the door. Appear to be a reasonable human being. That's the tricky bit. He sees her reasonable human being and raises her a lunatic.

— Why is it a certain kind of love brings out our worst selves? Flora asks.

— That's the real one does that.

— Why?

— Dunno. It's like a poultice. Draws it out.

— The madness?

— Aye! If love can heal us then first it has to pull all our demons right up to the surface, no? How can we slay what we can't first see?

— I think you're right, she says.

Flora's eyes glow with her own brightness.

— You know what happened to Robert the Bruce's heart? the barman asks.

He pushes olives in a fancy glass jar over to her and she ignores them as they lean closer together.

— No? What happened to Robert the Bruce's heart in the end?

— They cut it out, cast it in iron and gave it to Sir James Douglas to wear in a metal urn around his neck day and night.

— Why?

— To take it on a pilgrimage to the Holy Land, Robert insisted.

21

— The dead ay! So fucking demanding. Why the Holy Land? Was it the only place able to purify his murderous heart?

The barman nods.

His eyes have flecks of gold in them.

He lights another cigarette for her.

A double flame in his eyes.

He taps the packet and lights his own, touches her hand as he drops the flame.

— I know someone with a heart like that, Flora says.

They are still too close together. She holds her cigarette in long thin fingers. They can both stay warm in this glow for a wee while more. Ignore the lawyers behind them, filing out the front door.

— Did he make it to Jerusalem?

— No, he didn't, the barman shakes his head.

— Of course not.

— I don't think murderous hearts should get absolution that easy, lady, do you?

Flora takes a long drag — leaves a rim of red lipstick around the cigarette, tries not to smile back at him.

— What happened to Sir James Douglas?

— He died fighting in Spain along the way. They boiled the flesh from his body. Took his bones back to Scotland alongside his mate's heart — in its iron-clad box.

— Fucking hell.

— Such is the way of love.

He opens the cellar hatch. Someone rolls barrels in from the street.

There is a sound of chickens, or maybe a goat.

Flora triple-drags her cigarette.

Such is the way. It's like a disease. Love: 80 per cent proof. Risk of death if you drink it. Can send you mad, bad, blind and delirious. It is nothing like the no-risk companionship of loving a close friend. To decay without passion together for eternity – the traditional way. Flora would rather die than do that. She'd rather die alone, upright as a double bass, tuned to her own vibration. Companionship is for pets. Flora is not a pet. She's a wild creature. All for the kind of love that can kill you. Now that is living! Baśka Murmańska knew what that was. Flora meets her own eyes in the bar mirror. It's an uncomfortable feeling. She doesn't know why but she always looks away again quickly. Forces her gaze back. Why should she not like to look at her own reflection? Her eyes are grey and wide with long lashes. Her hair is blonde and shiny and neatly bobbed with a perfect curl on her cheek. Smoky eyes. Reddest lip shade she could find in Jenners. She is prettier than a woman should be. So what – her jaw is a little too long, her nose indelicate. These new knee-length skirts and dresses are more than favourable to her legs. A man walks into the bar and slides a pamphlet across to her.

TO WORKING MEN & WOMEN

"The Anti-Saloon League: of the United States" — which has now changed its name to "The World League Actions Against Alcoholism": has sent a number of skilled organisers and speakers to our country to help the misnamed "Temperance" Associations to:

ROB YOU OF YOUR BEER

The League is supported by millionaires, and has enormous funds. Its hirelings are paid a minimum of £60 a <u>month</u> and expenses. Will you allow these Aliens to:

DICTATE TO YOU, INTERFERE WITH YOUR LIBERTIES, CLOSE YOUR PUBLIC HOUSES, HUSTLE YOU INTO COMPULSORY TEETOTALISM?

What right have they to meddle with <u>our</u> affairs. What would "Yankees" say if we sent over a swarm of paid men to lecture on their habits, and interfere in their domestic concerns?

SHOW THESE FUSSY ZEALOTS THAT YOU RESENT THEIR IMPERTINENT INTRUSION. WRITE TO YOUR M.P. AND TELL HIM THEY OUGHT TO BE DEPORTED.

BEWARE OF LOCAL "OPTION."

– Nobody is forcing me into teetotalism, Flora wags her finger.

She takes out the phial as he walks away. Has two bumps. Dabs a little on her tongue and it tastes like petrol. That's how they get cocaine into the docks, in barrels. She puts the phial away. Emboldened she turns to check herself out from every angle. Sips just one last cocktail before she hits the road. It has been exactly eleven months now and she can still feel what it's like when he steps behind her. His breath on her skin. Can still picture his eyes in every detail. It is so utterly annoying. The cellar hatch slams shut and she jumps.

– So what happened to Baśka Murmańska in the end?

– Villagers killed her.

– Why? If she was no threat to humans, Flora, they should have just let her be?

– They found her swimming in a river and they didn't know. Her soldier got her when she was just a cub, he was trying to woo this woman who was into this Italian officer who had a white fox. This soldier wanted to top that and impress the woman so he goes to Arkhangelsk Market . . .

– She still prefers the guy with the white fox?

– Aye!

The barman shakes his head.

– Brutal.

– I know. The regiment keep Baśka Murmańska, they train her up, she gets a food allowance, sleeps at the bottom of her soldier's bed until she was older. Do you know a polar bear's skin is black underneath?

– No?

– Aye. When they absorb sunlight it goes through all the

shafts and follicles of the fur which make them look whiter than they are but their hair is just like – light tubes!

Flora has hit a slight slur.

Sit up taller.

A sway to her hips – even whilst seated.

– I should probably eat an olive.

– I wouldn't, they're rank, he says.

– I know, they are mingin' ay? Rich people have no fuck-ing taste.

The barman laughs and lights a tiny cigar she's taken out of her purse. She takes a drag and points it at him. The barman is wearing a white shirt, waistcoat, red tie, flat cap. Flora is aware if she doesn't leave on the next drink then her night is going to unravel.

– You see the Murmańczycy, to go back to it they get their polar bear because of infatuation, but they raise her on love!

Flora hiccups.

– It can go far that stuff, ay?

He holds her gaze for longer this time.

– Corporal Smorgonski tamed Baśka! Highly unusual man! They arrived on the *Toloa* ship. 27th September 1919. It was the last day I ever dressed as a boy.

Flora crushes the cigar out.

Exhales.

She stops lowering her eyelashes and looks back at him again.

– You are far too pretty to be a boy.

– Don't be nice to me.

– Why?

– I don't like it.

Flora peers into the mirrored bar behind him. Dabs at her eyes. It's taken a long time to get this look right. She is not going to smudge it. Many components were involved! Heated eyelash curlers – they're a bitch to use. Maybelline mascara. Cotton-wool balls from Woolworths to smooth foundation because her fingers make it too greasy. Dior blush from Frasers – that cost a bit more: fingernails just so, so red: carefully oval tipped with a sharp point, the new kind of varnish that they use to paint aeroplanes.

– My invite was hand-delivered in a brown envelope with two roses.

– Invitation to where?

Flora taps her nose.

– Do I look like I'm going to my own execution?

– Aye. Pretty glamorous execution though. You'll be needing another drink fir that?

– Best not.

Flora is far more tanned than last time her ex saw her. Why her mother whitens her skin she has no idea. Well, she has plenty of ideas but she doesn't agree with any of them. The more colour Flora has in her skin the better she looks, so she thinks anyway. Fuck anyone who doesn't! One more twist and turn to admire herself. She loves this new dress. It's silver. Fringed. It catches the light and dapples her face nicely.

– What perfume are you wearing, Flora, you smell amazing.

– Mitsouko, it's new.

– So, the bear went home to Poland and got killed after such a huge journey!

– I waved the soldiers' boat away from the docks, Poland

was just newly independent. They were so happy to go back after the war! Baśka Murmańska was on the top deck. I stood watching until the boat was only a speck. When it was no longer a speck, I still stood watching. When the sun fell I pulled my auntie's fur coat around me and lit a cigarette. When the darkness came I still just kept watching the horizon.

— What were you looking for?

— Evidence of the unbreakable bond of true love.

— You found it?

— No, not yet anyway.

The two of them laugh, the delicate relief of it loosens her spine.

— Go on, Flora, get yer guy, ay.

— Thanks fir listening . . .

— Any time, lady.

Flora leans over the bar and kisses the barman on the cheek.

Up onto the street.

She goes into the shop for two packs of cigarettes. Then down into the close. It is so familiar. Even just to step onto the damp cobbles hidden out the way down here. It makes her hard. Raises the knot in her shoulder. The first-floor landing is jammed by two young men pulling and pushing at a huge old piano.

— Can I squeeze by?

— Aye!

They tip it up and she flattens herself against the wall to slip past.

— I'm Archie, I'm moving into 5F5, sorry about the piano!

— Nae bother!

Flora runs ahead up the stairs, she has to get there before

anyone else does. If she can speak to him for just a little while on their own – she'll know whether to leave Scotland for good or not. 2F2. Tap lightly. He answers like he's been stood there waiting ever since she left. There he is. Just like that. Eternity. His eyes are still just as familiar as her own.

– Flora, I didn't know if you would . . .

– Why?

They both know why.

He lets the door swing wide.

Go past his arms. Heat. The flat smells exactly the same. Apples and oiled wooden floors. Scented baths. Copious pots of tea. Under all of that there is the smell of him. His skin. A memory of his mouth on hers keeps her eyes averted. She does not want to think about how every time she tipped over the edge he would kiss her with his tongue further into her mouth and somehow dirtier than any of the other kisses they ever shared.

– Is your wife coming?

– Don't be crazy.

– How many guests do you expect for your private drag ball, señor?

– A very select sixty. Will you help me with the drinks?

– That's why you asked me to come?

– No!

Flora looks around the flat, remembers places they have fallen to the floor, held each other asleep, there is still a small chip on the kitchen doorframe where she threw a plate at him one time. He's finally started doing the place up though, it's not so bare as it used to be.

– Where will everyone get changed?

– My bedroom, I've put a little hanging rail in there, a mirror, it's – nicer.

A grin.

– Have you missed me, Flora?

– No.

– Thought about me?

– Not once, you?

– No, he says.

– All moved on?

– Completely.

– New girlfriend?

– Aye.

– Does she have a nice cock?

– No, she does not have a nice cock.

– That's a shame.

Flora smiles despite herself.

– It is, he says.

– She's not like me, then?

– Nobody's like you, Flora, and fine well you know it.

Music is playing. He holds his arms out to her.

– One dance? First . . .

– You need to get the place ready.

– We have a few hours. Come here, Flora – please.

To step back into his arms. Follow his feet. He always was the better dancer. His stubble up close. Resting her head on his chest, he pulls her tight toward him. Falling – just like that, heart aching. Photos on the dresser in the lounge – his wife – their kids. Glasses are set out for Tom Collinses. His secret drag balls are the best. Select men and women across the city will be leaving their professional worlds. Dresses and suits in bags. Sparkly headbands.

Strap-on belts. Nipple tassels. Stockings and fishnets and hats and eye masks and whips. All of them keening for the glitter and the release – much as she still does. Her ex-lover pulls her waist. She is as up close to him as she can be. Looking for the first time in too long into his eyes.

– No, Flora whispers.

– No?

– Not a fucking chance.

He spins her out and back in toward him and on instinct she raises her leg and lets her head fall back.

Levi (31)

the bone library

I WORK in the bone library now, my dear brother, and they have done a few things differently since this war began. Just the other day I got into work to find they have built a shooting range in the basement of the veterinary college and the vets' practice down there and I suspect they are often drunk – which for armed men with little talent for shooting is deeply unsettling. It made me feel antsy so I went down for some target practice and walked out to silence behind me. That showed them! I will not be going back down there again. It's impossible to hear any sound from the basement so they can shoot off as many rounds as they like. There are a great many parts of the Royal Dick veterinary building that are like that. My good friend the postman told me there are 550 rooms – he is deeply boo coo but I like him. The postman drinks at least as much as me. He needs to. I need to as well. We all need to really. The postman went home with one of the vets' wives last year and she now has a child as ginger as he. It is not mentioned by anyone on the staff and we are all just real polite when she comes in to visit with the baby, we don't say a thing. I guess I am learning how to be British except as it turns out this is another

country altogether but I will get to that later. There are dissection rooms in the building and lecture theatres and a cafe
but I am not into what they cook, they don't dress their
sandwiches well – it's almost a tragedy, I don't think they've
seen a po' boy in their life. I'm missing gumbo filé, can you
send me some? I got me a serious envie for shrimp too –
pinch the tail and suck the head! Fuck me, brother, I am
homesick. Anyway, tonight I need to get some groceries! I
will cook something back at the apartment. I'm getting better at cooking and it serves me well to fend for myself
on distant shores. You remember that new zydeco band
we danced to at Breaux Bridge near Lafayette? Crawfish
races and dancing, they don't do it like that here but in
wartime everybody really wants to party, the Scottish can
totally pass a good time and then some – I'll give them that.
I get interest from some of the girls here but I am still a
Southern gent. Well, I am most days. This building has its
own bar and distillery and there are rooms full of tiny
cracked sinks with sheep's heads decaying in them. Since
I've been here they've dissected a zebra, two cows, one bull,
a gazelle, and a bear – there are dead snakes beautifully preserved and there is a wall of giant moths pinned to black
cloth. There are countless boxes of bones. The bones are my
primary concern. I don't let no one else deal with them.
They can stay the hell out of my business. I file the bones
and sort them numerically by size and species. There is a
maintenance room with a boiler bigger than all the fires of
hell, there's rage in that boiler. I don't want to be killed by
the damn thing so I go nowhere fucking near it. If it ever
blows up we are all going straight to hell with it. In the
Cube building across the way there is a room registered to

Egypt. Whatever they do in there, it's not legal in this country. Folks disappear through a plastic sheet, then they shower apparently, I have to find out more about it. Lectures take place most days. They treat hundreds of animals here every week. Mary Dick is the boss's sister. She's the one who really keeps this place running. Nobody wants to disappoint her and if anyone is disgraced it's her office they have to go to and nobody wants to do that – she is quite a woman, I like her a lot. Mary founded a scheme to treat the animals of poor people free of charge and it makes me glad to see animals go out mended. There have been two racehorses in here this month alone and each of them was worth more money than we will ever see.

It is hard to know you are all so far away.

I miss you.

Don't tell Dad or Mom but I don't use the name Wolf any more. As if it isn't hard enough being a young black man – what was Mom thinking? It's not like she called you Gazelle or Bear or Wildcat. No, you got the name Leo and I got Wolf. She thought you'd be a doctor and then three years later she looked in a crib and saw a child – to change everything. I know how disappointed she is that all she got was me. I go by the name Levi now. Don't tell her. My middle name just suits me better. I'm more of a philosopher than a wolf – more of a Ptahhotep or Plato or Aristotle, lofty unrealistic aspirations maybe, I know. Mom may not have wanted me to be anything less than a lawyer but all I want to do is think. It is a transgressive act. We need much more of those in times like these. The sons and daughters of hatred make me weary. Remember how we were all so bemused when Hitler got into power, weren't we? At first it seemed like a joke. Couldn't take it seriously and then inch by inch he brings in the Dictation Act, four years of free rein to do anything he wants – then the Sterilization Law, hundreds of thousands of people will be sterilized without consent, anyone who is considered mentally ill (if you don't support the Reich that is evidence enough they say). I'm still more interested in law than I'd like to be. Where is fairness? Where has it ever been? I find real people so very disappointing at times. I get comments here, of course I do. Where are you from, I say I'm from Louisiana and they say – no, where are you from really? I miss being able to walk down a street without a second look. It is hard for me to think about what is going on at home. I know you will write to me about it and as my elder and better brother I know you will still be more political than I ever was. I have no doubt Dad will still be hanging the signs on Main Street – I see them in my worst dreams. *A Man Was Lynched Here Today.* I can still hear those signs creak. I'm not sure if that is why I ran away. I have nothing but respect for what Mom has done, yet all I want to do is drink and paint and chat up the girl next door. I think of my niece walking home though. I do. I know she looks like she has not a care, but she is tense under her smile even in broad daylight. Along beside her on a thousand other roads are other girls just like her, hands held loosely by their sides, heads up, clothes pressed and fitting just right. Fear steps right in beside them don't it? It accompanies them every bit of the way. I hate that I can't check on her at the end of the day. See what words got snagged in her hair. Pick them out for her. Make her a flower chain. I'd like to sow the field behind her house with yellow poppies and listen to her tell me about how she dreams of zombies eating the brains of the precious poor and how chalk is the greatest invention. I miss her – Leo, I have sent her a parcel, I forgot to put a letter in though, will you let her know it is from me? I pray for her every night as I fall asleep. The building I live in here is strange. It smells odd. It is very tall. It ain't nothing like our shotgun houses at home. You access it down a tiny street they call a close. I wish they built them wider because they stink of piss, apparently it used to be even worse back in the day – all the narrow streets running down from the High Street (all called closes) were ankle deep in shit.

They used to throw their piss and shit out the windows.

Once in the morning, once at night, they'd shout a warning for anyone below to get out the way, gardyloo! They are still doing it in parts of the city so I hear say, or they use outdoor toilets, but if they throw it out the windows it's kind of an organized thing – the daily shit slinging.

Hours were allocated so you would not take a walk – while hundreds of pots of crap were tipped out the windows. People must have been real happy on the High Street when it rained back then to get the streets a bit cleaner, apparently the shit flowed downhill toward Nor Loch, then they'd hang their laundry out of the windows to dry – anyway, that's you all up to date on what they do or did after taking a crap, the building I am in has toilets and it is nice, No. 10 Luckenbooth Close is as tall as a skyscraper.

They call it a tenement.

There are nine floors in our building, plus a basement and an attic, there's other buildings nearby that have a good fourteen floors and the basements are damp. Most of them don't lead into catacombs like No. 10 Luckenbooth

Close does. Mr Udnam says the entrance way is boarded up down there but if you go into the catacombs under this city from any other access point (there are some under the arches in the train station) you won't be seen again. This is no exaggeration. They used to take bodies through the catacombs to sell to lecturers at the Royal College of Surgeons. I don't know how much they got per body. I don't know how many bodies they wheeled under these fine streets but I hear it was a lot. The poster boys for murder-to-order trade in bodies were Burke and Hare. They have a pub named after them now. As you may be able to tell the sense of humor here is dark. Even Princes Street which is so grand and pretty would have bodies getting wheeled underneath it, the good medical students needed corpses to cut up, they are mostly rich kids and if they need dead bodies to dissect then that is what they will get. Education is a big industry in Edinburgh. I do not use the word industry incidentally.

On the way to work today I saw a fishwife.

They are all over the city.

They come from Newhaven.

It's down by the sea.

They say it's the sea but it is not, it's an estuary, a big river, kind of sea-like. You couldn't call it an ocean. The fishwives are tiny, they carry huge wicker baskets on their backs with a strap on their forehead to hold it in place and they wear such old-style clothes it's like they are existing in a whole other time alongside us. They wear long skirts, shawls, they spit, they smoke, they pray, they swear (all at the same time). I wouldn't fight one. A fishwife marched past me today going up a hundred stairs twice as fast as anyone else and not only was she carrying a basket (about at least as big as you) filled with fish – she was knitting! I think she was about a hundred. Fast as hell. Her hands just battering away – double stitch, pearl and whatever. I was so impressed, I called after her to have a good day ma'am and she raised a hand and kept right on walking. When people talk here they sound angry even when they're not. I've gotten used to it. Every morning I hear water being poured upstairs in a sink, a little while later the stair door closes below, everything arrives and departs at No. 10 Luckenbooth via the stairwell – news and gossip, fear, post, furniture arrives, or is taken out, lots of bags of coal. The stairwell steps are made of stone and they are worn with footsteps from decades of wear, so many people have lived out their lives here, children, old people, friends, lovers, unwanted relatives, a dog on a string, a doctor, an undertaker. How many bodies have been carried out over all that time? How many babies born? As the building gets higher the apartments get smaller. The residents less wealthy, I should be on the top floor, I'm only staying on the third because my employer leased it to me whilst his nephew is away. Further up the building they have four apartments per landing. If you took off the entire front wall of No. 10 Luckenbooth Close you'd see the basement, stair, floor, room, light, ceilings and repeat for nine floors. None of us would be surprised by the others' habits. The man on the fifth floor (as he is doing right now) plays his piano on a Sunday, his wife's parrot is allowed to fly around their apartment, there would be different wallpapers, at least twenty-three beds, a few tin baths, fireplaces, rugs of assorted design – there is a prayer group meets on the sixth floor on a Wednesday, a card game is run from the landlord's fancy apartment on the first floor, he is paler than bread – except for his nose which is red as claret. I walked home last week and found him carving a pictograph at the front door, it is a tiny goat girl, he was drunk and it's his building! I guess he can scrape goat girls into stone if he wants. He is getting work done on the building just now. I chatted to the stonemason just the other day – a nice guy, his name is Jim Kane, he plays records in a local bar on Wednesdays, he said I should go in so me and the postman will go along for a dance and a drink there sometime soon. As I say I spend my time thinking but I also like to talk to a good-looking woman and sink rum and Coke and wake up with a feeling of over-whelming dread.

On each floor of No. 10 Luckenbooth there are patterns of behavior.

A kettle whistle goes on a stove on the fourth floor each day at 7 a.m., 11 a.m., 1 p.m. and then again at 3 p.m. Mince and tatties are cooked on a Thursday, it makes the building smell bad. Tatties are potatoes. Aye, means yes. Noh, means no. I dinnae ken, means – I'm so terribly sorry I don't have the slightest idea what you are talking about. I had no idea they didn't speak English here! Unless they are posh, the posh people speak English with an Edinburgh burr. The accent is softer in Edinburgh city centre than it is out of town. I went out there last week and I didn't understand a single thing said the entire time, I kept nodding and hoped I hadn't gotten myself into illegal gains of any kind. It is fish on Fridays. I stay out that day. I tried haggis. They store it in the stomach of a sheep. I have no idea what's in it but it's spicy and good. Everything smells of smoke in this city. Even my pants. Since the winter kicked in I find the woodsmoke smell comforting, I love building fires. I love wearing scarfs. I love closing the door on night-time and putting a lamp on and sitting down in a warm glow to write to you, or to think, or read. Mind you, it's still so cold each morning my fingers are numb. There is a woman in the stair (that's what they call living in the building here *she is in the stair* – means she lives here in this building and she does not in fact live in the stair but in her apartment), anyway, this woman – she fucks like a guinea pig. Or, so her husband likes to roar when he has had too much to drink! None of us can quite look her in the eye. What's really worrying is that her husband seems to know what guinea pigs fuck like. There is a child in the apartment above me who rolls marbles across the floor after school, the floors are wooden and it drives me crazy. I want to go up there and poke that kid's eyes out. It is not at all grown up of me I know. The child has a bath in a tin tub in front of the fire on a Monday and his mother doesn't like him, neither do I. I did feel bad when I saw her marching him down the street though, face pinched, hand clutched, dragging him too fast into his future so he'll just leave home and she can be miserable on her own again. I left some new marbles outside his door after that. These buildings tell their stories – in sound – like a well-oiled clock. Noises are passed from floor to floor like notes passed in school to inform tenants of each other's indiscretions, inabilities, or occasional talents. The hula-hoop girl in 6F6 thuds with her feet for an hour every day because she is keeping six hoops going, her waist is so slim I want to dance with her whenever she walks by.

The building plays us like an orchestra.

There is something deeply wrong with her tuning.

I have not figured out why yet.

I still like 'Minnie the Moocher'! I miss Louisiana. I miss our childhood home. I miss the heat and fireflies in Mason jars. I miss wooden porches. I even miss the glimpse of an alligator. It's strange the things we don't notice at home or don't care for and how they change so much in our minds when we leave – only then do we see home is not what we thought it was when we took it for granted. I miss a church that doesn't smell stale. I miss knowing where everything is, so I can walk down any street – without thinking about it. I miss muskrat and civet cats. Woodcocks and mottled ducks. I miss the Delta. I miss jambalaya made with anything, but especially boar. I miss hearing songs in Creole. I miss the coal skin and the slender glass lizard, I miss you, Leo. I smile when I remember us learning how to handle a snapping turtle and how to kill and cook them too, I didn't want to do any of that then but these things have changed in my memory now I am far away. I do not miss toads. I do not miss red fire ants. I do not miss the yearning to be elsewhere – that I always felt when I was home. I know if I come back again now I will feel like that again no matter how nostalgic I am from a distance.

Edinburgh often has the most beautiful skies.

Pale blue or pink and when cloudless it is breathtaking.

Sometimes the sky races in such a way it seems there are two skies from two different worlds entirely – rushing at each other in opposite directions, layers of cloud and dark moodiness — a hint of stars.

It is dizzying!

One day I will look back fondly on this ancient building. No.10 Luckenbooth Close stares down the city day after day like a slutty girl with a God complex, I know you thought I would find myself such a thing, no such luck yet. I would come home but I am not ready. It is difficult to travel because of the war and whilst I complain about Edinburgh, I like it here really. They say that makes me dour, it's Scottish for miserable bastard. They have a single word in Gaelic that means 'my eternal doom is upon me', I can't remember it right now. They are an old nation. They have a great wit at times. They need it to survive the damn weather. When it rains it comes down in sheets. Everything turns gray. Sometimes there is a yellow light through the gray like aliens are inspecting the cobbled streets. I think about aliens a lot lately, and if they came down I would go with them, gladly.

If it ever happens I advise you do the same too.

One of the women on reception at the Dick Vet talks to me a lot.

She is a member of a coven.

I like her.

She says all across Britain covens are gathering to spell-cast against Hitler, pagans and druids and witches, doing what they can. What is happening right now destroys me. All the news is bad. We are on the eve of destruction, Leo. Chamberlain is intent on making sure the Germans are stopped at all costs! Even the Canadians have gone to war against them! They never go to war against anybody! Why didn't they learn from the last world war? It's going to cost the lives of many people. The Spanish Civil War was bad enough. How long until we learn? How long did it take to get the KKK down from 4 million members to nearly 30K? Then the far right just lurch up. Why? Claim some new justification for their hatred. Why? I try not to be political. I do! I don't want to think about all of this! I try to do other stuff at least half of the time. I need to so I can cope with being stuck here on earth with so many fucking lunatics. I read the DC comics you sent. I'm so jealous that you went to the first World Science Fiction Convention in New York. I will write to you until I have no thoughts left in me, Leo. It could take a while. I am studying bones all the time. Maybe all any of us need to do is become an expert in just one thing? Also, I found out No. 10 Luckenbooth Close is called that because of an old word *lucken-buith*, it's what they called the first locked booths for trading, they used to drag carts to sell silver and other things but they'd have to cart them back and forth across the city and I tell you, brother, the hills in this city are no joke, if I wasn't a God-fearing man I'd say they were designed by a psychopath. Anyway, eventually those local traders asked the council if they could lock their booths and that's how the word came about. Also – a Luckenbooth is a piece of jewelry, worn either as a brooch or a ring that can be given to a fiancée – it is pretty – two intertwined silver hearts.

Yours,
Levi

Jessie MacRae (21)

the second day

FIRELIGHT DANCES around Mr Udnam's library. A rag-
time '78 spins on the gramophone. I am focused on both of
them. Her eyelashes are tinted. He has freckles on his arms.
His thing is huge. I don't want to stare at it but it is hard to
ignore. Shadows chase each other around the room like an
audience surrounding a deadly play. They lunge – then pull
back. The fiancée's tongue flicks. He moves toward me as
she holds me by the arms. Somehow it feels like the most
natural thing.

— I think you might be happier living somewhere else in
town, Jessie.

— When?

— After. You could visit the child a few times each year.

There is no word fir yes, or no, in my mother's tongue. I
have nothing and no one. She slips her dress off. Her waist
has two small indents above her arse. He touches himself.
She moves his hand away to do it for him. He wants me to
watch. It does something for him.

— You like to read, Jessie?

— Aye.

— We should give you books when you're in containment.

She pulls down my dress until I step out of it – my skin bathed in the glow of firelight. My nipples are erect and a darker brown colour and I can see blue streaks of veins on my arms.

– Touch her there, he instructs.

– Like that?

There is only this minute. It is all there is. Yesterday won't bother me here. He is inside me quickly, and she turns to kiss him, then me. His eyes have been taken out and replaced with hard gold coins. There is a perversity to the fiancée's smile. It makes me want to please her. I close my eyes, see a stile, tree, fence. Startling flowers. Tiny and yellow. Hard little breaths – through my mouth. We are so far out – in this warm glow. I could smoke that pipe forever! He arches up. Looks like he is dying. The nubs on my temple burn so hot – I want to take my hair down and trace my horns with her fingertips, I am losing time – all regret is gone.

What feeling is this!

Falling.

Chattering elves.

Shapes.

Bright squares, coloured light – the room re-solidifies around me.

There are only embers in the fireplace.

– Are you awake, Jessie?

She is whispering to me. I don't know when I passed out. Elise looks tired and wanton. They are either side of me. He snores like a rhino. I have the blanket up around my shoulders. I place my hand on my stomach.

It has grown hard already whilst I slept.

— It worked!

— Let's hope so, she says.

— Look!

Elise stares at my stomach.

— Is your kind touched, Jessie?

Worse than that.

I daren't wonder how much my father told them when he traded my body for a half-human heir. One he knew would be raised in wealth with the best education money could buy. His grandchild will be brought up in absolute privilege. I know why my father would want his grandchild to have that level of power. So it could go out and destroy this world – he has always envied the earth her beauty or maybe he just wants to make a point to her maker. He certainly didn't tell Mr Udnam my mother grew me in three days. My brother too. He didn't tell them most islanders refused to look us in the eye for all of our lives and the devil's blood does not need nine months. That's for humans and they are better than we. I hoped I was more genetically of my mother's human blood. I hid the tiniest of nubs on my head all of my childhood without anyone noticing, even when I started to bleed and became a woman – they got only a tiny bit longer and the tip more sharp but they were still never as long as this. Not until he died. Then they grew. I'd say they are almost three inches long on either side now. It is harder to hide them. I wrap them in linen, then I wrap my hair around them in two buns on top of my head and I wear a bonnet. If I'd had horns this sharp whilst he was alive – I would have staked him. I would have taken joy in that. I'd have staked him at least ten times. My blood can't carry his sins any more. If I can pay for him then I have to. I took the only action I could. He is not here now. My horns grew longer and now I can never truly hide where I come from and I could be exposed at any time. Anyone who wants to love me in this world, will not be able to – when they see me in my natural physical form – neither human or devil – yet somehow I am even more devil and human for being a part of each. Regardless I can only ever be me. I have human and devil blood in me in equal measures. More than either of those though there is my essence – that was born into me and it belongs solely to me – as it does for everyone. I'm not my father or mother. I am me. My natural essence is harder than stone. It is so determined. It will never let me give in, not even to the devil. Not even when he is the one who taught me how to use a knife and fork. Who taught me how to slaughter a goat or cow or sheep. Who had me steal an egg from an eagle. Who let me know I must never be afraid to cross invisible lines. Elise traces my cheek. As if to settle a child. Rests her head on my stomach – her hair falls across us.

– I could live in this library.

She giggles.

– I'm so glad you are here, Jessie. He—

Elise points and pulls hard on her pipe, nods at him.

– He insisted I read everything. So when we travel he can talk without being bored.

– You still bore me, he says, waking a little, eyes still closed.

– So far, I like Jack London.

– You liked Gertrude Stein.

– That's only because she was nice to us in Paris, and she has all those painters in her salon. I don't understand what she writes but she introduced me to a man called Picasso. They say he has invented some kind of new painting, something to change everything.

— Picasso won't do a fucking thing! He's in Spain with a lover, not painting!

Mr Udnam takes the pipe.

— I like Baum — what's it called, that book? Elise clicks her fingers.

— *The Wonderful Wizard of Oz*! What a bag of shite.

— No! It's a great story! I don't rate all the things you like! Sudermann, Apollinaire, Henry James. All tedious as fuck if you ask me, darling. Chekhov, I suppose, had a few decent stories, I don't see what the fuss is about him personally.

She says it to me, not him.

— What have you read, Jessie? He looks at me.

— The Bible, three times in full and a chapter every Sunday, sir.

I stand before them naked and curtsy.

Mirth dissipates.

They both gaze at my stomach.

It has grown four inches since I slept. Noticeably round. A fine dark line trails down from my belly button. I am not sure how they are going to take this but I am pretty sure the child will be here by Wednesday morning.

— Did you hear the Earl of Bute is going to fly a plane? He designed it himself.

Elise is trying to distract him.

— We're not meant to fly. Think of Icarus. Jessie . . . what's happening?

My stomach rises half an inch.

— How long? Mr Udnam roars.

He pours a brandy and looks at me with red-rimmed eyes.

— You're a witch?

— No.

I am close to tears. It is so unlike me.

His fiancée steps away from him and holds her hand out to me. His eyes blacken.

— We'll sleep in the lady's room.

He nods.

I am led down the hallway like a feeble child.

Inside me forms a heart. Legs. Ribs. Feet, nails, skin, a brain.

Elise's hand is cool.

— Come on, into bed, that's it, rest on the pillow. I've wanted a baby for so long, we won't let him ruin it, okay?

Nod.

She takes a seat in front of three mirrors on her dressing table and opens a pot of cream.

— It's almond oil and benzoin, I use spermaceti and lanolin to make my skin clearer too but you don't need that, do you?

My belly button pops out.

— What did your father die from, Jessie?

— The consequences of evil.

She glances toward the consulting room. There are loud crashes. She takes a small key and locks the door as if she has done so many times before.

— He'll pass out soon!

Elise opens talcum powder and dusts some into the palm of her hand and then combs it through her hair.

— I wash my hair once every three weeks, it's why it is so shiny!

The dimple in her cheek disarms me. She lays down on

the bed beside me. We sleep and wake. She sends the maid
out for food and has her deliver it to our door on a tray and
then she is dismissed. We hear Mr Udnam go out and Elise
keeps him away from me and I watch my stomach grow bigger. I am trapped now. Can't take it back. Life finds its way.
On the third morning she wakes me with coffee and places
her hand on the bump. A small elbow or a foot slides on the
underside of my skin.

— Three days ago, Elise, I took a bottle of tinct iodine —
washed it out and stoppered my secrets.

— Aye?

— Aye. I placed it in the sea. I like to think my secrets will
be passing under migrating whales in a bottle right now. I
hope they turn under the moon. Or the shadow of hammer-
head sharks twist below it. I hope an albatross crosses it
with her huge wing-spanned shadow. I hope barnacles adorn
its bottle neck. I hope seahorses swim below it in shoals. I
hope they are giant seahorses with ornate trunks! I hope
someone finds the bottle. Sees that it is pretty. Takes out my
letter. Puts flowers in it and drinks tea from a china cup and
saves my secrets in a tea tin for someone else to read in a
hundred years.

— Did you have a funeral, for your father?

— Aye. There is an order to things on the island though.
As soon as someone dies you snap open the window to let
the spirit out, then close it again so it doesn't come back in.
Then you throw a blanket on the mirror so they can't stay
and preen themselves. Spirits are vain creatures. You tip
over all the kitchen chairs so the spirit cannot sit and refuse
to leave like a child in a huff!

— What else?

She is rapt now.

— You stop the clock at the time of death.

— Why?

— The dead's time is done, time won't move on for them again.

— Harsh!

— Press white wooden teardrops into the front door, so the funeral crier will be notified by a passer-by. He calls out. Seven women leave their homes. In our case, the women only came to host his waken out of goodness. The men only took him on their shoulders to make sure he was gone.

My stomach strains and a clear foot outline passes under my skin.

— Women prepare the body?

— Aye. Twin fates. Life and death. Women's work. We bring life into the world and we take it back out again. One woman brings the dead rags, we wind them around the body after cleansing — every area, knotted rag up his arse, so he doesn't leak! If the dead person is liked, they get sung over tae the other side.

— Did they sing for your father?

— No, he's lucky they weren't swearing at him and sticking needles in his fucking eyes!

There is a thud from the consulting room.

— He's passed out!

I want to take down my carefully wound pompadour. Show my horns. I have two heartbeats inside me. Four eyes to see. One set for this realm and the other for the underworld.

— Then you bury them? she asks.

— No, then we perform Kistan. We lift the body — as

one – into the casket. During the waken we take turns to watch over it so the devil can't take their soul. In my da's case that was only really carried out fir the facade of tradition.

– You think the devil didnae want his soul?

I smile at her, bitterly.

– Three days later the women do first lift. Take the casket on our shoulders and carry the body out feet first so the soul can't come back in. Then the men take him. They're drunk by then. They've been drinking fir three days. Sometimes they get in a fight on the way to the kirk. Sometimes they lose the body and can't remember where they left it. They dropped my da's body over a clifftop. Left him looking out across the North Sea. I'm pretty sure they were just trying to make sure he was irreparably dead. We all were, really.

– Your stomach is hard as rock, Jessie. The skin has stretched. Do you think it's coming?

– Soon.

She takes a long drink and stares at me.

– What are you thinking about?

– The taste of flesh in my mouth.

– What else?

– How my horns grew the minute my father died.

– What else?

– There was still soot in the grate.

– And?

– I was glad he was dead.

– How did you know the men dropped him down the cliff?

– I went to find him.

– Why?

– So I'd know he wouldn't cause chaos any more.

– That's what he did?

– Aye.

A hard kick to my stomach and I bend over in pain and sweat pours off me. The contractions are like having my insides torn apart by a thousand rats at once. I don't know how anyone lives through this.

– Help me stand!

Elise pulls me to my feet and water sloshes onto the floor.

– Let me get towels!

– I can taste blood.

– We'll get through this!

– What if the baby has no face, Elise?

– Stop it.

– What if he's no head because of me?

– Why would the baby have no head because of you?

– I've done a bad thing!

– It's okay, the baby will have a wonderful head and it will have a face, and a head to put the face on and a neck below that. It will have everything! Head, face, neck, the whole fucking kit-and-caboodle. Dinnae panic, Jessie! The baby will have all of the things. Are you listening to me? It'll have aw the fingers and all the other stuff too, toes, teeth, everything – I mean the teeth will come later.

– What if it has horns?

– We'll hide them under a bonnet!

– I'll nurse him! You've not had time to get a nursemaid, let me nurse him?

– It's a girl, Jessie.

– How do you know?

Elise looks back at me and I realise the pretty witch in this apartment is not in any way me.

There's an animal roaring.

A beast.

Cloven hoofs pace underneath the city as I grab onto a metal bed frame.

— Bear down, Jessie. Push!

— What if I want tae keep the bairn?

— Part your legs further, Jessie, come on, stay upright, it'll make it easier, I can see — a crown, it's coming!

She has not mentioned horns. That's good, she is not coming out horns first. I don't want my little girl to come out horns first!

I could weep.

Crown!

It's a crown she can see.

Something is stuck and my body judders.

Elise's arm is inside me then — turning the baby — I am screaming with pain — begging for death — her delicate hands do not falter; they belong to a woman made of steel. I have never been so grateful for another woman's presence in my entire life.

The baby whooshes out.

There is not a single solitary sound except for my ragged breathing.

— Smack her feet, Elise!

— What?

— She's purple, smack her hard!

The baby is bloody and she has wrinkles.

A nose.

A perfect Cupid's bow.

Squashed face, wrinkled fat, tiny fists unfurl and Elise smacks her feet and I cannot hear a single thing until the baby wails.

We are both crying!

– I am going to cut the cord, Jessie, is it okay? I don't even know what I am doing, do you just cut it?

– Aye! Are the scissors clean?

– Aye.

Elise turns away from me with my baby in her arms.

Does she see something?

There is blood on my thighs and my hands. I glimpse in the mirror and it is on my face – she wraps the baby in a towel.

– She is so perfect!

Elise does not want to let her go. We eye each other. Mr Udnam appears in the door. He is as high as all the kites.

– It's a girl?

– Our daughter!

The two of them inspect her.

I bite down hard on my lip and try to think of reasons not to stake them.

– The renovators will be in soon. They are stripping out the flats above us, Jessie. I own the building, you do know? We can put you in another flat once they are ready. All the walls are open just now. I need to find a way to tell people that we have our baby!

Eyelashes long and dark as her grandfather.

– I want my child.

My arms ache, my breasts. The baby turns her head looking for me, she can smell my milk across the room. There is only one person who she wants. If they don't give her to me I will kill them both.

– Give her to me, now.

– It won't be appropriate for you to hold her outside of feeding time though, Jessie.

– Oh, no?

She does not belong to him yet.

I have not taken a fee.

I take her in my arms – she smells clean – skin like velvet. She suckles like she's done it all of her many lives. This is not the first time we have met, her and me. I settle down into the little parlour chair with wings. Elise takes a tiny hat out the drawer for the baby, booties. She has been waiting for this moment for years. It hurts her to leave the feeding to me. Run my hand over my daughter's fuzzy dark hair. It looks like a gentle caress but if she has what I have in her blood then we will have to go as soon as she's done feeding.

I would have to steal my own child or they would kill her and me.

– How can it happen in just a few days like that? he asks.

– It's a blessing! Elise replies.

– Is the infant cursed?

– No!

As they argue in the hallway I sing quietly to my daughter. I won't live in another part of town – visit once a year! My mother didn't ever lay with my father other than to have us. She said it was worth it only for that. He went with women on all of the islands. Fought their husbands. Burnt down barns. My mother had no fear of him in the end. After he beat her she went to lay with the priest. The priest loved my mother (witch or not) and he was the only man my father ever feared. She came home and taught my brother and me what she learnt in his library. I can't think of my brother even now without a hot spear of loss. He would have adored the baby so much. A niece to love. To wiggle his ears at. My mother soaked up everything she could about maths and geography, history, philosophy, religion, English, art, chemistry, physics. Her most passionate subject was women who do extraordinary things. She must have known. A granddaughter was coming. My mother read to us at night. Tales of Ching Shih, the Chinese female pirate who commanded a fleet with 80,000 outlaws, Boadicea and Joan of Arc, the Virgin Mary, and Eleanor of Aquitaine, Jane Austen, Ada Lovelace, Angela Coutts, Mary Wollstonecraft, Josephine Butler, Mary Shelley, Mary Seacole, Cleopatra, Elizabeth Fry, Mary Anning, Catherine of Siena, Hypatia, Sacagawea, Nellie Bly, Catherine de' Medici, Isabella Bird, Aphra Behn, Artemisia Gentileschi, the Pankhursts, Sarah Breedlove, Prophet Deborah, Mary Somerville, George Eliot, Murasaki Shikibu, Clara Schumann, Beulah Louise Henry, Aisha, Yeshe Tsogyal, Sophie Blanchard, Émilie du Châtelet, the women on this street, on roads at night – all of those women were beloved to my mother.

I can see her looking out of the croft.

Watching those skies – storms coming in low and high at the same time.

My father hammering coffins together.

Sheep up on the hills.

Rock grey and hard and rubble and all the earth a hard unforgiving seedless place.

He is still in that crevice.

Staring out all the way across the North Atlantic swells.

My coffin bobs on the docks.

I've got blood on my mother's only good dress.

Elise will have to loan something to me.

My hands pause caressing the baby's head.

Two nubs!

So small – only I know they are there.

I will call her Hope – she is so warm and perfect.

She lays heavy and happy on my chest, sleeping, dreamless and fed.

This will be the most blissful sleep of her life.

Those tiny fists make me hold my breath.

In Elise's three-way mirror – I see them both watching me at the door. My own horns grow long as my child wakes to suckle again. Sharp and curved they bend up toward the light. I feel them heavy and strong on my head. I dip to kiss my daughter and they glint. It will be some time before Mr Udnam tries to take her from me.

Flora (33)

After — everyone arrives

SHE SHOULD not be sitting at a party thinking of a dead polar bear. It could make her appear pensive. It will be bad for her cheekbones. Each knock at the door makes her jump. It's not the police! It's not a raid! They are not being dragged to the cells in their finery. If they were they'd be the most glamorous prison population in the country! It's a risk. They all know it. They all come anyway. Such a beautiful thing! The courage to turn up. Everyone in here has it. Flora grabs a handful of peanuts. She has to eat. Alcohol meets truth. Not something to peddle before midnight. Her ex-lover is chatting to another woman. Why did he even want her here? Love is a cage. If there ever was a key, he swallowed it. Love as a trap. Love as a fox fur. Love as a riddle. Love as a contract killer. Love as a shadow. Love as benzocaine. Love as novocaine. Love as cocaine. Love as a light bulb flashing on and then off. Love as a hummingbird. Love as a leather glove. Love as a recurrent dream. There is nothing that can be done about it. Feelings are fucking hideous. Flora hates them. Just one more cocktail before she lays on the floor and weeps for eternity. She eats three pickles. That has to constitute a meal somewhere. She feels a tiny bit more able to keep drinking now without ripping off her clothes and screaming until the building falls down. No. 10 Luckenbooth Close has a melancholy that fits her psyche usually. None of it is apparent tonight. It shimmers with dancers and lovers and thinkers and friends. She can't move for bumping into a writer, or actress, or comedian. Flora far prefers her local with her pal Jock. His most consistent earnings are from putting a six-inch nail up his nose for a pint. Jock hasnae paid for a drink since 1903. Her ex glances at her across the room. Despite the injuries accrued it appears she still has a heart and it is beating.

— Hi, mind if I join you?

— No, hello, I'm Flora, you don't need to introduce yourself — you were just acting at the Theatre Royal, in Glasgow?

— Aye!

— I've seen you so many times, you're amazing!

— Thank you, is that Nan?

The actor's eyes flit around the room, he fluffs up his purple wig.

— I think so. I've never met her.

— Her poetry makes me die every time I read it.

— What's the new director like at the Theatre Royal? she asks him.

— Cruickshank, he is efficient! He's partner in his dad's builders firm, they built King's Theatre.

He sips champagne.

— Were you in the Cameo last week, Flora?

— Easy Virtue?

— Aye!

— I knew I'd seen you somewhere. Are you still in touch with . . .

– Clara Bow?

He raises his fingers to his lips. Someone calls his name. Flora reclines on a chaise. Behind her there are four women in suits, no bras, breasts on show when they lean forward. The glimpse of a nipple and laughter to turn her head, a flash of white teeth. Each is smoking. They have perfect real-looking little moustaches on. They sit with their legs spread wide. The way men do. Mr Torrance has admirers gathering. A small group of men flutter around him. They all wear leather. Eyes sparkle. People arrive in twos, threes. Some of them go into the bedroom to get changed. There is a long trail of glitter down the hallway. Stockings are pulled on. Lipstick is blotted. High heels stood up in. Legs elongate. Cheekbones materialise. Eyes pop. Tits rise. Over in the corner a circus vixen – in a diamond-encrusted bikini – flirts with a girl in a half-moon hat. Rubies dangle either side of her ears. Three jewelled strands sparkle between her eyes, heavily lined in kohl. There's a girl in a pumpkin mask and orange striped stockings. She has a promising bulge. Could do with bumping up against her later. Cleopatra starts a hand jive. Lips red. Shiny black hair. Her ex-lover is at the door, saying hello as each person comes in.

Flora watches him the way she used to.

The social butterfly.

A maestro.

She wants to go up and touch him. Kiss his cheek. That is not allowed, no, no, no!

Flora goes to the bathroom.

Takes a small bump of cocaine to help her stay awake.

Another to sparkle.

One for luck.

A fourth for our Sainted Mary, Mother of God.

Two touches for the Father, one for the Son, another for the Holy Ghost.

There's no reason to be cheap, is there?

She does one for Snow White and another for each of the Seven Dwarves.

It takes a long, long while of gripping onto the bathroom sink before she stops feeling like her heart is going to explode across the walls.

— Done too much! Done too much! It's okay. Just breathe . . .

She whispers to herself.

His bathroom is like something out of a magazine, that's what to think about. Just keep counting the things around her until she has an actual heart attack, or — goes out to dance until dawn. White floor tiles in small hexagonal shapes. Black ones line the edges. Sink with turn-on H + C taps and a tiny faucet in the middle. Two silver poles hold up the basin. Plant on the side. There is an art deco lamp on wooden towel drawers. Flora twists her signature curl around her finger repeatedly. Lays it on her cheek. She looks good though! A pout and a pose then she turns to the bathroom cabinet. He has no idea. All this luxury! Her area is still going through the Leith Improvement Scheme even now! It's endless in Leith. Rebuilding! Old businesses closing down! Men from the council walk around with clipboards being total fannies. They won't stop until all Leithers are out ay Leith. They'll keep hiking up rents until that's exactly what happens. It will be this city's total shame when it does. Flora rearranges bottles. There is a massive bottle of One Night Cough Syrup. That looks useful.

Ingredients include: alcohol (less than 1 per cent); cannabis indica, F. E.; chloroform; morphia, sulph. Half a teaspoon three times daily. There is Farben Fabriken's – heroin. What a very pretty bottle! He's brought that back from New York. How many coughs has he had lately? Cocaine tooth drops. He has never before complained of toothache! Her ex once got a bottle of vintage Vin Mariani. 11 per cent alcohol and 6.5 mg of cocaine in every ounce. Leo XIII gave it a gold medal. Robert Louis Stevenson wrote *Dr Jekyll and Mr Hyde* during a six-day binge. If it was good enough for Jules Verne and Conan Doyle and Queen Victoria and the Shah of Persia! Before the war her ex's mother, no less, used to get a kit in Harrods called *A Welcome Present for Friends at the Front*. It had everything! Cocaine, morphine, syringes, needles. Of course it has a touch of the bad reputation about it now, harder to get a hold of, which makes it all the more fun. There is a tin of Johnson's baby talc. Perfume by Yardley and hair clips. Close the cabinet door. Flush the toilet three times – just for the novelty of it. There's a cough and a scrabble and a snigger.

Flora pulls back the shower curtain.

– Did ye do too much, hen?

– Bite me.

The taller man pushes the other one down onto his knees and takes his cock out.

He pulls Flora over and kisses her deeply.

The man kneeling in the bath runs his hand up her leg and caresses her arse.

She shouldn't!

Although . . . Greig will have had countless women and men in the last eleven months.

Flora parts her legs. It's wrong . . . which is why it feels so good.

On the way back down the hallway she fixes her dress.

Flora looks into his empty bedroom. There are so many pairs of men's shoes. All lined up. Suits neatly hung. It looks like a fancy shop changing room, not someone's home. The vanity is covered in debris. All his furniture is stained green. Her hips move. It's jazz riffs. Need to dance! Glasses clink! Move down the hallway back into the lounge. She is more than buzzing. The last seven bumps definitely were not necessary. It's a fine line between sparkle and psychosis. She's tipping.

— Can ye lock the front door, doll?

— Aye, why?

— I just had to pass some neighbours in that stair, I got dressed before I came — it was, just a time thing, I'm sorry!

Flora double-locks the front door. The doppelgänger of Josephine Baker but far taller and even more lithe takes off her coat and is absorbed by a group of women hugging her and cooing over her figure and her clothes. The gramophone cranks up louder. A girl is doing a striptease on the kitchen table. She swivels her hips. Turns to show a real pony tail high up on her arse. A man in a top hat puts a bit in her mouth. An armchair is writhing with arms and legs – a sexual octopus of subversion. Flora can hear Greig arguing with somebody.

— MacDiarmid is a genius! .

— Away and shite.

— Yer away wi the fairies, Paul — he is the best writer in the country!

– Nobody wants tae read writing in Scottish, Greig! Get a fucking grip ay yersel!

– Whit about Burns then?

– Tepid. A complete pig as well.

– Well, MacDiarmid is ahead of his time, I quote him like this: 'the Scots vernacular is a vast storehouse of just the very peculiar and subtle effects which modern European literature in general is assiduously seeking . . . it is an inchoate Marcel Proust, a Dostoevskian debris of ideas – an inexhaustible quarry of subtle and significant sound.' Stick that in yer pipe uhn double-drag it ya fucking prick! Come on! Then he writes Sangschaw! Fucking ay! Don't tell me he doesnae ken exactly what he is talking about.

– Are you quoting me?

– The man himself, Chris, I didnae see you there!

Her ex-lover's voice has so much tinkle when he sees the writer that the chandelier grows visibly depressed. The writer moves right on of course. Instantly bored. Girls in flapper dresses mix Tom Collinses, bras stuffed to the tip. Greig is behind her then, she feels his breath on her neck before he touches her waist lightly.

– Flora.

– Hello, Greig.

– Are you enjoying yourself?

– No. I should have known all the writers would be here. The literati only ever come here to feel bohemian, you know that!

– Always so harsh, Flora. They come to have fun.

– No, they don't. They come to forget that they are cardigan wearers. They think that we are just queers and cocksuckers whilst they are geniuses and thinkers and never the twain shall fuck. The twain don't fuck. We don't, do we? Greig? Why are you looking at me like that?

— What about all the queer ones?

— Those ones are good, they are ours but you are all over Chris or Hugh or fucking whatever he wants to call himself lately, and he has no time for you! It's embarrassing. You know that.

— Are you jealous?

— No! I could handle any of them being here if they sucked dick half as good as I do — or in fact at all — but they don't. This isn't a zoo. I am not fucking interested in voyeuristic day trippers.

— You are jealous!

— Dinnae flatter yerself, Greig.

— You think of me, don't you Flora, when you . . .

— No.

— Liar. Every single time I still see your face . . .

— Every time you cum you see a different face, Greig, that was always the problem.

— I'm sure you're not doing sexual sobriety, Flora.

— Of course not, why should I?

— My beautiful girl, come here.

— I'm not yours, Greig Heatherly, and don't you forget it.

— You've always been mine.

He leans back, crosses his legs at the ankles.

— Oh fuck off, and the Scottish Literary Renaissance — can suck my balls. You are all over them like an upright citizen! Middle-class people drive me crazy. You're all so fucking two-faced. It's fake. It fucking is!

— Come on, Flora, you know where this kind of fury leads us . . .

— I'm not going to bed with you.

Realising the whole time they have been talking they have moved further in toward each other.

Their love is a carousel.

Endless circles.

It has been this way now since forever. Who can change it? Unlike him she can do solitude though. Always could. Flora was brought up in a small flat with many people. She knows about the anonymity of a beating heart. He has never been alone properly in his entire bloody life and he is totally incapable of doing so.

— Where were you?

— Flora, don't do this again.

— When I had to tell my officer — where were you?

— Baby, please.

— They examined me with ten men in the room!!

— I know.

— They put me in the nuthouse because my body scared them!

— I hate them for what they did to you.

He has tears in his eyes.

— Where were you?

— Here.

— That's right. You were right here, with your nice bed-sheets, or at home with your wife to look after you and the kids, and her family, and your mum, and your brothers and your sister and everyone else to make sure you were okay like they always do! When I needed you, you weren't there, it's always about everyone else being there for you. You've never done anything on your own in your entire fucking life! You have no idea what it's like for people like me.

— What do you want from me, Flora?

His eyes blazing then.

So easy to ignite that, just ask anything he can't answer. All around them the party swells and pulses. A girl grinds down on another woman's lap. The men in leather trail off into the bathroom. Someone runs the shower. He cups her face in his hands. Kisses her cheeks and nose and forehead and then her mouth. He traces her lips with his finger until she bites. He places one hand around her throat with just the exact right pressure. Everything is spinning — the flat, the people dancing and touching each other, the bar — the entire Luckenbooth rotates its way through night like a disco ball with them all — safely contained — for a short time, in the glitter.

— I thought you were never going to sleep with me again, he whispers.

— I'm not.

— I can see that.

— I hate you.

— But you miss me, don't you?

Him pulling her in, holding her — their hearts beating right next to each other again, want like this doesn't go away — no matter how much she might want it to, it won't.

— Fuck me.

She whispers into his ear quiet as a spell and just as true.

— Gladly.

There is a hard bang at the front door. The record is slid

off. There is a pfft-pfft-pfft pfft-pfft sound as the record table rotates with nothing on it.

— Oh, fucking hell! Sssh, everyone! Be quiet, shut the fuck up, for a minute, please!

Greig holds his hands up for everyone to be silent.

In the door he has drilled a tiny hole.

So clever.

He walks over barefoot and elegant and feline and he looks quickly to see if it is the police on the other side.

— It's MISTER UDNAM! Open the door now, Greig, or I'll have the police here in minutes!

— Let me, Flora says.

She pulls her dress down at the cleavage, leaves her stockings on show — she opens the door.

— Flora, why are you here, what is going on in there?

Keeps her body in the crack.

Everyone is stood up against the wall behind her but he can't see them.

— I am so happy to see you, Mr Udnam! My ma speaks so highly of you — she said your charity helped us out so much. Do you remember visiting North Fort Street? You came after those fires. Spent lots of money. The community was so grateful. My ma said a man like yourself changes the world only fir the better, Mr Udnam. I need your help, to be honest.

— You all know who I am!

Mr Udnam strains to call it out over her shoulder as the entire party holds their breath.

— I am an upstanding member of the community and a CHRISTIAN!

– I can see that, Mr Udnam, truly!

– I won't have sin in my building!

– No.

– I do remember your ma. What's a nice girl like you even doing here, Flora?

– I know, it's just, I have had such a terrible time, trying to – better myself. I try to pray, properly, across the road, at St Giles' but I just can't quite get the words right. Would you, help me open my heart to Jesus?

– Yes . . .

He seems uncertain.

Flora grabs the first fur-lined coat she can find.

– You want to go now?

– I fear, Mr Udnam, that the absolution of ma spirit – depends on it.

Everyone in the room is covering their mouth trying not to laugh. Arts types are so useless. How many of them have had to act because their actual life depended on it? Fucking wankers. That's what they are. Every last one. Flora closes the door firmly. Steps out into the cold echoey stair. Mr Udnam glares into her then. His eyes are rheumy. She feels colder by the minute. He turns and walks downstairs slowly. Flora follows him in silence.

Levi (32)

the four horsemen of the apocalypse

WELL, DEAR brother — if my workplace hasn't gotten stranger! They load animals in the back courtyard and I work to the sound of chickens, dogs barking, cats, elephants, zebras, odd birds, even the odd bear going down the hallway. There is blossom on the Meadows in pink and it flutters across the paths — it's so pretty, students go there to sit in the summer and I am told it is a graveyard for plague victims.

Remember I told you I found a room in our building registered to Egypt? I heard the staff go in via a big blue plastic sheet, after that they can't be seen. I found out more. They remove their clothes in a sealed room, shower, then get into boiler suits, then go through more sealed spaces — to get into a laboratory. I have looked into it and when they are in that room they are definitely not working under UK law. They are working under Egyptian law. What is more acceptable under Egyptian law? I am no expert in that legal area specifically but what kind of work also requires people to remain in a sealed unit and to have a full shower on arrival and then again when they leave?

It is cloning.

I think they are trying to clone the first animal.

In the cafe the workers from the Egypt room have their own table. They don't talk to the rest of us. If they find a way to clone animals, then next it will be humans – it sounds like science fiction but it is going to happen. What next? No humans needed? Just machines running the whole world? Machine horses. Machine penguins. Mechanical animals performing sacred rituals? Cloned humans working every job and telling the great un-cloned that we were merely the makers of bad history and now we are to be replaced? They are playing God in that room in the Cube building and it is a dangerous game. Why would you clone a human when you can't even look after the humans who already exist? I have been reading about futurists and the lost generation. Apparently futurists attended your first World Science Fiction Convention this year in New York and they thought they were better than everyone. If I had met them, brother, I would have shook each one of their hands and informed them that no geek is better than me – I can out-think all of them. Did you see them there?

I've found somewhere I can buy the *New York Times*. I cannot believe the dust bowl is so bad again – in Texas it's blackening the sky. I remember how bad those dust storms were at the start of the decade. Do you remember one deposited 12 million pounds of dust on Chicago? Red snow in New England. They say 3.5 million people have had to migrate already, they are always going on about migrants, about identity and colour and race – it's almost as if the universe did not create us all from stardust!

No?

I say words out loud to soothe me.

Osteomyelitis, osteitis, acromegaly, multiple myeloma.

There are whale bones at the end of middle Meadow Walk.

I am beginning to think this entire city creaks and groans with bones.

I have this feeling, Edinburgh will dispose of each of us once she has had her use – drank all the energy and talent and money and vitality and then she spits out the bones. Hungry city!

Subsists on human souls.

I am ignoring what is going on in Cube and the rest of the world this week and having nothing to do with the dark soul of my current home – I am getting on with my work.

Sort of.

At the end of my bone library there is a door to the Dissection Room. There have been lectures in there all week. They have a massive Highland cow hung up on a great big fuck-off hook. Also – they shaved him. Somebody took six bags of cow hair through my library. I have been picking out hairs from everything. I am still studying bones all the time. Did you know they had oracle bones in China? They would engrave questions of the day on the bones and then when they split it was thought the spirit world was divining answers. Oracle bones were mostly oxen scapula or turtle plastron, they called their form of divination pyromancy, scapulimancy was the term they used if it was an oxen scapula and plastromancy if it was a turtle, they would carve in oracle bone script, asking deities to bring answers then they'd heat them up until they cracked and the diviner would read answers from the cracks. They mostly used oxen or turtle but human bones were found too. I think about human bones in relation to animal bones. Did you know if your finger bones got longer and longer you'd have a similar bone structure to a bat? If you took out human leg and arm bones, we would have the same skeletal structure as a snake. I spell out words with bones, I drum with them, I draped jewelry around a beaver skull. I am filing the skulls I have found most fascinating, they include:

Crow
Horse
Bugle bird (I don't know what it was doing here)
Red fox
Bobcat
Bali starling
Black stork
Grey-legged douroucouli
Lowland Nyala
Hamerkop
Scottish wildcat
Waldrapp ibis
Red squirrel
Deer
Seal
Swan

If only we could find a real unicorn skeleton! It's Scotland's national animal which makes me like them more. I want to see a wolf skeleton. In my bone library I have to keep lots of collections in sturdy brown boxes. Did you know owls regurgitate entire animal skeletons? It's a thing! I arrived in the bone library minus my heart. Isn't it always the way? I wasn't sure how I had ended up in a place where bones are so insistent on rigidity, it made a mockery of my click-clack vertebrae.

I have been building things I shouldn't – when the professors aren't looking – specifically, a mermaid.

It is the most majestic thing I ever made in my life!

I used whale bones, a dormouse, half a dog, a lot of weasel, cat, a few horse bones and if the postman is right in what he says – there are human bones in her tail. I am sure it is not true. He was so drunk he thought it was a real mermaid, he is so drunk he thinks he's still in the navy. I like to think about the 260 human bones – skull, jaw, cervical, thoracic, lumbar, sacrum, ribs, breastbone, scapula, clavicle, humerus, radius, ulna. Sometimes I hang bones out to dry and they clink in the breeze.

I slide the drawers closed in the bone library.

It is very satisfying.

They glide, you see – then click shut. A fine cabinetmaker built them. My filing is immaculate.

When I fall asleep at night I am always thinking of carpals, or metacarpals, or phalanges, or tibia, or fibula, or tarsals, or metatarsals. I dream of a piano with long bones as keys. There is an irregular bone in every single one of us and it is not for conforming with the rest, brother, mercy, mercy, mercy! There are osteoblasts, osteocytes, osteoclasts, osteolite. I've been dreaming lately about a man who has finger bones for teeth and he bares them like a whale in the great blue deep. I could have felt bad about building my mermaid out of bone but – some kind of siren is calling to me. I can feel her in No. 10 Luckenbooth Close. Each night as I go to sleep it feels like I am being lured out to the rocks by her singing.

I have begun to do things without thinking.

The other day I bought a bunch of medical texts on the

human skeleton. I have been looking at it. I feel a density every time I lay down lately. I feel a gentle indent at the foot of my bed as I drop off. If I was superstitious I would say someone is sitting there watching me sleep.

I try to think about good things because the light feels as if it is fading.

There were penguins in the Dick Vet today.

I had to rebuild a horse.

The skeleton is going into a cabinet downstairs. I became obsessed with him. Two hundred and five bones. The skull alone had fourteen major bones. My favorites: temporal bone, zygomatic bone, palatine bone, parietal, sphenoid, vomer, pterygoid. I have built a skeleton horse so good he could win the damn Derby. My horse has evolved over 55 million years! They carry foals for eleven months and that four-legged elegance comes out walking and whinnying and running from day one. Don't tell me we are the most evolved species, we are just the most upright ones – with irrational levels of delusion.

They should put horses in charge.

I am sure it is a glitch of evolution that we are dominant.

When you think about it horses were the very first animal to give us our personal freedom and what happens to them? I sat with my horse skeleton most of the night and I cried, Leo. Something in this place is getting to me. Since I moved into No. 10 Luckenbooth Close I have gradually felt more and more weak. I thought about my horse getting up and galloping across this city, I thought about my ghost riding her over to the other side, I thought about how our animal instinct is something any horse can smell, how we can't hide our fear from them and how they recognize it on sight.

My boy is a Trojan horse.

I found out that they used to call trains curious little fire horses!

We calibrate our machines in horsepower.

How much weight can a steam engine pull?

What is its horsepower?

A long time ago people could only date someone on their road. Or a village they could walk to, or across town on foot.

It was only when the first wild horses were tamed – that love and humanity and all the humans in the world opened up a much wider map. The circle of our hearts' hope grew exponentially.

I have traveled far.

Perhaps it is because my person was not anywhere near our home.

She is waiting for me.

It was our ability to travel on horses that allowed us to lay in places far and wide. The DNA of the human race began to change. They dragged us into the future.

The Four Horsemen of the Apocalypse are coming, my dearest brother.

They have set divine judgement on the world and show us the apocalypse and how it will begin. We are already there, are we not? Right at the start of it? The prophecy said each horseman represented one part of the apocalypse. There was Pestilence, War, Famine, and Death. A white horse whose rider spoke of people in constant war. A red horse whose rider had the power to make men slay each other. A black horse whose rider spoke of famine. A pale horse and its rider was Death. Hades was behind him. He spoke of plague upon the wild beasts of the earth. What plague is coming? Is it one we ourselves are setting in motion now? I told you that a girl who works in reception here has begun to talk to me. It turns out she lives upstairs at No. 10 Luckenbooth Close. I don't know why but I want to tell her about all of this.

I am going to send this letter to you today. I will write again as soon as I can. I can verify now, thinking is the deepest act of transgression. We can change everything in our mind: synapses, programs, ideas, thoughts, false histories, unobtainable futures – it is dangerous and it is not good for me but I won't stop doing it, not for mermaids, or sirens, not for dictators, or racists, or creeps, I won't stop for Mr Udnam, or Mary Dick, or the army, or God himself, I have set my mind to it now and I won't stop thinking as deeply as I possibly can, for nobody.

You are in my best thoughts always,
Levi

Jessie MacRae (24)

the conclusion

THERE HAS been no two-room croft to clean. No byre to build. No drywall to stack. Malevolent skies do not roil toward each other violent as a cauldron. Endless fields do not remain barren each morning. Winter does not last a whole nine months. There are no islanders to watch my every move. The paths are not littered with sheep skulls. No blackened gorse to snag my skirts. No fallen rocks to stumble over, or worse, draw blood on the way home. What starving animal might catch the scent of such a thing? At night-time the light does not come only from stars or oil. No smashed eggs stolen from eagles' nests to incite my wordless fury. I don't have to feel my mother's unremitting sorrow. Giant birds do not circle me on the way home. The empty coffins that my father built, used to sit outside our kitchen window so we would see them each morning – now they are all gone!

Elise's sisters have accepted the child as hers. The pipe is always filled. There is a choice of not one but several fine sofas in our apartment. There is art in all of the rooms. I often stand barefoot and look at it with a glass of wine in my hand, or gin, or whatever it is I want to drink. Mr Udnam's library has more books than a person could read in a lifetime. My child sleeps on Egyptian cotton sheets. I should be grateful.

I am not.

Roll a cigarette.

The smell of Elise is still on me and it is more than soothing.

I have taken to standing in the hallway in the morning with my horns on show so he sees me when he comes out of his room. He hates it. The maid has been told to only come into the apartment and clean when I am banished to our parlour. I have been naive. Elise has kept the worst of it from me. I see more what Mr Udnam is capable of and that he keeps her (and everyone else) in check with the fear of murder. He has men work for him all over this city who would do anything requested at his bidding. We all know it. He has all the keys to all the buildings and every one of them is bloodstained. While he parades through restaurants and newspaper interviews and city council meetings and fancy balls – his adulation is underlined with the scent of fear. I spit out a strand of tobacco. Put our little tin back on the bedside cabinet. Light up and inhale so deeply my throat burns and there is almost no smoke to come back out. Hope is asleep. She is so beautiful. A cherub with fat fists and a smile to heal the weary. Lay my cigarette into the ashtray and attend to my hair. Smoke curls up into the room. I can hear the maid sweeping the hallway out there. She will be gone soon. Usually Hope is out there with Elise in the mornings, or she is visiting in the consulting room with Mr Udnam for a short while, or they are off across town for a morning walk. Today they are both at home with me. He has done it to appease us.

Last night, he dragged Elise down our hallway. Locked himself and Elise into the consulting room. There was not a sound and that put fear in me more than anything. I paced. I held Hope until she slept. I considered trying to kick the door in. The clocks in our hallway have never ticked so hard or so loud. When she came out this morning she couldn't look at me. I made sure not to cry. I filled the washbasin and added her favourite lavender oil. I washed her body as gently as I do with Hope. I combed Elise's hair and kept my breathing steady when I felt her wince. He must have pulled her hair nearly out of her head. There is a clump missing at the back. I combed her hair over it. I put ointment on the areas that would bruise later on. I held her until she fell asleep. I lay awake. I listened to her breathing. I tucked her in and kissed her forehead then I got up and stood at the window. I hated myself for not going through immediately to kill him. I stared out at a dark city. Felt the creatures that walk underground getting restless. They could hear me if I called to them. I know it. I would not give my father the satisfaction though, I can't, I am better than him. It's what Hope needs me to be. Whilst I am tempted lately to give in to the evil I could call to me in his name, I won't give in. I am scared of what will happen to us because we still keep trying to play fair. Good people are always at a disadvantage. What can we do to Mr Udnam when he is willing to torture anyone who gets in his way and then lie about it and parade himself around this city like a hero among men and so many important people would absolutely protect him by their presence and approval and money and time – all so they can bask in the reflected power he wields.

None of them would help us even if we asked them to.

Elise and I cannot continue this way.

He won't touch her again.

This morning the scent of tobacco seeps into lavender that the maid liberally doused on our pillows. I have a white rage in me. It is still as a great lake untouched by the wind or even the ripple of a fish. I imagine a great white lake that is the shape of a giant tear. In the middle of it, a single drop of blood unfurls and disappears.

I bury my face into Elise's hair and breathe deeply.

She sleeps beside me, fitful and tear-stained.

Mr Udnam keeps his eyes trained on Elise at all times now.

We eat dinner in silence each night.

It has been three years.

He is so very far from good and it will never be in him to see that remotely – let alone closely.

Mr Udnam has a truly terrible sense of his own greatness.

He has the serenity of a man entirely without conscience.

There is no end of other people for Mr Udnam to blame. That is all he does. He will pay, bribe, bully, cajole, he will tell people anything they want to hear about how great they are – so they will like him, or he will do them favours so he can get as many people as possible to owe him publicly. The more he can hold over other people and the more publicly he can masquerade as a decent human being, the better. His self-wonder borders on psychopathic. It leaves no ripple in the water. I can see that great tear-shaped lake in my mind's eye and it has a coffin bobbing at the side of it.

The police do his bidding.

Lock doors for him.

Make sure people do not go down corridors he does not want traversed.

Elise has pleaded with him to not make me leave so many times now and my daughter screams like she is opening a portal to hell each time I am sent away. If they send me away I'm pretty sure Hope will open a portal to hell. All the creatures I have chosen not to call upon would come to her aid.

There is no nursemaid who can soothe her when I'm gone.

She is mine.

Nothing can change it.

I kiss my daughter's forehead.

Close the shutters.

Select an ornate umbrella from the hat stand.

The maid has clicked the front door shut. I ease it open quietly.

No sound from the consulting room.

Mr Udnam is passed out.

In the hall mirror my horns shine now.

Rubbed with oil.

So pretty.

They have neat ivory rings all the way up them.

Deepened into a blue-black shade at the base.

Like sheep or goats' horns, they will keep growing for the rest of my life. Most species only have horns on the male. I tip my head this way and that. Such a waste – when a female wears them so well!

All down our hallway are stags' heads.

He is hunting with a frenzy.

They are mounted with glass eyes.

Long antlers.

I put my bonnet on.

It deeply bothers me each time I do it now. I am less myself than I was a second ago. I won't meet my own eyes in the mirror when I have it on. There is a huge long picture frame opposite the stag heads. It is filled with butterflies.

Gossamer wings.

Some are so fine they are see-through!

All staked through their body.

Pinned to black velvet.

They have been collected all over the world. I have learnt to read the names neatly printed below each one. Tortoise-shell. Swallowtail. Red Admiral. Blue Morpho. The Mourning Cloak. Admiral. Peacock. Dogface. Queen Alexandra Bird-wing! Montezuma's Cattleheart. Trans-Andean. Dead Leaf Butterfly. Glasswing. Viceroy. There is a Giant Owl butterfly right in the middle. My brother used to catch beetles. Put them in a glass jar. Freeze them in the stone store then pin them to the outside of our croft.

— What are you warning the winds against, little brother?

— You.

— I'm not the one we need to worry about!

— I'm not worried what you will do, Jessie, I am worried what he is going to do to you. Da is scared of you, you know that, so they . . .

He had pointed at our croft with beetles pinned all over it.

— urr the eyes of the dead. They'll see what's coming before we do and they'll tell me first.

— What will you do?

My brother had looked at me so levelly.

— I'll kill him.

84

Bang, bang, bang!

The front door is being hammered so loud the ornaments rattle.

I don't want them to wake Elise or Hope!

I yank it open wide.

– Hello.

– Alright Jessie, we urr here tae see Elise.

There are five of them, red-haired, they stand shoulder to shoulder, short to tall, the complete spit of their sister.

– She's asleep.

– Is he in?

– Aye.

– Can we see him?

– No.

– How long are you going to watch ower fir them, Jessie?

– I'll leave when Elise bids me to do so.

The little one steps forward and looks up at me – whilst the eldest lights a fag.

Every one has identical amethyst eyes.

They are not the kind of girls you'd want to fight. Elise was not wrong when she told me there is not a posh bone in her – truly, in the best possible way.

The girls crane their heads to try and see down the hallway.

– Where is Hope?

– Elise is letting her sleep in the big bed with her. I've an errand to run, youz'll huv tae go.

Pull the door firmly closed.

I don't let them into the apartment ever and barely do they get even the briefest sight of Elise.

– Is ma sister okay?

85

— They are both fine.

— Are you?

— Aye.

I go down the stairs slowly enough to make sure they are trailing behind me.

It is a magician's trick.

Look at this hand! Over here! Look at me! Don't go in there and look at them.

They are even worse than ever, lately.

Fighting.

Elise can't have been off the pipe a day since last October. The girls march away home. They eye people suspiciously in this part of town. I walk up the High Street. Breathe in clean cold air. I love mornings like this. The errands must be done while they are sleeping. Everything is on account. I never pay. I go along George IV Bridge and then down Chambers Street and cross over into James Thin's bookshop. I like it in here. There is a parcel of books waiting and I've nae time to browse. I wish Elise and I would have a tiny bookshop somewhere. It would have four cats and a pot of tea always brewed and Hope to play in the aisles and talk to customers at the till. Then when she was bigger she'd take the place over and Elise and I would tend a herb garden with things in it to cure everything. We'd make jam and kiss each other and be glad for each of our days together.

I have got all the messages my love will need when she wakes. An orange, freshly peeled, so she can smell something good before she opens her eyes, a tiny perfume bottle, her books and then just a brief stop at the candy man's basket – Elise has the sweetest tooth of anyone, she is like a child in a woman's body.

I pick up a small box of Turkish delight.

– Flavoured with rose!

– Braw.

It is the only thing I pay for with cash. I hurry back down the close. The building is almost finished now. He's been years at it. I hurry into No. 10 Luckenbooth Close. Run up the stairwell. I tip my head back every time – look up at the cupola all the way above me. Imagine all the people who've walked these stone steps. For hundreds of years, people going round and round the stairwell like the cogs of a clock. Past and present and future passing each other by. The dead, the living, the barely living and the cowards and the ordinary and the brave, all winding round each other through time.

I love this stair.

Now I'm just a part of its history too.

The devil's daughter and his grandchild, passing through, like all the other people who have gone before us and who will come after. Mr Udnam has put lamps in. Gas is out. He has ripped the building apart and put most of it back together. Soon tenants will come back. It was far better for nobody to be here, so Elise could go into hiding. Then bit by bit she began to go out until everyone around them has just seen Hope as her own. He has left a few of the walls open though. They will need to be closed up. Perhaps they are still open for the plumbing; they have that all over the New Town.

I go in and click the door shut.

The apartment is silent.

Lay gifts and messages by Elise, kiss her cheek, take Hope and lay the child heavy onto me. We have a fancy stroller for her; she walks most of the time but it's handy for busy streets. Elise insists I bump her down the stairs when we go out. Keep my coat on and settle our girl. I bump her down the stairs so carefully she doesn't feel a thing. I will let Elise rest awhile.

Hope wakes up on the High Street.

I offer her my hand to squeeze.

The child wraps her fist around it.

It's all she needs to descend to the underworld. One hand to hold onto like a balloon back in the real world. It can lift her back out again should she need it to.

We turn right onto Victoria Street.

Pass the cheesemonger, the tailor's, the lace petticoats and linen, wooden brushes and down toward Bow Well – the smell is rank.

I need to be somewhere old.

The city has stood her ground so long and today I need it to hold me. Hope can no doubt sense all the executions that happened at Bow Well. They even hung the hangman in the end. Locals lynched a captain. A hundred Covenanters had their spines snapped right there. Maggie Dickson got hung then woke up in her death carriage! They hung her for having a baby without a father. It is how it is. Men decide what goes in women's bodies and what is taken out. How and when and in which way those things occur.

At least the law couldn't hang Maggie Dickson twice.

I want to be in the most haunted place that will serve me above ground level.

The spirits will protect Hope and me a wee while.

We duck into the White Hart.

Nod at the barman.

Let the wee one eat a bit of orange and then she falls asleep again. A feeling that the winds are coming in. All the way from my father's croft to here. Think about my mother. I couldn't protect her from him. I won't make that mistake again. What to do next time Mr Udnam does it? My ma said: only love a man who reads books and understands them properly. If they don't read books don't go to their bed. Ever! It wasn't them she wanted, it was what they knew. My mother thought if she found out enough, one day she'd come across a way to turn an evil man good.

I know better.

A small glass is slid across the table to me and I smile without looking up.

Pick it up and drink.

— I have a dagger in my stockings if you want to kill him.

— What are you doing here, Elise? I left ye asleep. Yer sisters called.

Elise kisses me.

She peeks at Hope, joins me at my side of the table, nods for two more drinks. Elise takes my hand and places it on her thigh. There is indeed a dagger. She grins so wide and wicked that I may have to marry her before sundown to save our immortal souls.

— We'll have to go this time. We can't let him do that to you again. I mean it, Elise.

— I know.

— Are you sore?

— I'm okay.

She is lying to me so I don't feel her pain.

— Where will we live?

— In a boat, middle ay the sea. Ye got a boat, Jessie?

— Not a boat really, I wouldn't call it that, no.

— What ye got?

— More like a small vessel. If it's still there after all these years.

— Grand.

— I'm not sure three of us will fit in there, Elise.

— We can squeeze up!

— It's not appropriate fir raising a respectable young family, this vessel.

— It's the right one fir us then.

Elise is looking directly into me. We have both been avoiding the truth of our situation. He numbs us with things to smoke and wear and sleep and eat and time passes. We think of Hope and how to provide for her somewhere else and we stay another day.

— It can't go on, Elise, I won't let it.

— I know.

Elise's eyes are purple until the iris and then they are navy blue, like the line of the horizon. I can see us sailing into that blue in my old coffin. No white teardrop lake with spirals of blood. It would be clear skies. One healthy, funny, crazy toddler and Elise up front, catching fish. I would show them tides and moons, skies and seas.

We can seek another shore to take us.

Three policemen in uniforms appear at the front of the bar. Mr Udnam's spies.

We can't ever tell who will say if they've seen us.

Elise pulls me quickly through the back and the dish-washer man lets us out into an alley. The back of Edinburgh Castle looms way above. Hope sleeps, her feet splayed. We take an end of the stroller each and lift her up the steps. Elise's pretty mouth offers words – proclamations – spells, incantations. She is speaking in tongues, ranting at all that is wrong, her soul focused only on escape. In the apartment she unwraps the binds around my horns, then settles Hope into her bed, returning.

Brandy.

Pipe.

She tastes of alcohol and smoke, pulls me in toward her, slows all of time. Her fingers trace the fine points of my horns. I slip down onto my knees between her thighs. We do it quick and hot like this. I feel that same complete exhilaration as Elise moans out.

He pushes the door open.

Stands.

I look up at him.

Unsheathed.

The way he least likes me.

I haven't seen him since last night and he doesn't even look guilty. Elise is up fixing her dress and saying she is going to get Hope who is awake again and screaming like all of hell has opened and every spirit is rushing out toward us.

I see the knife then.

It is silver.

Mr Udnam turns it one way, then the other: a practised move.

— You can't kill us.

He points the blade toward me.

— I'm not going to kill them. I'm going to kill you!

— Why?

— You are an abomination, I knew I would have to do this ever since I first saw those!

He points to my horns.

– Don't come near me.

– Hope is old enough now, she doesn't need a nursemaid any more and neither does Elise!

He gestures toward the top of my head again and I wish I had bound them this morning, I was stupid to think he was getting used to it. Every time they are exposed or commented on by him, I fear for the nubs on Hope's head. I can't believe my daughter shares blood with this man and for a minute I know exactly how my mother must have felt.

He steps forward.

All the spirits in the building and the underworld flood across the city.

They flow up the stairwell.

Into this room!

All to see the devil's daughter fight a mortal man.

It is not in my want to kill any more, though. Elise's love has dissipated that in me. If I kill him even if he is a bad man then I am no better than my father. If I act from anger or entitlement or bitterness then I am no better than him. I chose to kill because of what he did to my mother and brother, to the people in our community, for those exact reasons.

I've always had a choice to make – to be me, or him.

I can't be him.

I realise this at that moment, with great embarrassment and disappointment in myself because if there was ever a time I should be protecting my own this is it. I can't kill again and still think that I am a good person. Every atom of my being is screaming at me for it!

It is in my want to cure him.

I know I could do it if I had the time and focus and energy. Who could be a greater healer than the devil's child? One who has true evil running in her veins but who won't ever turn to it. I know now that I won't use what my father did. I made my choice when it came to evil. I made my decision. I will not back down no matter what the circumstances are – I am better than him, I am better than I ever knew I was and it is so sad it has taken this moment for me to know!

My heart is pure.

Still, I have a woman who loves me and who I would one day make my wife if I could and we have a child to protect.

I lower my horns and look directly at him.

– What the fuck are you doing, Mr Udnam?

He points the knife at me and it is sharp as anything I've ever seen.

– I don't want to do this, Jessie. I have no choice! My fiancée lays with you in that bed, my daughter turns to you, every corner of my house vibrates with your energy. The whole building does! I am taking it back for me, for my family, for my future tenants. Luckenbooth is not your home any more. You have horns on your head! It reminds me every single day that you, Jessie MacRae – you are evil!

I laugh.

– What are you laughing at, Jessie?

– It's fucking ridiculous, Mr Udnam. What you are is, what you say other people are – over and over again.

– Liar.

– You've left bruises on her, you've hurt her again and again. Now you want to do the same to me. Don't pass this off as some fucking mercy mission, Mr Udnam! I'd advise you not to touch me, in this life or the next.

– You're a witch!

– No, your fiancée is the witch, she cast a spell on me

without even trying the first time I saw her and there is little she can't cure given the right herbs. I am not the witch,
Mr Udnam. I'm the devil's daughter and I have no fear of
evil, not of my father, or of you!

The child cries out.

I turn to tell Hope to go back but she is already running
toward me down the hall and there is fear in my gut as I turn
back around to stop him going near her.

He is right behind me.

Mr Udnam jabs forward and stabs me as hard as he can –
right through to the heart.

He grunts.

Fat red hands shake with rage.

The knife is still in me.

I turn to look into his eyes and he looks triumphant, then
afraid.

Hope runs into the room barefoot. Tiny feet thud, thud,
thud. Blood billows across the floor at my feet as if I have
spun around with a crimson gown on a ballroom floor and
the lights are coming down so pretty and light. Mr Udnam
pulls the knife out with some effort and in full view of our
child he plunges it back into my gut.

I whisper it low . . .

– I curse you and your precious Luckenbooth for eternity.

Elise runs toward him with her dagger raised.

Hope has got hold of my skirts. She is tugging and roaring, her face red.

– Mama, Mama!

I fall to the floor just as Elise stabs him once from behind
but she has missed any vital organs, just grazed him, he pulls
the knife out of her hands and turns and stabs her over and

over, again and again. Hope screams. My hand reaches out. I have to hold her back from running to Elise. Her heart is gone. I feel it as my own flickers out.

The toddler shakes with rage looking from Elise to me.

My father appears at the door.

Mr Udnam raises his knife.

I see Elise's spirit rise up from her body as our child's throat is slit.

— You can't ever have her or us, better we be in spirit than stuck with you here!

I roar.

The building shudders.

All the limbs of Luckenbooth lock together to try and contain my rage. I curse him, and everything he touches to eternity. I curse those who protect him. I curse those who demanded my silence for his favour. Rain batters down onto the streets. The skies darken. My lover's skin is still scented from her morning bath. This man disgusts every single fibre of my soul. This life is not all there is. Our actions don't end here. I have always known that to be true. I rise up out of my body. Turn to see it laying on the floor behind me.

Hold my hand out for Elise to come to me, away from him.

My daughter has stepped out of her body, just as easy as if she were getting out of bed.

Children don't need to question it. They are so close to the other side anyway, so newly arrived, going back in this other realm is not so hard for them.

I lift her up.

— What did you do, Jessie? This is your fault.

My father says it from the door.

Still I roar, I roar and I roar. A noiseless vibration to take down all things. Timbers are shuddering. In the body of the building insects appear in larvae. One day they will take this entire building down. I won't stop until all the structures fall and are rebuilt again. I put a sickness into Mr Udnam. I don't even look at my father but before I turn I note there is a cavity still – in the centre of his chest.

– I want her head!

He shouts it at Mr Udnam and then points at my body.

It lays on the floor surrounded by a red-black sticky moon.

Skirts billowed.

Every wall spattered in blood.

My beautiful horns are even longer and sharper now in death – than they ever were in life.

1928

Flat 2F2

Flora (33)

It's not my cage

THE CHURCH is so pretty. Flora has not burst into flames. Because it is late, nobody is there to hear the young minister's sermon. He appears earnest and clever. Candles are lit all through the main hall.

Mr Udnam gets on his knees. Prays. He prays for so long, Flora fears he must be praying for the absolution of all their souls one by one. Candles flicker. Saints look down on her. Like they are so perfect! Jesus holds his face up to his mother's breast. Eventually, Mr Udnam gets up and sits back down next to her. The pew creaks.

— Have you prayed already?

— Yes I have, Mr Udnam. I prayed for forgiveness.

— For what?

— Everything.

— Good. We need to keep our house in order, give them less filing to do when we get upstairs. Did you know I'm going to make No. 10 Luckenbooth Close the first housing association in our city?

— What does that mean?

— Cheaper rent, maybe even a tenancy agreement.

— A noble cause.

— That's what I do. I support others, to better their lives.

— So I've heard.

— I've founded seven charities in this city now, all under one name.

— Your name?

— No.

— What is it then?

— Hope.

As he says this, there is a flutter of cold air. Flora turns around and sees that the door to the cathedral is closed.

— I am on the board at eight organisations.

— How fortunate for them to have your expertise, Mr Udnam. I hope they appreciate it.

Flora turns her head to the left; looking in her bag on the side furthest away from Mr Udnam, she takes out a phial. While Mr Udnam fixates on his own might and benevolence, she inclines her head and sniffs a bump off the back of her hand. She has got so good at this; even the Virgin Mother looks impressed.

Flora puts the phial back in her pocket.

Picks up her glass.

He didn't notice her carrying it all the way down the stairs.

Only sees his own name in history. Nothing more!

She sips her Tom Collins. It is so good. Extra strong which is exactly what she needs. The minister looks down toward them and she half-raises it. Cheers to him and his fancy black frock! The things some men have to do to feel comfortable in a dress.

— I am the most moral, upstanding, philanthropic, God-fearing man that has ever been known in Edinburgh. I could call the police on that young man and have every person at that party locked up. I can do anything I want. I know his father. I know everyone. You can't move in this town without someone who knows me and admires me! I am not bragging. Only failures do that. I am just telling you how it is. Those parties have to stop. I will give him an eviction notice! I do not want the authorities . . .

He coughs until his face turns purple.

— I don't want them . . .

He wants police in that building even less than we do.

— Don't worry, Mr Udnam. We won't do it again.

— I can't . . .

— I know.

— Do you hear me?

— Aye, it won't happen again. I promise!

There is spittle around the edge of Mr Udnam's mouth.

Mr Udnam will get his statue to himself in this city, of course he will.

He stares at Flora like the fires of hell are in the pit of her stomach and only the power of God will put them out. He glances at the minister. Looks straight ahead, to the front of the church. There is a feeling stronger than repulsion. Flora feels like she has to leave immediately. It takes all her will to remain seated. The man nods at the minister going out as a new one comes to takes his place.

— Can I smoke in here?

Mr Udnam shakes his head at her in disapproval.

— But the incense . . . they'd never even notice.

She puts her tobacco back in her purse. Windows cast tunnels of moonlight down the main hall. The moon is so big out there tonight, illuminating every crevice of this city.

It makes her feel wanton. There are huge pillars. If God were to design a house, it would be filled with stone arcs and archways like these. People can't even see how much they can achieve just through their own talent when they put their minds to it, without any ideas of God having anything to do with their creations, just sweat and hard work and design and what people can achieve is so extraordinary.

— You know *he* designed you, just perfectly.

— What?

Flora gets a shiver down her back.

The minister has said it in passing as he leaves his shift.

Long chandeliers of candles hang from the beams. Light flickers and jumps in the eaves. The ceiling is painted a spectacular blue. Like the skies on the day she saw Baśka and met the only man she has ever loved. The holy man is right. She was designed exactly as she was meant to be and there has never been a thing wrong with her mind, or soul, or body — what a thing to realise. She feels peaceful, like there has been an epiphany that will change how she feels in all the coming days.

— Will you remarry, Mr Udnam?

— I never married. My fiancée left me and ran away to New York with our maid.

— I'm sorry.

— I'm not.

He booms that out.

The older minister looks at both of them from the pulpit.

What is he doing up there?

He's not making a joint — she's pretty sure of that — although God knows they could all use one.

— My fiancée and her maid were wicked women, delusional types, liars, it is only themselves they deceived, not me! I serve God and this city and its residents without distraction now. It is better this way.

— I'm sure it is, Mr Udnam.

— Women are different these days too.

— So I keep hearing.

— It's since you all got the vote, Flora.

— Amen.

— Not in a good way, young lady. It was bad enough when we let you vote over the age of thirty, but you weren't happy with that were you and so now any woman can vote! That's the problem. A woman doesn't even need to be educated or have a husband or be God-fearing to vote now. It isn't practical. It helps society in no way whatsoever. Then there are women walking around dressed — like you!

Flora nods.

— Amen.

Mr Udnam closes his eyes and he is opening his fat slick lips in silent fervour and prayer.

By the smell of him, he's already doused in spirit.

He will be here for quite some time.

Flora gets up and tiptoes away.

She needs to walk for a little while.

Mr Udnam won't go back up to Greig's again tonight. He won't call the police. She doesn't want to go back until later, either. Outside she lights up. Goes down past the Tron. People are out, eating and drinking. Across the road and up past Old College. She goes onto Nicolson Street then down around the corner until she can see Arthur's Seat. It is the best big, dead, old volcano that could ever be right in the middle of a city. Her favourite time to see it is when the sun is going down against the crags. They look like they are on fire. The entire thing turns rose gold. Then it disappears and the clifftops are black and moody again. Lean against a building. Light a smoke. There are advertisements all over the wall opposite. Camp Coffee. HP Sauce. Sunlight Soap. Those crags look like the jagged faces of ancient men glowering across the city. They always have done. They always will. Once this was all water and ice and then plants and animals and eventually people and cars and motion and fashion and food and those that have and those that will never have. Those crags have watched over it all. Up there to the top of the crags: that's where she is going. Hard rubble underfoot makes her unsteady but she knows this path too well to stop and she knows what she wants.

Flora's thighs hurt. Her shoes are so wrong for this.

She doesn't care. Right up to the top of the crags is where she can see again. The sea is a steady dark blue in the distance. It is dark but she knows exactly where the island is. Big ships will be sitting out there on the Firth of Forth. Sailors will be drinking in the Port of Leith. Flora can see all the church spires. One for every pub they say. The outline of Edinburgh Castle and Holyrood Palace down at the bottom. Flora climbs the rocky path of the crags until she can see the whole city skyline sparkle before her. The lights across Edinburgh are tiny dots – like human souls. Like each soul has it in them to ignite another one. As if they really are all linked, even if it rarely feels like it. Like all the freedom they are trying to find in the twenties is just a light that so many other people will snuff out. Greig is in among those lights, in his tenement, dancing. The whole city sparkles best at night. It is when she comes into her own. It is worth the risk. All of it is. The drag balls – they need them. Where else can they be properly free? Greig used to go to drag balls in Harlem when he was working in New York. He told her sodomy stopped being punishable by death there in 1861. After that you got life imprisonment for it.

Flora rubs her hands on her arms to try and warm herself. She begins the descent. Thinks of how in 1885 they changed that to Clause 11 of the Criminal Law Amendment Act or the Labouchère Amendment – to protect girls from prostitution with a side clause against sodomy between men specifically. Two years in jail, with or without hard labour. Flora nearly goes over on her ankle and picks her way down more carefully. What kind of a world locks people up for loving? Hard labour for sodomy or oral! Oscar Wilde got three good years for it. Flora does not want to be touched like Greig does, though she'd defend his right to be touched in any way that makes him feel good – as long as his partners are of legal age and willing. What act is really perverse then? None is; sexuality is weird and ugly and strange and terrifying and real and beyond the realms of actual reason. But right now she doesn't care about any of it. All Flora wants is to get into bed and be held. To read quietly next to him and to make a cup of tea in the morning and sit together in silence.

It has taken no time to get back.

Through the front door and straight to the bar. The perfume smells stronger than it did before and cigarette plumes have coloured the air blue-grey. Lights are turned down lower. A circle has formed around the walls. Another circle inside it begins to rotate the other way. Flora meets her ex-lover's eyes across the room.

Still that gladness to see his face.

— Baby, come here.

Over to stand beside him, an arm draped around her shoulder. A drunk poet to the right points at a man in a black suit.

— Is he from the Spec Society? I thought they only met at the university. There's another two over there . . .

— He is, Flora says.

— How do you know? the poet asks.

— I fucked him in the William Playfair room. Afterwards he cried like a baby. There are no female members in the Spec Society, unless they are visiting for some other reason you'll never see a woman in there.

— No, the poet says approvingly and skulks away.

The room is beautiful. Deep teal wallpaper. A woman is down on her knees now. Another is strapped to a chair. Legs parted. The whole room is a mass of flesh. A man is having his cock sucked while another woman kisses his neck and a woman dressed all in black fucks her with a strap-on. Another woman steps over the man's face and sits down casually, as if she were in a fine dining room.

Greig's fingers slide up her legs and he is licking her. She arches her body toward him despite herself. He looks up from between her thighs. Flora drags him up by the hair.

— You're such a hideous prick, she says.

— I am, that's true.

She takes him by the hand over to the bar, flushed, both dress straps down, stockings gone, lips red as her cheeks, she takes two clean glasses and a small silver spirit measure.

– French 75, ta, doll!

Flora adds three parts Edinburgh gin, one part fresh lemon juice which she squeezes out by hand, a spoonful of sugar powder, then champagne. Tops both glasses until they fizz. It is so cold and crisp on the tongue. The feeling of her ex-lover's kiss on the nape of her neck pulls her in again. They kiss – hot and cold, lemon and gin, champagne and tobacco.

– Come on, into my room. I've got it clear, just for you.

He unlocks his door and they disappear into the familiar dim. Sit down on the edge of the bed. All the shoes and suits are gone. He looks sad. Concerned.

– I'm unsteady without you, he says.

– No, yer not.

They lay down, face to face, noses touching, small light kisses.

– I've done worse than just hurt you, I know. It doesn't feel okay, Flora. You are not someone I will get over. Not ever. Not now, not in ten years, not in twenty. I love you so much I don't even understand it. I know I wounded you. I did much worse than not turn up.

Flora can't speak.

They have never done this conversation.

He whispers to her so quietly.

His eyes are blue-black in the dim light.

The city is falling asleep around them.

All those lights, from all those souls, are just so fragile – they need to be tended to, protected, cupped in two hands. A huge moon slides down toward the horizon. The glow of their lights reaches out to each other always. From one part of the city to the other. Even over the sea. Through time. The light people come from – what souls emanate and society can't yet see — is what they all reach for and miss when it is gone. When a person's own light is dimmed. When a soldier takes a polar cub to a woman to try and see light in her eyes but she has already found her light in another. Or when a polar cub protects the light in hundreds of soldiers — is able to restore their light to them or to keep it flickering longer — until they go home to their children who also hold their own light. When someone lays in a bed with the wrong one and they miss a light they feel they might never know. But sometimes on a street — or in a bar or in a bedroom — those first bits of light separated out — find each other again.

Levi (32)

fear fir the mermaid

DEAR LEO, something bad has happened. Strike that – a series of bad things have unraveled. Do you remember I said there was this indent on my bed at night? Like a ghost comes to watch me sleep? Well, there are two. Actually, I believe there are three. The second one is heavier and it feels exactly like when Mom used to sit on my bed holding you. I am not hallucinating. I drew three anatomically correct skeletons on the wall behind my bed whilst asleep. Two women, one with horns, and a child of about two or three years old in the middle. Every bone was marked and filed absolutely perfectly. I don't know what I was thinking! I'm damn spooked, brother. I can't remember doing it. When I went to sleep last night that indent on my bed was so pronounced. I fell asleep thinking of my mermaid and then no more thoughts until I woke up and stood at the end of my bed and saw the two skeleton women and the child drawn out perfectly – they were just looking at me.

I am not a superstitious man, Leo, but I feel too freaked out to sleep in that apartment again tonight and it is draining my energy even just to think about the place. Nothing in my life has been right since this morning. The Four Horsemen of the Apocalypse are pounding down my dreams. When I do finally find it in me to go back into the world of sleep, I fear I will fall so deep and hard I won't come back out. It does not help a man rest easy. I am tired and I pace. I feel like death is near me. I open the door to the stairwell and just stand there. I am missing something! I do not know what! It is driving me crazy. I am agitated all the time. I hide so many things. I am so used to doing it that I thought I had that skillset down to a fine precision. I didn't notice before but there is a basement in our tenement that has a big lock on it. When the air-raid sirens call we don't use our basement. We have to go down to the blackout bunker in Mary King's Close. It is like going back in time, Leo. The arches down there are damp and it smells of something I can't even describe. Tonight Mr Udnam came to me and asked if I still study law and I said no. He said he needed my legal advice so I better look out my law books. What choice do I have? My options are limited in this town right now. I looked at him like a man who had just been found by the head of the highly esteemed Dick Vet College in bed with a bone mermaid . . . oh, it is so bad, brother! I made the mermaid. She is mine. I won't let the other men take responsibility. I can't, I'm not that kind of asshole.

To be honest, it is hard to tell what kind of an asshole I am lately.

I need to grow up.

Something has taken my soul.

No. 10 Luckenbooth Close is the reason I cannot sleep.

Even as I write this, can you see my handwriting is getting so much smaller?

That day started much like usual. In the morning at the

Dick Vet there was a group of penguins walking down the corridor, they are cute as anything. We had a lot of budgies in, there were the usual dogs and cats getting treatment, some spiders, a mouse, three chinchilla rabbits. It was happy chaos. It always is in the Dick Vet. There was a sun bear from Edinburgh Zoo. It was also the beginning of a series of lectures by a professor who was up from London. They were set up to be held in the room next to the bone library. The professor wanted to see how I file bones, he wanted to see all the books where they are accounted for. I had to hide the mermaid when he was in so I just threw a blanket over her.

I was harassed — you may as well know that from the start.

Things have gotten hard here and I should have gotten out weeks ago. That's why I have not written.

It all started with this old woman who was drunk and screaming at Mr Udnam about her daughters, says she had six and that they are all dead because of him, all red-haired girls apparently. I didn't know what was going on and Morag who lives upstairs knocked on my door so I invited her in for tea. She told me a lot more about it. Apparently one of the red-haired sisters, the eldest one, had left home to become engaged to Mr Udnam; Morag said it was years ago but her aunt had known the girl Elise quite well. She told Morag that Elise disappeared one day and was never seen again, then a year later — her five sisters started a petition to find their missing sister. They go to the newspaper and the story is printed, then the very next night, they all die in a house fire. All of them. The smallest were just girls, younger than our niece! The mother of all those girls (the missing and the dead) is the drunk woman, so Morag says — and she was out on the close shouting and shouting. Mr Udnam got into her face and said something and then she ran off. I swear his eyes turned black for a second. Half an hour later we heard the sirens. The woman was found dead. Back broken. At the back steps to Waverley Station. It was a busy day. Nobody saw her jump. I just kept thinking — I don't even want to write it down — but did she jump? Did she? I don't think she did. I have seen what humans do to others. You know I have. Mr Udnam was going back into the stair and I swear he had shit himself, there was fear on his face.

I didn't see it at first. There are two cities in Edinburgh. There is one above ground and one below, one in the center and another on the outskirts. The one in the center seems to be able to do anything it wants and the one on the outskirts can only take whatever is dealt out to it; it all seems so damn familiar. There is the Edinburgh that is presented to tourists. Then the other one, which is considered to be the real Edinburgh, to the people who live here. There are the fancy hotels and shops and motorcars and trams and places of work, then there are the slums, starvation, disease, addiction, prostitution, crime, little or no infrastructure, no plumbing, no clean water, no rights . . . if the council want to go and take their homes down, they do. This is all on streets just ten minutes' walk from the fancy city center. When will these things change? Everywhere? When? All fur coat and nae knickers. That's a phrase the postman told me. It embodies this city. They keep children without families in a home on the other side of town and they train girls up as maids and sell them into the households of the wealthy. Boys get trained to sweep chimneys and then they get sold too. I had no idea! The area where the sisters died in the fire is notorious for early death rates – although not often from something as horrific as that.

I thought my day couldn't get any more awful, then my neighbor Greig in the flat below begins shouting – his wife has turned up! We didn't know he had one. She accuses him of living with a girlfriend there, which of course he has done for a long while. But none of us knew he had another home with a wife and kids that he lives in half the time. The wife then tries to stab the girlfriend with a fork! Police come out. They take the wife and girlfriend away. A reporter got a hold of the story from an ambulance attendant who was paid a few quid. Mr Udnam has a fit! He thinks the police are there for him! He stands at the door shouting that he helps the poor! That they are not getting into his building. He reels off every important person he knows – he is frantic! I've never seen a face so lined with guilt. I stayed watching from my window in the tenement as it all unfolded.

Then the police just leave.

Greig packs his things, hands Mr Udnam his keys, says he won't be back in this fucking city again. I don't think he will be either. He walks off shouting about Indonesia and sending for Flora.

There is a sick pulse in Luckenbooth and crazy things do happen around the full moon and right now we have a moon so big it's making the entire city feel like a film set. I have déjà vu every second of the day and I won't be able to sleep in that fucking building ever again. Do you know how long rats can go without sleep before they die?

Thirty-two days give or take.

I am a lot bigger than a rat but I can't see me making it beyond a month.

Since all that happened I was trying to drink myself unconscious so I could sleep at work. I hoped to pass out and crash for a week in the bone library but I didn't have a chance to do that because they fired me.

The bone library is no longer my domain.

I am heartbroken.

Don't ever go see a mermaid on the tip of a blood-red moon.

Far less after the Buckfast! It's a drink made by monks — those drunken cunts know what they are onto. Each barrel has a sediment and the lower you get in the barrel, the stronger it gets. I think me and the postman got through four bottles each, as potent as could be. We didn't know what we were doing, Leo. It's the weekend, most of the staff were away, we were singing, then we went into the labs and turned the taps on. We let some rabbits free, they went off hopping down a corridor, we had a quick turn at the shooting range, went to the distillery for more supplies. The postman took a photograph of me surrounded by sheep heads — not yet decomposed — all of them smoking. I was found asleep this afternoon by the head of the Royal Dick Vet College — in bed with a bone mermaid. When he asked me what I was doing with her, I told him we'd recently wed.

I suppose in my inebriation I didn't want him to think she was a slut.

I don't know where I will be by the time you read this, Leo, but I am definitely going to try to sail my way home. I am thinking of offering to work for my passage — all the way to New York if I can, if I can find any ships down at the docks that will have me.

I have been thinking and it's far harder to tell you about that.

There are many ways to fight what is wrong in this world and I know I have them in me.

Bad men are always coming.

Especially for people like us – and we are the good ones!

I think a lot about all the invisible lines we cross because of white men.

Any car journey can change from just sitting having a conversation – to going over one of those invisible lines where white people police those of color. Those moments when we are just going about our day. Then we get that feeling. The constant unfairness and cowardice wrapped in racism is about to take an action that could alter our life. The conversation stops mid-air. You pull the car over. People on the street look the other way. They look the other way and that makes them fucking complicit, Leo! Does it not? If they maintain silence to profit from racist men like those I mention, that means they endorse their racism. We must pick our battles. I have more than one to fight. I want to come home. I will sit my bar exam and I will stay the fuck away from monk-brewed alcohol and bone mermaids.

What has this city done to me?

I will focus on inequality in education.

I will teach a class on ideas. And on ideology.

How ideology is sold to us as a fixed thing that every infrastructure is based upon . . . but they are all just based on ideas. And those ideas were created so people could find a way to control billions of other people . . . a way to profit, a way to order society, a way to warehouse humans. I will enter the system from the inside and work my way out.

Who says it can't be done?

We must file our history differently and put the false stories to bed. There are no different races of humans; there are only humans and we are all made from stardust every single one of us, we are children of the universe and we are one massive fucked-up race and there is no God – only good and evil and every shade of possibility in between. Who will listen to my thoughts, Leo? Wherever I end up over the next few months – on a ship, or in a cell – I will write to you. I will do it on this pad and if it is taken from me, then I will write in the dust on the floor with my tongue.

They say we are helpless, they say we are weak, they say we are nothing . . . they are liars!

Life is so short. Who would want to have blood on their conscience? Blood of humans, of animals, of the planet? Who would choose to arrive into the next world with all that blood on them? There is no God wants murder in their name. Not a single one. Humans made that up to compensate for our own bloodlust, to sanctify it, to make it holy, to refuse the gallows, to avoid the cells . . . We keep our silence and do not act in ways we should because men with money pay poor men to hold guns up to other poor men or women to keep all of us in line. They own the people who own the armies who own the schools who own the hospitals who own the police who own our homes who own our rights and who can do anything they want – to anyone. They lock us up if we dare to think too loudly, let alone speak. Well, I am thinking, and I am ready to speak. And not in a letter to you.

Not in bones and not in code. There can be no peace, or change, in silence.

I hope with all my heart to see you again one day, soon.
I love you,
Levi

Part II

Ivy Proudfoot (17)

the night witches

THE NIGHT WITCHES fly in formations of three. Yevdokiya Bershanskaya is the regiment commander. Serafima Amosova is her deputy. Irina Sebrova has flown more missions than anyone else. I am obsessed with them. I can't jump into a biplane like they do but I can still do what I can considering, can't I? We have lost almost all of our family. First it was the Spanish influenza. That is the main reason Mum still drinks so much. She was left in a small flat in Paris with the bodies of her grandparents, aunt and cousins. It is a miracle she was still alive. They watched people dying in hundreds, then thousands, then millions. Nobody escaped that pandemic untouched. Mum survived and grew up to be permanently tense. Then there were both of the World Wars. We are strong people. We want to do what is right. We didn't ask for any of these things and now the person we loved most is not here.

We don't say out loud what happened, there is so much we don't know.

Every morning I place a glass of milk by my brother's door just like I used to do when he was home. Dad drinks it every single time and then he leaves the glass by my brother's door for me to take away later on. Neither of us mentions it. I wear my brother's pyjamas at night and I bake his favourite cake, over and over again, badly. I take the cake into our back garden and put it on the wall where he used to have his lunch. The foxes eat it at dawn. My green-eyed brother was happiest when he was dancing. He would try to lie to our parents but he could never pull it off – I always could. I write tiny notes to him. Leave them under the chest of drawers where he kept his cigarettes. I've taught myself how to smoke using his stash. I do target practice every morning on a range in our back garden which Dad set up for him. My parents don't say a thing when they see me going out in my dressing gown with his pellet gun. I shoot whether it is sunny or raining. I have stood out there in sleet and snow. I shoot when my stomach is cramping from my period. I shoot when I am sick or I have a cold. I have become such a good shot it is scary. I am aiming for one person each time: the person who sent him to a camp. They claimed it was going to be a place for the men captured from his regiment to work out their remaining days in the war. This is not what they go there for. One person ordered that to happen. When I lift up my brother's weaponry, I aim between the eyes of that person.

My brother was the best part of our family. I am one half of a circle now because there was never a me without him. We completed each other, yin and yang, him light with a touch of darkness, and me – I suppose there is at least a touch of light and the best of it, it came to me from him. He was the one that patiently kept explaining right and wrong to me, when he could see I did not naturally get it. There are photos of us as kids all over the house. We look out at the present day with no idea what is coming.

My mother named me Ivy after a girl she went to school with back in France. I have brown hair and grey eyes. My teeth are uneven. I have a heart-shaped face. I apply make-up every morning, I sing out of tune and – it is true – I will never bake like a wife. I have urges other people would find horrifying. I have been working in our boutique in town for three years. I am seventeen, which means I am old enough to kill people. I'd say so anyway.

Outside it is clear today.

I polish up old brass keys on the till.

Boil the kettle.

Place a new mannequin (in a top and trousers) on display in the window. Ask anyone from here to Fountainbridge – I dress a window nice as the ones in Paris. My mother takes me there every year. We never go to the flat where she lived with her family. She still has nightmares about the Spanish influenza pandemic. She lost all of her friends. She said the government failed them all. Streets were like ghost towns. Medical workers died unprotected. The stores ran out of things people needed. Jobs and industries folded. By the end of it there was no family left for my mother at all. Because of this my brother and I mean even more to her. Whilst I do not feel certain other normal things, I feel my mother's pain. I do not know what to say to her. She says that it will not be the only virus to take out humans. She says this won't be the only war. I listen. That I can do. I don't know how to comfort her. I am better with mannequins. They appeal to me. I have stuck many bobby pins in their eyes and not a complaint from one!

I am not proud of my urges. I know they are bad but it doesn't mean I can't use them for good. Hundreds of thousands of people have been trained to kill other people all in the name of this war. Murder is legally insisted upon by governments all over the world. Why is it that young men who kill are heroes, but a young woman who has the urge to do so is reviled? I don't particularly want to serve my country, I think it's run by idiots. I don't see why the poor have to die for fights started by the rich. I want to avenge my brother. This is the way to do it. I want to see fear in the eyes of men when I take their lives. It may not be the moral high ground. I have little care for that. Killing will not be my official job description. It is what my main duty will be. I have read everything the recruiters have given me. Imagine, just a shop girl – in Paris, armed and drinking with Germans.

I exercise daily.

As should every aspirational killing machine.

I'll do what I'm told.

Whatever it is – no matter how dangerous.

I'm motivated by the killing, though – let's be clear on that.

I like dressmaking, yes, but I'd rather raise a gun.

Are there any heroic dressmakers?

There are bound to be countless heroic seamstresses in the world.

Girls are not meant to think like this.

So they say.

They never ask us what we actually do think – certainly

not without telling us first what it is we should be thinking. And if we are not thinking what they have said we should be, then they say our thinking is wrong. If we tell them (men) what we think, they correct our thoughts. Thoughts leave our brains, exit via our mouths, hang in the air, ready to be shot down by their artillery all day long! We say we think a thing and they (men) ignore it or they (still men) say we just don't fully understand it. Then they expect silence. Or an apology. If neither is forthcoming, they look away. Perhaps they walk out a door. They rewrite the words that come out our mouths by teaching us to edit them inside our brains.

No?

They train us to actually go into our minds and begin to rewrite the words – correct them – before we even think them. It's clever. There are sanctioned thoughts. There are unsanctioned thoughts. There is sanctioned body hair (your head), unsanctioned body hair (mostly anywhere else). Girls having power is not sanctioned. Until it is. When they need to use it, for example. The Night Witches are proof. Teenage girls have as much courage as any man. They would rarely agree (men). Even if they see us commit acts of complete courage and heroism . . . they will write it out of their mind immediately. Then, condescend us to fucking hell and back until they feel good about themselves again.

Everyone who is lucky finds out their true calling. I hope I have found mine.

I am slight.

Look innocent as a church mouse.

Not that pretty – so I'm told.

Rummage around in the shop drawer to find a measuring tape.

On a pad there is the word – *RETRIBUTION* – written in red a hundred times.

There is much space between the lines. I don't write in full sentences any more. Only single words.

HOPE.

GOD.

DEATH.

ANGELS.

EVIL.

RETRIBUTION.

Tonight, Morag and I will go dancing at the Palais.

Morag is the only hard thing to leave behind. If my brother was the best part of our family then Morag is by far the best part of me. She is my heartbeat. First time I met her she was standing at Cupid's Corner (they only sell fruit drinks but you do get a great view of the dance floor) and I was smitten on sight. She was with an American at the time who was trying to leave the country. He worked for our landlord. Morag and Levi had been seeing each other since he helped her bring a new bathtub home.

I danced hard that night to try and impress her; two weeks later I stayed over at her place and I've been there every weekend ever since. Levi is gone now. Our happy threesome of cards and drinking and hungover walks is over and he asked me to keep Morag safe and happy and I've done that.

But I'm bored of selling dresses. I have strength to spare. I am young. I am not stupid. My years make me braver if anything. I do not need my mind manipulated to replace my own thoughts with ones written for me.

Killing is a good vocation for me. I know it's not socially acceptable, but nobody can say it won't be useful right now.

I will be efficient and mercenary given the right training and just one or two people to believe in me. Luckily I have found exactly that. Death by Ivy! Why is a girl so rarely afforded to choose who she is? Am I getting it wrong? Are these faulty thoughts? Are they just another thing I can't possibly understand?

Life is a series of ever-smaller lassoes thrown by the thought police.

They land around our thoughts.

Drag them along the back of a truck until the thoughts are scattered so far behind us we can't see them anymore.

My mum is obsessed with amphetamines.

After my brother died she stopped getting up, or washing, or brushing her teeth.

She did nothing.

It was her most interesting phase.

The doctor came.

He sat down gravely in the living room and ate a slice of Battenberg.

He insisted there was only one thing that could help her.

Amphetamines – two grams per day – to invigorate her blood.

My mother's blood is very weak.

Not so any more!

They said the amphetamines would help focus her time and energy once again. It has done that and then some. She cut our garden lawn with nail scissors when the lawnmower died. She sleeps upright in the living-room armchair with a duster or magazine or cocktail in her hand. Our house is so clean it squeaks. But of course there have been issues. Yesterday I found her in the kitchen with her ear up to a silent radio.

— Maman, it's six o'clock in the morning!

— Is it? I should get up.

— Go to bed!

— Ivy, *ma chérie* — can you tell if this radio is the kind that gives housewives subliminal messages?

We both looked at the radio.

— I think they all do, Maman!

My answer did not help her agitation any.

These days she's thinner than a whippet and does a fuck-of-a-lot of brass polishing.

Maman only speaks in French.

She doesn't like Edinburgh. Or its weather. Or its people. Or my father. She likes smoking and amphetamines. Expensive shoes with very high heels. Brandy and plastic. She is very thin and very French. She could out-French anyone across this entire city. We do not have my brother's body. I want to bring it home and lay it at the back door for my mum so she might one day sleep again. So she will stop rattling around like a wind-up tin toy. I know it is a stupid want. Aren't wants so often that way? My dad speaks French offensively poorly and only to irritate Maman. Amphetamine truly is the ultimate patriarchal conspiracy. Men are cleverer than us — it is quite clear. We do the cooking and cleaning and everything else for them and it is all for free. Then they give out amphetamines to keep us thin and efficient and more neurotic than ever. Dad thinks I will just get married. He doesn't know how many of his papers I read, or

how many war journals. I read every bit of political information I can get my hands on. What girls are usually able to
do is limited, but right now we are holding down nearly
every kind of job in this country! The war is presenting a
window of opportunity. Dad talks about that. He talks
about the progression of science. He is a nice man – I won't
lie. Everyone we know says the same. Except Maman. Dad
would like me to find a nice husband and have children. It
is quaint. My aspirations are . . . different. Why not
become a deadly killing machine?

The shop door tinkles.

A woman places her brolly in the bucket.

Her coat drips on the shop floor.

Death.

Counterblow.

REVANCHE!

If good people don't kill bad people, then the bad people
will kill all the rest of us. Without guilt. No second thought –
that's a fucking fact – and then they win.

No?

The female recruiter always browses the tea dresses for
a good twenty minutes before she comes over to speak to
me. I like Violet a lot. I don't know what she has done in the
war because she won't tell me. Her footsteps in the shop are
my favourite ones. I have given notice to my landlord; in three
days' time, I will leave No. 10 Luckenbooth Close and not
return. I prayed to God to give me an opportunity and he has
granted it to me. My brother was sent to a work camp. It was
the recruiters who explained to me what that really means.
Now I can go to war with a clear conscience. I know exactly

why I want to do this. My brother is not the only person we know who is gone. We had an aunt who was building bombs in a factory in the Highlands. She lost her hair and then all of her teeth. Her skin began to blister. She died at the end of the summer. It has happened to a lot of bomb-making women in northern Scotland. Our neighbours have lost three boys. My old English teacher was killed in service. So was the man from the chemist. In Edinburgh (and across the whole country) we count up our dead as the year goes on.

Like water in a flood – the numbers keep rising.

I will be fine!

Other girls do this.

The Night Witches fly with two pilots, in formations of three planes.

There is no room for parachutes and they do up to eight missions per night.

One plane up front.

Another two either side, just behind it.

Polikarpov U-2 biplanes are made of wood and hold only two bombs.

They idle the engine on approach so only wind noise can detect them.

The Nazis say it sounds like witches' broomsticks overhead.

It's said they only hear them at the very last minute – just before a bomb hits.

They fly at a different speed to the Nazi planes – much slower – and it makes the Night Witches hard to shoot down. I wonder what they do after a night of bombing. Do they sing along to the latest record they love? Do they dance in the mirror? Does all that stop? Do they gouge little strikes for all of the dead on their headboards? I would. I will. I will tally my death count up on my headboard, or carve marks into the underside of my shoe.

The Night Witches are the 588th Night Bomber Regiment of the Soviet Air Force.

I am not Russian or Ukrainian so I cannot join them.

I am half-French though.

Raised to speak best in my mother's tongue.

It's why the recruiters came to see me. I can pass for wholly French, and I usually do.

They have sent girls from all over the country to live in France and appear innocent and pretty and find out anything they can from the Germans. Or – like me, take actual missions when they are sent. I go behind Violet and space out dresses along the metal racks. There are three new polka-dot designs. A dark blue Lindy Bop. Pockets on a peasant skirt. Seven mustard tea dresses. Two black halter-necks. Parachute-silk knickers. Seamed stockings. Four pairs of high-waisted jeans. Pussy-bow blouses. A-line skirts. Pleats, tucks and shirring. Shoulder pads. Candy tops with a sweetheart neck-line. Belts. An Evergreen playsuit that I love so much I would fly any old plane eight hundred times just to see it in my ward-robe. I am shallow. My brother always told me so.

Violet goes up to the counter with a top.

She looks like a normal person.

Every time I see her, I learn more and more how to do this.

I go back behind the till. She nods so I know we can talk quietly.

— Violet, what if Nazis want to sleep with me?

— Say you won't until you are married.

— Who will train me next?

— F Section will train you as a field agent. You've already been cleared for security purposes.

We continue to talk at the till — just a young shop girl talking fashion in a tiny boutique while the leaves on the Meadows turn ochre and passers-by go about their day.

1956

Flat 5F5

Agnes Campbell (63)

the fraudulent mediums act

SHE HAS ectoplasm in her purse. It is a thick, clotted, mucous-like substance. It came from a vagina. It mustn't be exposed to light (the ectoplasm) so she has to dispose of it the right way. It didn't actually come from a vagina – the fraud just kept it stuffed in there. A common scam. The 'ectoplasm' is paper and egg white, mushed down with chemicals. A fake medium swallows it and regurgitates at will during her seance but this one had no gag reflex. She had to be stopped regardless. It's hard enough for anyone with genuine skill to be taken seriously. Agnes is entirely with Houdini: track down frauds. Get rid of them. Agnes had thought she'd be sick at the table this morning. Pretending to be a sitter. Watching as the woman lifted her skirts and flung out ectoplasm, expelled it into a bowl, then brandished it around at her audience wildly.

Agnes stayed behind after.

– I am a member of the Spiritualist Society.

– Aye? What the fuck d'ye want?

Agnes is small but she was raised with nine brothers on a worse side of town than this one.

– The government has repealed the UK Witchcraft Laws, she stated.

131

– Fucks sake, does that mean they'll no burn you?

– To deter fakes, like you, they've passed a new Fraudulent Mediums Act.

– Are you trying tae say you've really got the gift?

The woman snorted and Agnes tried not to clench her fist.

– Members of the real Edinburgh Spiritualist Society are warning people like you – that practising as a fraudulent medium is now dangerous. They'll put you in prison for it.

– Where d'you live? I bet yer no in a slum. You go out on Leith Walk and take a look at ma sons! Only three ay them have shoes. Ye see that washhouse up the street? I cannae get in there without money to pay fir it! We wash with every cunt else in our tenement. I am sleeping with eight, in one room! How many rooms have you got? You got an inside bog? D'ye shite on yer own pan? I bet you dinnae have to go into the fucking outhouse freezing yer tits off every fucking morning!

– There are other ways to get money than conning people in their grief.

– Well my cunt's broken and my mouth is tired ay being nice tae men and I couldnae conjure up a real fucking spirit if you held a gun tae ma heid, the factory is full and I've nae other fucking skills, hen. In fact every single day of ma life I wish ma useless husband was dead – so I dinnae have tae worry about him coming tae ma door at night and battering me up and down in front ay aw the bairns – so what exactly does your Spiritualist Society want me tae do? Conjure money like fucking magic?

– Getting put in jail for a fraudulent medium charge isnae going tae help any of yer kids, is it? Here, take this. And no, don't think I'm rich. I'm in a housing co-operative and my husband's sick but I bring spirits to me all day long even without the will to do so – it's just how it is. You girls are taking our trade and making it unsafe for us tae practise. I dinnae want tae go to jail cos you cannae stop tricking people and then they think I'm as bad as fucking you are.

The woman put Agnes's coins in her bra and lit a fag.

She'll be practising again but maybe a bit more canny with it.

Agnes is glad to be home after this morning's events. She heads down the hall to the kitchen. The ectoplasm has to be disposed of in the exact right way or she is for it this time.

She places it on the bunker, uncertain of what to do next.

– Is that what I think it is?

– Aye, Archie.

– If you block the kitchen sink with ectoplasm one more time, I'm fucking leaving ye!

She surveys her husband coolly. He is ten years younger than her, still in his very late midlife crisis. A bright crimson Teddy-boy coat is draped over the sofa and creeper shoes kicked off by the telly. She sets down a Peter Allan bag. Agnes has got some treats for her nieces, a few boxes of sweetie cigarettes, four Atlas comics and brightly coloured yo-yos. She can give them the gifts when they come over tomorrow for their tea.

– Do you have to do another seance, Agnes?

Agnes puts the kettle on.

Her husband is in his armchair staring at a blank telly.

– The telly is off, Archie.

– I just like tae look at it! Is that alright wi you? Fucks sake.

He tuts and inhales his cigarette furiously, keeps staring at the black screen.

He has a newspaper beside him.

— Another news story on the city planners. Agnes, they are shagging this city up the shitter, making it a wee toy town fir tourists. Edinburgh isnae a big city, it's a large village. There are already too many cars! That city council should listen tae me. They'll end up getting smog deaths ay, like they did in London four years ago, how many died there, Agnes? Thousands!

He triumphantly concludes his point by grinding his cigarette out.

Archie's quiff is lacklustre.

There is a half inch where his trousers ride up and expose thick white socks and very hairy ankles. Agnes looks at him in despair and once again dreams of a man who, like her, listens to Miles Davis and John Coltrane, one who buys her silk headscarfs and bracelets that jangle, one who takes her to bed after a brandy in the early afternoon, one who is not as hairy as a bear.

Someone who could make her feel . . . seen.

She wants a man who really, really — looks at her and *sees* her.

Men go after women with such conviction and then when they have them they discard them in plain sight. And just like Bluebeard, they keep the bloodstained keys to their women's souls hostage — while, of course, coveting any other women they now think they'd like to lock up in their make-believe tower. But the one at home better not go anywhere! Her days as a free person are done. Agnes feels so discarded by this man with whom she is legally bound to spend her entire life. He won't even leave her. She just has to live with being nothing to the person she is most often around. Agnes has to go to spirit lately – just to feel like herself.

    – So is the fake medium gonnae stop her Fraudulent Medium Act whatever it is then?

    – No. I blame Helen Duncan.

    – I blame Winston Churchill.

    – You blame Winston Churchill fir everything, Archie! Even our blocked sink.

    – The man's a fucking Druid!

    – I have no issues with Druids!

    – Aye, but we dinnae need one running the fucking country – do we, Agnes?

    – Helen Duncan should have stopped practising when they tried her under the UK Witchcraft Laws. She'd been at it for years! Churchill was right to abolish that law. Getting tried as a witch in the 1950s! In Britain! All that cheesecloth and theatre makes a mockery fir those of us who genuinely huv the gift! We've had the Fraudulent Mediums Act instead of the UK Witchcraft Act fir three years, Archie! The fakes ken they shouldnae be practising. I've had e-fucking-nough ay it!

Agnes roars at the kettle and she hears his silence grow louder at her outrage and frustration.

    – Frustration just has to come out, sometimes, Archie.

    – Aye! It does that.

Her husband hovers over his telly buttons with a haze of smoke around him. Even though it is early there is already an empty tin of lager by his slippered feet.

    – Any jobs this week?

    – No.

— Are you just gonna sit there watching *Billy Bunter, Andy Pandy* and the news?

— *Gies a fag!*

— Did you have to teach the fucking parrot to say that?

Agnes pulls her headscarf from the parrot's cage. His eyes are pure black with a bright yellow ring around them. He has a plume of vivid blue feathers which he preens most of each day. He pecks at her through the bars.

— I'm only keeping myself amused, Agnes, fir fucks sake!

— *Fir fucks sake fir fucks sake fir fucks sake* . . .

— Say pretty boy, come on Ovid, say pretty boy — fir Mama!

— *Fir fucks sake!*

— The seance will only take an hour, Archie, something is trying to get through hard this time. I can't stop them.

— Aye and I can tell you're nervous or you wouldnae be shouting in our fucking kitchen like that, so, who's coming from the real world?

— Dora Noyce.

— The Queen of Danube Street! The most famous madam in town, ay, visiting our wee flat! What an honour.

— Dinnae pretend you're no going down there, Archie. We both ken you do.

— Only fir tea and sandwiches!

— Aye, and the place really is just a YMCA with benefits. Okay then.

— Can you blame me, Agnes? The last time you touched me was in 1932.

— We did it in '47!

— Aye, and we were on those funny tablets yer pal gave us, I dinnae think it counts.

Archie hunches back into his chair.

Ovid pecks at seeds.

Drinks as noisily as he can from a glass tube.

The wind carries sounds down the close – buses, trams, people, all going about their day. Ovid wobbles his head from side to side and steps from claw to claw.

Agnes places two tapered candles on the table.

She unwraps a soft velvet black cloth and takes out a heavy crystal ball.

– Seers were just like chemists or mechanics in their time, Archie. I don't know why ye make a fuss.

– Bollocks.

– We just provide a link between this world and the other one. Sometimes it is required. Like your trips tae Danube Street.

– It's dangerous, I have to put up with how much it wears you out. We have to worry about whether the polis will come and convict you. I ken you dinnae think I care but I do, Agnes. Is this the last time?

– Aye, it's the very last one, Archie.

She opens the drawer and takes out her Ouija board and says the words only to soothe him and it will work for a wee while. Agnes places the Ouija board centre of the table. She arranges the planchette (a teardrop-shaped wooden pointer) in between YES and NO. There are two semicircles above. The first has numbers 0 through 9. The second holds the letters of the alphabet. GOODBYE is at the bottom of the board.

– It was the Fox sisters in New York who first made these, you know, Archie, in 1848! They asked the first board what it should be called and it spelled out OUIJA. When they asked what it meant it just spelled out GOOD LUCK.

— What time will Dora be here?

— Any minute. She's been tae London to visit a painter called Bacon who brushes his teeth with Vim apparently!

Agnes talks a lot before it happens and they can both feel it already. It's a wee bit like the few times they tried getting high — a buzzy coming-up sensation that something is started and cannot be stopped for a while.

The spirits never stop visiting Agnes in 5F5 No. 10 Luckenbooth Close.

Not since they moved here over thirty years ago.

Even when she doesn't host a seance for months (to appease her husband), they're always waiting, trying to get her attention. Perched on his armchair, or sat on the mighty unshared loo that Agnes is so ridiculously proud of. When she drags out their tin bath and fills it, spirits get in before she does.

The door goes as someone chaps on it then there are footsteps down the wee hall.

Archie hangs up Dora's lovely fur coat and settles himself down in case they need him.

In his cage, the parrot starts clicking, head bobbing.

Agnes settles herself at the head of the table.

Dora sits opposite her, the Ouija board between them.

The wind picks up outside.

The wooden shutter slowly creaks itself half open.

— Are ye good, Dora?

— Aye, Archie, I am, and you?

— Great, aye, nice to see you and Agnes doing the . . .

He makes a circle with his hand in the direction of the board unable to pronounce its name.

— I'm hoping fir a message, Archie.

— We're aw hoping fir a message, Dora. It's God himself who decides what we get!

Agnes tries not to visibly despair at her husband's verbal shite.

She takes Dora's hands across the table.

Their hands form a circle around the board. It's nice to do a board with Dora. They've known each other forever and the woman is so intuitive — she just lets Agnes do it. Agnes can feel herself drifting part way into the universe already, collecting particles, to a place where all things are bodiless. She imagines her husband turning on the television and seeing her out there, gathering different-coloured strands of energy. A feeling of luminosity is replaced by impenetrable darkness — it raises a vermilion flush to Agnes's cheeks.

Blindness in one eye has never stopped her seeing.

There is always the other one.

Her third eye too — it can look right out of this world and into another.

Agnes is so adept at it, and — has been since she was a little girl — that there is a long queue of people from the other side — who know of her — or who have spoken to her before and often try to come through again. Dora Noyce opens her eyes and looks over at Archie and he blushes deeply. The women hold each other's hands even tighter and Dora closes her eyes again. Agnes ignores her husband's guilt.

She begins to shriek.

It's like an alarm.

Higher, higher, louder, louder!

Archie knows better than to touch his wife at this point.

The planchette spins around. The energy in the room is so dense that Ovid's cage is beginning to rattle. Archie forces himself across the floor to see what the Ouija board is spelling out. The two women are staring at it in silence now. Agnes's shriek still hangs on the air like a harbinger of what is about to come.

The letters spell out the same thing over and over.

J
E
S
S
I
E
M
A
C
R
A
E
I
S
C
O
M
I
N
G
S
H
E
K
N

EWOURSISTERSHEHASSOMETHINGTOSAY

There is an almighty hammering on the front door and Dora is alert then, as ever – for the police. Archie is down the hall to tell whomever it is to fuck off, but it is Mr Udnam, wheezing at the door. The old man shoves past Archie and comes down the hall into the living space where the women are sat at the table. His face falls as he looks at the board and back up at the women's faces. Dora looks up at the man with a clear dislike. Neither of the women moves and Agnes does not look at all surprised to see him.

– They're just playing, it's a board game Mr Udnam, can I get you a drink of water?

Archie tries to distract the old man.

– Are the sisters coming?

Mr Udnam asks Agnes but she says nothing. His answer is spelled out on the board.

Y
E
S

– Dear spirits, this is Agnes, I want to thank you for coming. How many are there of you?

F
I
V
E

– Is there anyone else?

Y
E
S

— Do you need to ask something?

Y
E
S

Agnes opens her eyes and looks straight at him.

— I have some people here who want to speak to you, Mr Udnam.

— I can't.

— If you don't speak to them through me, they will come straight for you. It will be less pleasant for you. There are five red-haired sisters in the room.

— Jesus Christ.

The board rattles violently.

— There are others on their way too, I can feel a few more. They know you are here.

Pipes clang low down in the belly of the building.

Mr Udnam begins to pray as the front door locks and bolts itself.

— The sisters are all barefoot. The youngest is six years old, the next is twelve years old, the third is nineteen years, as are the fourth and fifth. Let me listen . . .

The planchette spins.

— They're looking fir their eldest sister and she is twenty-one years old.

— Elise?

— Yes.

— I need to sit down, he says.

Archie pulls out a chair for Mr Udnam.

— The sisters say there was a fire, Mr Udnam.

— Liars!

The coal embers in the open fire glow bright red.

— They say you sent someone to light a fire at their home to stop them from finding out what happened to your fiancée — their eldest sister, Elise?

— They're fantasists!

— I don't believe they are, Mr Udnam.

— Delusional!

— They say you ken fine well exactly what you did to them.

— Wicked liars!

— If you don't tell them exactly what happened to Elise, they won't let ye leave here today!

Mr Udnam claws at his shirt like he can't breathe.

The two women at the table are in a deep, deep trance.

Agnes's eyes are clear as a Highland seashore.

She nods her head slightly as one by one five sisters appear in spirit and through the depth of his guilt Mr Udnam is able to see them too.

They are all barefoot, in cotton nightdresses, with identical long curly red hair. They hold hands and stand in a row. The youngest steps forward and scuffs her foot. She raises her arm and points at Mr Udnam — she is going to be the first to speak.

1963

Flat 6F6

William Burroughs (49)

the basement

BILL CALLS this his Rothschild suit. He is smoking. His spectacles are thin-rimmed. His shoes are worn at the heel and the leather is cracked. One hand rests in his pocket. It is a grey three-piece. A thin black tie; bright eyes; lined face; pointy chin; slim outline. Long fingers and a fedora. He is ashen as the city. Sea haar creeps along the streets until they disappear into its dense fog. Edinburgh is relentless in her gloom when she chooses, a city of endless night. In this mood, the ceaseless grey is enough to numb an optimist. Pea soup! It is hardly an inventive description. Those who describe Edinburgh's vampiric soul as thus are not his kind. They are no starry angel-headed hipsters! Twin-souled city. All the darker for the light and to find himself back here in secret is thrilling. He just wanted to come back and hide for a few days.

Bill keeps doing it.

Hoping to find himself somewhere else that makes sense.

So far it is not working.

Tendrils of sea mist wisp around a corner. Off to eat another street, and just like that the grey lifts.

A sky appears above in blue as if it has been there the whole time.

He can return to his young man soon.

Can't stay away too long.

Who would want to? So few have his kind of soul. Rarity is sought by the poet – in intimacy and in art. His young gent has no reliability or money. He has little airs or graces: he is, in fact, uncouth but he has never short-changed Bill on the muse.

First the poet will attend to what must be attended.

Morning rolls.

It's a thing they do here.

Soft, warm blackened bread things and sometimes it is eaten with flat sausage. The poet does not eat often. Simplicity in food appeals. The other revelation is a white pudding supper from Brattisani's seasoned with salt and sauce. Local chippie sauce is particular to Edinburgh – he has discovered it this time around. A brown sauce drowned in vinegar. That meal is enough to keep an addict going for some time. It is good, at intermittent occasions, to refuel. Of course, he has not gone to the baker's for rolls or milk. The milk cart and horse trundled by some time ago. It was the money exchange he was after. No.10 Luckenbooth Close hovers over him. An old spindly stone giant. The poet counts out four notes. Places the rest in his back pocket. He pushes a scuffed front door open. His favourite graffiti is still there. It's a pictograph of a devil child. Bill takes out a knife. Adds a cigarette to her slender fingertips. He is bereft without a decent gun at his side. At least he can still carry good hunting knives here. The lock on the front door does not click closed behind him. A skylight at the top of the stair is cracked. Leaves cling sodden to the glass. It looks like a child's dolly pram is on its side up there too. The weather – mercurial as it is – had one of her hissy fits a few days ago. Rearranged the detritus of this city on a whim. She has been known to rip stone masonry from buildings. A waitress died from such a thing. Quite a temper the weather has here. Once a year there are winds so strong a lamp post will be hauled down, or the Forth Road Bridge on the Firth of Forth closes itself to lorries.

Bill is most at home in a storm.

He stands on the bottom landing, torn.

Go up or down?

Sobriety is less illuminating than supposedly educated people insist.

He pushes the basement door gently.

He's not hiding this from John, per se.

Just best to do his own business in private.

It's his way.

They met last year. After the International Writers' Conference. Bill always smiles remembering that one. Writers leaping up like jack-in-the-boxes declaring themselves homosexual. Demanding one cut his long, long hair off. Someone asked Trocchi (onstage) (in a rammed room) what his inspiration for literature was.

– Sodomy!

– Trocchi, you beautiful creature . . .

MacDiarmid nearly spat all his teeth out when that was said and Bill fell a bit in love with Trocchi there and then. Afterwards on his way home – through streets with puke and takeaway wrappers and empty bottles (excessive people here) (he likes that) that would be cleaned before the tourists woke (there had even been a pair of man's pants covered in shit) – he walked to Mary Queen of Scots' bathhouse.

He considered moving right into it and writing a book.

Not that anyone would let him!

Bill would have lived there forever though.

William Burroughs, Fairytale House, Holyrood Palace, EH – fucking – whatever.

Does the queen have a postcode?

The old bathhouse is tiny, ancient, with a crooked chimney and small barred windows.

They could just pass him drugs and cigarettes through the bars.

Across the street, a young man had been asleep on a park bench. Bill sat next to him. Lit a cigarette. The man woke. Smiled. Held his fingers out for a cigarette. It seemed that they were already part way through a very long life together when they met. The awkward part of getting to know each other – never occurred.

There will be time to climb up the worn stairwell after he's sorted himself out.

His love will be drunk as a long-eared owl.

Intoxicating to have him to go to!

That time with one you want to be with more than anything else.

He never thought he'd feel like this again!

Bill has left all he has ever believed in or cared for – many times. Arriving is a form of leaving. He cannot seem to quit. Finding a way to leave behind everything and start over again – has become a way of being.

Non-attachment: authorities don't like it.

Who wants crooks and drunks and junkies to seek tendrils of free thought?

Send them out multiplied.

A relentless octopus of free thought to descend all depths. Gain incandescent light! Grow more pods. Become a deity with sharp tiny teeth. Grow ever longer tentacles. The great octopus cult of the future! Authorities would not like that one. Bill has known for a long time: endorsed crooks, drunks and junkies have one label for their power only. They call themselves – government. That single word seems to be used as a get-out clause for literally any old degenerate selfish behaviour. Those crooks and junkies and drunks – dispute the right of any other human – to think in any way that could be considered free. There is a click behind him as the basement door closes. Bill descends. There is a dim light. The air grows mustier. It is laced with urine and something darker he does not want his psyche to even detect. His nose (finely tuned) seeks out a faint vinegar smell, an odour like vitamins. Sometimes there is no smell – other times it is weirdly like Band-Aids. His nose is always trying to detect it.

The basement room has a low ceiling. Rubbish and needles litter the floor.

She is in the corner sat in lotus.

Wizened as a monkey.

She looks up at him with luminous eyes.

– Bill.

– Little Mama!

She grins with darkened teeth and eyes hunched under bone. A jukebox glows merrily beside her.

– We hacked into the electrics since you last visited.

– I see, more lights and music!

– Someone's electricity bill upstairs will be huge for this! We made sure it was ran off the council's bill. A just retribution, no?

Bill nods.

Picks his way across to her.

His hat skims the roof.

He takes it off and holds it in front of himself respectfully.

Holds out the money.

It disappears.

– Pick a tune, Bill.

He goes over to the jukebox. It has circles glowing in blue light under the glass dome. Puts a coin in. The record arm drops down. 'The End of the World' by Skeeter Davis – lilts through holes in stone walls and travels off down into the catacombs below the city.

– My favourite young poet. Just a blink of an eye since you were last here, no?

– It feels like that, Little Mama.

– Doesn't it?

– Always.

He's walked out that door and had a year elsewhere. Or that was just the dream and he has been here all the time. That's how it feels. He nods. He wants to do it here. Little Mama gets her accoutrements together.

– Are you living here now, Little Mama?

– Aye, still got the same supplier. They live up in the gods – seventh floor. They take their cut, and stay out of the polis's sight. I stay high. Win-win. I fall asleep here sometimes. I've got a flat down in Granton.

She waves her hands around the basement like she is in the Los Angeles Hilton.

– Did you go back inside, Little Mama?

– Twice.

Little Mama looks like a child fixing up.

— You remind me of my ex-wife.

— Aye? Why d'ye think yer back here then, Mr Burroughs?

— All things happen for a reason, Little Mama. We live in a magical universe.

— We sure do, kid.

— I got love in me.

— Oh really? For me? I hope you don't cut yer wee finger off tae impress me?

Bill smiles.

— That's sick.

— Why, thank you, Bill!

— It's why I like the people of this city, you are nothing if not dark-humoured. You know, they say I cut it off to impress my lover, but it was actually demonic possession. They would have locked me away for longer if I'd told them. Why do you think I got so good at scrying?

— You really curse those who cross you?

— Damn right I do.

— I bet you do a good curse, young man.

Bill sticks his stumped finger up at her and she laughs with glee. He selects another button on the jukebox with it. 'Be My Baby' by the Ronettes spins.

— When ye going back to London, Bill?

— Probably in the morning, or maybe Sunday, or Saturday, I don't know — it depends on what happens before then.

— Be careful, things are tight in Scotland just now. They're clamping down on all crime hard.

— Is that right?

— Aye, they just hanged a man.

— Where?

— Aberdeen, few weeks back.

— What for?

— Killed his girlfriend. She had a husband and a kid, it was a bad scene, Bill. She goes back to the husband so then the boyfriend kidnaps her back, drags her away on some hell car ride, and fucking kills her. Men, youz can be such absolute cunts.

Bill sits down next to Little Mama and takes his coat off.

Rolls up his sleeve.

As she cooks, candlelight hooks her nose and crags the caverns of her eyes.

Little Mama empties the needle into her vein.

Inhales deep.

The spoon is hot and ready — it glides toward Bill.

He drops his needle into the liquid.

— He killed her for going back to her husband?

— He killed her because he was a psychopath, there's never any other reason than that.

— Sometimes there is.

— Aye, well, they hanged him in the new gallows. Two hundred people waited ootside. The thing is, Bill, and you know this — wealthy men make mistakes. Working-class men commit murder. Then they get hanged. Not as a deterrent tae murdering women, noh, they have little reason tae try and deter that — fear ay that and rape helps keep women in oor place, it's why they hardly ever convict them firrit. They killed that man to warn the great unwashed — to warn other working-class men — watch yer fucking step ay. We can just fucking hang your kind!

— Excessive.

— Isn't it?

— Yes, ma'am, it is by far. So, my precious, wonderfully dark Little Mama, why are you still wasting yourself on this place?

Bill gestures around.

— What am I gonnae do, ya great big arse? Be a poet? What wummin poets are you little Beat boys supporting?

He laughs, eyes crinkle.

Little Mama is the only woman Bill has ever met who relentlessly calls him out on his bullshit. There is something highly comforting in a woman seeing who you are — without judgement. Just saying how it is, and not compromising on clear sight. Little Mama is a warmth in the glow. They are in the place beyond. No usual constrictions on a human mind. Hours pass. Songs spin. Walls breathe. They cook. Spike. Nod.

— I can feel this building, Little Mama.

— Aye, ye will.

— Dangerous isn't she?

— Aye, something in her history that gies me the creeps.

Little Mama points over to where an ancient workbench sits, above it there is a rusty double-toothed saw nailed to the wall.

— If only I could translate the language of an ancient building.

Little Mama shakes her finger at him in warning.

She is yellow.

Nods in lotus.

Eyes closed.

Bill gathers his coat, puts his hat back on, bows to her — unseen.

Up the stair, to the door of John's rental place on the sixth floor.

Knock softly.

— I thought you'd never get back. Where's the rolls?

Bill kisses him on the cheek.

– What a blessing is a barely dressed angel for a wretch like me, on days like these?

Follow him down the hall. Bill discards clothes as he goes. Shoes off. Socks gone. Wriggle long bony toes. Hairy line on a concave stomach. All around the floor are cut-ups. Words circle their feet. Snipped out from newspapers.

– No rolls.

– Fucks sake, what do ye want fir breakfast then, Bill?

– To get high and fuck. Love, lust, want – what a way to glide through the cosmos!

– That's it?

– After that – just words. It's all I want. Words. I want to infiltrate and disorder meaning. Rearrange the fabric of existence in twenty-six letters of the alphabet. Twenty-seven if you include the ampersand.

Newspapers are stacked up.

Pages gape where whole sections are missing.

There is a round white plastic television in the corner. Two aerials stick out the top giving it a humanoid appearance. A brand-new tape cassette player sits on a low wood-effect sideboard. It has seven tapes. Bill brought them from America. This young man commandeers his space, time, location with ease. Two egg-shaped armchairs face a sash window. It is a tall window three panes wide. The living room has been cut in half with a cheap partition wall. There is a narrow bedroom and long living room out of what must previously have been a good-sized lounge. Bill places a glass on the floor and lowers his ear to it.

– There is a sound coming from under the floorboards.

Downstairs there is a low repetition of words and hymns

and curses and ancient secrets that could be recited by a human.

— Voodoo?

— It's a parrot. It belong tae ma neighbours Archie and Agnes, down the stairs, they've lived here for years.

Bill is laid out, spreadeagled and naked – on top of the words all over the floor.

He appears to be wearing Marigolds.

The poet cannot remember putting them on. Marigolds are a new thing. He supposes, at some point, he must have been offering to do the washing-up. Time is strange in this city and even more so with his lover.

— Why does a parrot go on like that?

— It had a psychotic break, after what happened tae Archie's wife.

Bill nods.

His young man is handsome in an unkempt way, and he's dark-haired with a voice to die for. John is getting him to stroke his skin with Marigolds on. Kink. Plastic, oil. He must have placed these on his hands whilst he was nodding and Bill is not going to judge him: he's going to fuck him.

Later, when the buzz eases.

John is very naked.

He is the most naked young man Bill has ever seen.

His eyes have flecks of real gold inside them and John is bending over him on the floor. Bill wonders if he took too much – his racing heart!

John is going to speak.

Waiting for something to come out of his mouth is terrifying.

— Are you okay?

— There are 3.136 billion people in the world, John. We could count up how many legs that is, how many livers, how many arms and fingers and toes. Of course we'd have to account for all the toeless folks, it does no good to ignore them.

— It's too many, Bill.

— Fir what?

— Democracy.

John lays down beside Bill.

— I took some LSD, I put some in yer tea unnaw before you went out. It should be working. Bill, how can all of the people on this planet have a consciousness?

John curls beside him soft and gentle as a cat.

— Some of them don't. Not my neighbours back at home. Or their dog.

— Consciousness radiates fae you like fire. I uhm sorry ye've been cursed with so much of it.

— I am too.

— It's like loving a volcano, a sage. One day you will be very famous, Mr Burroughs, and I will still be an undertaker and we will still be living through the strangest days. You think I'm using you but — my love is true.

— I know. I'm sorry.

— I'm not.

— What we need to do is devote a day solely to thinking up new inventions, John.

— The world needs that!

— A day that should be spent considering science — not poetry. I am a poet and as a whole we are a suspicious people. What we all need to look at is the antimatter.

– Bill, d'ye want a cup ay tea with just sugar in it this time, nae LSD, maybe milk and two?

– Do I want one? Would I like one? A question, I see. You are going to brew, tea?

– Aye.

– At a time like this?

– Like what?

– Well, we are declaring our feelings are we not? It always seems to happen to me in Edinburgh. Like last year, all the writers gathered publicly. They spoke and fought. Arrows have been slung – there will be repercussions.

– Are you talking about the Writers' Conference, Bill?

– That does indeed seem to be what I am referring to.

– Do you take sugar?

– I do, John.

– How many?

– At least ten, or eight if you're running low.

– Do you like it strong, or weak?

Bill stares at him.

– You probably don't even know how the hippos were boiled in their tanks, do you, John?

His lover comes back out of the kitchenette. There are cut-up lines of poetry and prose Blu-tacked all over the walls. John picks one off the wall and reads it.

– *Telstar Marilyn!*

Ivy Proudfoot (17)

cupid's corner

CLIMB UP onto the kitchen table. Adjust the rope above my head. I tie the rope tight. Pull on it to see how much weight it could take. Turn it over in my hand. If I placed it around my neck, the rope would burn. If there comes a time when I have to do this, would I choose rope or a bullet? I'd take drowning if it came to it. There would be no memory after that. No. 10 Luckenbooth Close has some kind of purple memory vibrating through it like an endless hum. A little girl wanders the entire nine floors every night. Only I can hear her. I let the rope go and the laundry maid swings above me, free of skirts. It's breezy in the kitchen. The windows are old and rattly. At least it helps things dry. There is a fruit cake in the cupboard which I made on Sunday. For someone who can barely bake, I'd call it a triumph. Morag and I will have some before we go out. The wood on our kitchen table is unvarnished and it is rough under my bare feet. We have laid plate after plate on this table, teaspoon after cup after pot after saucer. Wine and vodka. Cigarettes and purses. We have laid each other down on it and all the other things. I want to leave just one more memory here. Whilst I wait for her to come back, I splay my toes trying to touch all of those memories so I don't lose them.

Morag opens the kitchen door.

She leans on the frame and smiles at me.

I pull up my skirt just a little.

Slowly, inch by inch, so she can see my thighs appear. Then further.

Turn to show her my legs from the back and then turn back around. Sway my hips, pull my top down a little – she likes when I dance for her on the table. I'd do most anything for that look! She is smoking. Always. Her blonde hair is curled and bobbed short and almost dark brown at the ends. I like to think of her in the cinema with all that light on her face. To me she always looks like a silent-movie star.

– Exactly what are you doing, Ivy?

– What does it look like I'm doing Morag, *ma chérie*?

– It looks like you are hoping to seduce me?

I pull my skirt all the way up now. Nod with my breath held like it always is just before she touches me. She places her hands on my thighs. This will be our last time.

Morag pulls my knickers to the side.

I tilt my hips – up to meet her tongue until I have to grip the rope hard in my hands.

I've dated boys and not one made me feel like this.

I think of words left behind in closed rooms.

In drawers.

Single.

In groups or clusters.

Help me – I need you – I don't know how to love.

Her tongue is warm and fast.

I like it when her fingernails dig into my skin.

Thoughts do as they will. I see another woman step behind her. The recruiter — Violet. It's a fantasy I shouldn't have and so I have it all the time. In my mind's eye she straps on an antique dildo and fucks my beautiful girlfriend from behind really slowly — stroking her thighs as she does it, kneading her arse. I feel Morag's tongue quicken as if it were true. I am helpless in that moment — I would agree — to anything at all. I can feel the orgasm building and I try to catch the feeling. I imagine I am bound to a chair with my legs parted so wide I can't close them — the recruiter sliding her hands down over my nipples from behind and kissing my neck and pulling on my hair. I imagine Morag kissing the recruiter with tongues. It makes me jealous and she knows it. So she buckles up and tells me to open my mouth and suck her pretty dick. She tells me to do it well, looking down on me the whole time . . .

— I'm going to cum, I'm going to . . .

Morag pulls me closer in.

I shudder all the way down my back — my legs are shaky.

Lean down to kiss her.

She is cat-like.

My girlfriend is beautiful and strange and sweet and innocent.

Like some underworld queen.

God has no problems with our love. He created it. The church holds issue. It's why I don't go there. Morag pulls over a pot of strong tea. It's lukewarm. Pours it into the saucepan. Takes out her old make-up sponge. We always used to get ready like this. It's how it started between us. Levi watched the first time she did this to me, before when we couldn't get stockings – we will get ready like this tonight for old times' sake!

Morag dips the sponge into the tea.

– What shade do you want?

– Light brown.

– Do you think women will do this in the future?

– Stain their skin? I don't see why. They'll have cheaper tights then.

– Is it the last time, Ivy?

– No!

I lie to her so easy it's like my tongue was made for untruths. Morag leaves a lipstick ring on her cigarette. Smoke spirals up toward me. The radio plays quietly. 'I'll Be Seeing You' by Bing Crosby.

Rain patters off the window.

– It's the longest night of the year, Ivy!

– We should light all the turnips when we come home. I can't believe you carved all of them for little me!

– Of course I did! Aye, let's light all of them, definitely.

– It's creepy enough in here half the time, Morag, you'll need the candlelight when I'm gone.

– I know! Did you see Mr Udnam is putting up a new housing association plaque? Aye. There's some big honour being bestowed on him by the city. I keep seeing him getting all these things but how come he's doing this housing association or charity work or whatever it is he does, and we *still* can't afford to live in Edinburgh? One day nobody will be able to afford to live here but rich people. And they'll live elsewhere most of the year! It'll be an ancient city that's just a playground for posh cunts. We'll travel in by bus sometimes to look at it. The buildings will all be empty. They will be full of silence.

— Imagine us marrying men and living on the same street, Morag.

— Raising our children together?

She taps my leg.

I turn.

Watch the rain.

Say nothing.

We can do pretty much everything without speaking.

She is my favourite quietude.

Both of the recruiters came here to see me the second time.

Commented on how innocent I look.

They said Germans like French girls who flirt. I acted it out. They seemed satisfied. Left. When Morag came home she had no idea who had been sat here a few hours before. She fell asleep. I lay with my hand splayed on the bedroom wall. I imagined that little girl's hand splayed on the other side of the wall.

I knew then.

I won't come back to No. 10 Luckenbooth Close.

I will live out my life somewhere else after this war.

There will be an after! There has to be. I look over at the sideboard. Our Halloween turnips are so pretty! Acorns are strewn around them. Some have been carved so they have tiny ornate flowers blossoming all over them – a miracle. Turnips are hard to carve! Another is covered in tiny moons. One turnip has a long root at its bottom like an elephant trunk. Morag has drawn eyes on it and topped the hairy turnip lid with a tiny bowler hat from the shop. She painted three small turnips dark green with silver stars. One turnip has been painted black and hollowed out and inside it she has made a tiny scene. There is a forest floor.

A little carved turnip wolf is stood on a miniature boulder. He howls at a fingernail moon. There is moss on the turnip floor and long twigs make it look like a forest at night. Drums begin to pound down low out on the street. Hundreds of them! Pagan drummers marching down the High Street. It is Samhain. The white witch will be given her ritual sacrifice on Calton Hill. The Green Men will protect her on the journey. There will be fire breathers up on the hill and a bonfire and tiny sparks of light flying off it.

— What is that?

— Beltane drummers. Did you see that new guy for a lunch date today?

— Might have.

— Morag, you are so cheeky. How many of us are you in love with?

— Just you! We can fit in one more film before dancing at the Palais, Ivy, please? They are playing *Pride and Prejudice*, Aldous Huxley did the script.

— Maybe.

Shrug.

She sharpens the kohl.

I turn to face the window.

Morag runs eyeliner from the top of my thigh all the way down to my ankle. Straightest line in the world, it is even more perfect than a silk-stocking seam. She does the second line so my left leg matches my right.

Images flash through my head.

A dog barking at me in a river. Walking across empty fields covered in snow.

Soldiers in pursuit.

— I fucking hate this war, you know that?

Morag never swears. Has she guessed where I am going? I have caught her reading my books. All the papers Dad has in his office that I took over here to read without worrying he'd catch me. The worst are so hard to read. Eugenics and racial cleansing was the focus of the last one I found her going through. It's horrific. She cried a lot that day. Morag would not be against it if I told her what I want to do or where I am going in the morning. I know she wouldn't. But she would worry about me and I won't have that for her. I hope she stays in this country forever and lives out her days — happy and beloved to someone. I love her more than time. If I can take even one action to keep someone as good as her safe, I will do it.

— Nothing has been right since they took France.

— I know.

— Do you know what I heard, Ivy?

— No.

— That it says above one of those camps — ARBEIT MACHT FREI — Work Makes One Free. Those people are imprisoned by others, and they are working them to death, aren't they? I've heard even worse things. They are doing experiments. Trying to work out how to create a perfect human and then sterilise everyone else. It is so creepy. There are kids in there! Families! How can they do it, Ivy? How can anyone do that to another human being? What is wrong with them? Do you think it is true?

She is crying.

I am numb.

I hold onto her and rock her gently and stroke her hair as lightly as I can to soothe her.

— I don't know, Morag. Some people make no sense what-soever to me.

I want to tell her about the tickets in my purse and that by the time she sits down to Christmas dinner, I will be in France. I have heard so many worse things about what they are doing in the camps. My brother went into one and he did not come back out again. I feel rage in my stomach, like the beginning of a kettle whistling. I swallow the lump in my throat. I am not telling her one thing. All we do in this war is worry. Everyone does all the time. I will not add anything more for her to feel sad about.

— That man is insane, Ivy!

— I know.

— Why do the papers publish his propaganda?

— I don't know.

— Why is he allowed to have that much power? He is just one person! Is it because they agree with him? No Jews! Whites only! An Aryan race? Are you kidding me? We got through one World War already for this? The world better not let anything like this ever happen again, Ivy. I can't take it. Please don't leave me and go away. I don't think I can take that either. Why can't you just stay here? Why do you have to go and help a friend in London of all places? Do you know how many bombs have been dropped down there?

I kiss her on the lips.

— Have you written back to Levi?

— Aye.

— Is he okay?

— He's good, or he says he is anyway. I can't believe you are both going to be gone now!

– Don't worry, you'll be okay. And I killed the mouse.

– You did?

– Yes.

– It wasn't a bad mouse.

– You can't know that, you never met any of his friends. That mouse might have been a total psychopath and not in a good way, I suppose there isn't any good way to be a psychopath . . .

I glance at her.

– But it was so small.

– Small mice can be psychopaths too, Morag, and it was riddled with disease and it was sitting on the back of the sofa last night when you were sleeping on it, it stuck its finger up at me!

– Mice don't have fingers.

– Aye, they do.

– How did you kill it?

– I put a glass bowl on top of it, but then it tried to shoot its skinny arm out with that little pink paw thing and I slammed my hand down on the bowl because I thought it was going to get out and it broke its arm, snapped it, clean in half. It was bleeding on the floor.

– Gross.

– So I lifted up the bowl and I took the broom and used that to stand on the mouse. It crunched a lot for such a tiny thing.

– You can be so cold, Ivy Proudfoot.

I smile with a fleeting touch of pride despite myself.

She has no idea.

I don't tell her I watched it die.

It lay on its side and its heart was beating so fast the whole ribcage was just a huge indent of oxygen going in and out and in and out. She wasn't asleep either. She was in the bath. I was as quiet as I could be so she wouldn't hear anything. At least I know that I can kill something now. Everyone has to start somewhere, a little thing and then a bigger thing.

— What we need is music and dancing, have you got your ID cards, Morag?

— Aye! The polis from St Leonard's asked for them the other day. I asked him what he was looking for and he said they had to check to make sure I wasn't a spy, Ivy. A spy! He was flirting with me, but really! Have you heard anything so ridiculous? Do you think I'd make a good spy?

I return her gaze, light and easy. Kiss her on the cheek, tuck her hair behind her ear, run my fingers down her neck.

— No, but I think you'd make a fucking braw wife.

— Oh, well, fuck you very much.

— Morag! You are not built for things like that, you're too good.

— Right then, Rudolf Hess! Just because you worked on the SOE listening stations, and you're a trained FANY wireless operator, just because you're going to live with your new friend down south and get all qualified to do things I don't know anything about, there is no need to get all above yourself, Ivy Proudfoot! Is she cute, your friend down there?

— No, she's hideous.

Morag smiles.

I go through to the little bedroom because I don't want her to see me almost cry.

Archie is playing his piano upstairs.

Someone is cooking meat. It smells like three weeks' worth of rations are being blown on one massive meal. It makes me hungry. Fruit cake and tea! Maybe some cheese and oatcakes and peppered mackerel and pickles or just a boiled egg with salt and a tomato, then a brandy, or a sherry, or a gin and tonic or two before we get to Cupid's Corner at the Palais. I will need at least a drink or two if I am to do what the recruiters have asked of me. I touch a phial of poison in my pocket. I didn't know my mission would start before I even left this city.

– What time are you leaving in the morning, Ivy?

– Early.

I go into the wardrobe and pick up my bag. Its bottom is false.

When I got this after graduating from Training 1, I knew it was becoming real.

All the items are there.

In my head I only speak in French already.

For me it has been like that for months.

I dream in it. I will not speak one word of English after I leave here tomorrow.

Not even through final parts of training.

All those years with Mum speaking only in French at home and she never knew one day I would use it to go and make some kind of vengeance – of even the smallest kind – for what was done to her son. Morag and I have slept in this bed nearly every weekend for a year. Flirted in the same bars. I have had her back. I held her when any man left her. I've been here whenever she needed me and even when she wanted to share me with Levi, I was happy to be shared – to his delight. He sent her a letter. I know they miss each other.

I will hold her later. Naked, held close – it is the best way to sleep. Then later, I'll be able to reach for her in the night. My favourite kind of touch is when we are both half asleep and we kiss each other blindly, fall into an abyss where it is only want and touch and sweat and both of us warm from sleep. All those hours together during blackout where we didn't go down to the air-raid shelter. Just closed the shutters, curtains too, not even a line of light coming from any window. Our whole apartment felt totally closed off from the entire world – what a way to love!

– Life is now, Ivy.

She stands at the bedroom door, nails painted, dress on.

– You look stunning.

– Are you going to miss me?

– Every single second.

There is a lump in my throat then. I have to turn away because we won't ever do this again. She is so dear to me. You truly never really know how much you care for someone until you are about to walk away.

– Can I write to you where you are going, Ivy?

– Aye.

– Will you leave an address?

– I'll send one.

– I love you.

– Stop it!

Morag laughs. My inability to deal with emotion! A man is not a mouse but the principle of murder is the same. I can do this. The recruiter said he would be at the Palais and they have shown me a photograph. He will be talking in English and covering his accent to pass as a soldier from down south. I had no idea I'd have to do this tonight until just this afternoon. I am exhilarated and frightened that my urges will not see me through. That they are just the terrors of a child scared of its shadow. Maybe I will be unable to kill him in public without being seen at all and I will have failed my attempt at becoming an assassin. I mean, the recruiters don't call it that, they just say it's a mission.

Morag goes to finish getting ready.

I love the sound of her wandering around our flat.

I have memorised the codes I need.

I know how to tap in the night, in tiny rooms – to send out messages on (hopefully) unassailable waves. I will ride a bicycle in France. I will go out to a railway line at night. My job will be less about spying and more about sabotage. To hinder Germans in any way possible. To send back any and all information. I met three other SOE women on Training 1 and each of them was clever, funny and brave. Two were such good actresses they could hide the pain of leaving a child behind. I admire them with everything I have. The recruiter has not pretended. We will have a survival rate of roughly 50 per cent, except wireless operators for whom the percentage is much lower. The pipes in the walls clank hard again. The little girl in the walls is warning me. I ignore her. Always have done. I open my bag, and check it again. I can do this. I place my travel case back under the bed. Ignore a feeling that the little girl in this building is watching me begin my mission. That it is her, clanking those pipes in the walls, warning me not to go.

Morag walks back into the room, putting earrings in and I am trying not to get emotional but I am so sad that this is our last time together, and she doesn't even know why.

– You really do look totally stunning.
– Thank you, Ivy Proudfoot.
– I love you, you know that? You know I always will?
– I do.

Take my girlfriend's hand so we can go out for one last time together and open the door – ready to meet the night.

Agnes Campbell (63)

the sisters

BLACK CLOUDS race like warhorses pounding the sky. Pink electric lightning splits the darkness. Luminous clouds roll under darker ones above and there is a low roar of thunder several miles away.

Lights go out.

Archie clicks the lamp on at the plug. Nothing.

Mr Udnam laces his fingers together to pray. Dora gives herself completely to the seance. She and Agnes have gone through so many of these now. The parrot steps back as far as he can into his cage. The room sheds its floral wallpaper. It is bare and empty. There is a chunky wooden joist exposed as the ceilings are being replaced. The workmen have placed it on top of two big metal barrels ready to put up later. The girls are fading in and out from vision before they settle more solidly in the room. The first girl is standing on the left of the beam and she kicks her bare foot to and fro at least five inches above the table below.

Agnes and Dora look like they are praying before dinner.

The child is tiny. She doesn't look six years old yet but she is.

Her name is Mary.

She holds out her hand and another appears from the ether to take hers.

It is followed by a pale freckled arm attached to the body of a boyish twelve-year-old Olive who has curly hair and a pointy chin. Four bare feet swing now. Along to the right of the beam a third girl appears, nineteen years old, her name is Rose. All three girls look beyond her expectantly. Two girls appear. They are also nineteen years old. The twins were born the same year as their older sister. Long curly hair down their backs. The same simple cotton nightdresses as the others. The last two girls stand on the beam and look directly at Mr Udnam. The twins are called Bessie and Clementine.

His face visibly pales.

Over at the table, Agnes's one blind eye turns white.

Her blue eye is luminescent.

Archie grips the sides of his armchair.

— May I ask if there are any sceptics among us?

— No, Agnes, we are with you, Dora says.

Archie nods his head reluctantly.

— I welcome the dead into my home with the same warmth and respect I would offer the living. It is the positive energy of the sitters that is required to maintain this connection.

Dora squeezes Agnes's hands.

The planchette moves slowly around the Ouija board. A glass on the table falls over, water drops onto the wooden floor. Agnes keeps her back as straight as she can and takes a long slow breath.

– Spirits, we urr here to receive you.

– Amen.

The sisters reply in unison.

Agnes can clearly hear them, as can Mr Udnam who is now crossing himself and praying in nonsensical mutters. The smallest sister shoots a paper aeroplane from the spirit world toward him. It is always the tiny children who can see everything. Like children and animals in the living world, they are still so close to the other side that they can flit between the two with ease.

– What we have here today is highly unusual. There is not one presence in the room as of yet but five.

Archie rolls his eyes and slams his fist on the armchair.

The twins swivel their heads around to look at him but he can't see them.

– I welcome each spirit into my and my husband's home. May we serve you the best we can.

– Amen, amen.

Dora falls deeper into some kind of alert sleep.

– We wish to speak to those blessed with light.

– Mercy.

– We hope you may communicate with us today in truth. If you are present in the spirit world can you indicate your intention?

The piano plays five high notes all by itself.

– I feel a powerful presence in this room. Dora, I have to ask if you are ready to continue and I need your assurance that you won't break the circle no matter what occurs.

– I am ready, Agnes. I'm here to support you.

Archie has tears in his eyes.

There is an electric energy in the room.

Agnes appears beatific. Kind and ageless, this is where she is most herself. The bells at St Giles' Cathedral toll up on the close. Rain thrums hard. A steady rumble of thunder moves further away now as black clouds race toward hills in the distance. Mr Udnam takes off his jacket, his hat, his tie, loosens his shirt: he looks like a caught man. One who always hoped his past – and the truth – would never catch up with him.

– There are five sisters with us in the room. Dora, Archie, I want you to send these girls only love and light. I can see them in the middle of this room, back some time ago when the whole building was being renovated – that's what it looks like – am I correct, Mr Udnam?

He shrugs but the veins on his hands are pulsing and purple and his lips are red and his face is sweaty. Each of the girls stands up on the beam and jumps on it until he shudders and he looks up at them. His guilt is an energy the girls can use and they do.

– The building was renovated, yes, in 1910.

– I know you girls have been trying to reach me for some time. I have felt your presence.

– Agnes, are you sure you want to do this?

Her husband hisses across the room and the girls look back at him. He can't see them but he can feel their intent.

– I knew I had to be ready to receive what you have to say.

– You won't be . . .

Mr Udnam mutters and sits back in defeat.

– I have seen the youngest sister before.

– Mercy, mercy.

Dora crosses herself as well.

— I have heard your treads on the stair behind me for years and I am ready now to listen to whatever you have to say. Let us begin.

Mr Udnam has his head in his hands.

Each of the girls' heads swivel toward him in one motion. Ten green eyes blaze.

— Who lit the match, Mr Udnam?

Mary leans toward him, her spirit calls him to look at her and he does.

— Mr Udnam, may I ask if you can hear the girls for yourself or do you want me to repeat what they are trying to say?

— I can hear them.

The empty water glass rights itself on the table.

— Are those of you in the spirit world in distress?

— Aye.

— Has a wrong been committed against you?

— Aye.

— Is the perpetrator of that wrong in this room?

— Aye.

— Can you point that person out for me?

Agnes looks up at the wooden beam and offers a soft smile to the girls who are standing on it looking down at them. She has a silk scarf wrapped around her head. Agnes does not cover her all-white eye but occasionally she blinks to see them more clearly again. Her skin is soft and lined. Archie's face is wracked with worry for his wife. He cannot intervene but he can tell this is far beyond the normal Sunday seances they have held in their home and some of those knocked her out for weeks. Dora Noyce's face is set with determined strength. Each of the five sisters raises her right hand at the same time and points directly at Mr Udnam.

— Mr Udnam, the girls are pointing at you. Can you see this?

— Yes.

— The message coming through today is for you. Are you willing to receive it, Mr Udnam?

— No, no, no, no, no!

The old man shouts at her. The parrot pecks at his bars — he is wide-eyed and pacing.

— Mr Udnam, you only have one chance to hear the truth.

— I don't want to.

— We do it in this world. Or, we do it in the next . . .

— I'll wait.

— If you do it in the next when you've been offered a chance to repent in this life, you will be treated far more harshly for your sins.

Archie intervenes on his wife's behalf.

— Can you afford that, Mr Udnam? How bad can it be? Just take the message. This is causing my wife distress. Her health suffers for this!

Colour has drained from Mr Udnam entirely.

— I don't know what to do!

— You are an old man, ready to pass soon yourself — do you not want to show you have at least tried to hear the truths against you before it is your time to seek the light?

— Yes! Okay . . .

He spits blood into his handkerchief.

His chins wobble down to a long turkey neck.

His head is bald.

Partially spotted.

Mr Udnam's eyes are sunken with folds of skin in a darker shade underneath. Dark age spots mottle his cheeks and he coughs into the handkerchief again. The girls note this. Nothing goes past them where he is concerned. Agnes struggles to contain the huge energy radiating down from that beam. If she does not keep it together right now, the haunches of the building will lock into each other and glide upward. An undeniable sense that this whole building wants to stand up and walk away. Unendurable sorrow. Mr Udnam's eyes grow even darker. It is clear to Agnes that if he doesn't hear this he will pass from here to limbo. The man is too frightened to open his heart. Worse still he sees no wrong in his soul.

— We have been following you for years, Mr Udnam, one of the twins says.

— Who lit the match?

— Our mother was asleep.

— You had us murdered in our beds because we kept coming to your door, looking for Elise. Did you not, Mr Udnam? All five of us would come here smartly dressed before church on a Sunday and again on a Tuesday, sometimes on a Friday.

Bessie says this quietly.

— We only ever had one question.

He looks over at Bessie and Clementine.

They hold hands.

Watch his face for a reaction.

— Our mother was the only one who survived the fire. Did you know she couldn't pay for our funerals? Had to bury us as paupers? It was in the Edinburgh paper that week. You know our mother jumped from a bridge not two minutes from here because you murdered us, don't you?

– I am so sorry, Agnes whispers.

– Her son went first in birth, then five daughters and another missing.

– Our sister left home before us, Mr Udnam.

– She was beloved to us all.

– We didn't want her tae go, we missed her.

– She came here to live with you.

– Engaged tae be married we heard.

– To the very Minister of Culture. Our mother was so proud!

– A step up, that's what she said!

– All the steps up!

– She lived here with you downstairs and you had her dresses made fir her and her hair done at a fancy place and you did everything you could to make her look like a lady, but she couldnae bring you a child could she? That's why you got Jessie. Did you think we didn't know?

– What did you do to her, Mr Udnam?

– Is that why you killed us?

– Because we kept coming to your door to ask questions?

– You were scared we'd ask them on the street. Where's our sister?

– We will not stop following you until ye let us ken what happened to Elise, so ye might as well dae it right now!

Olive slams her hand on the beam to emphasise her point.

– Where is our sister, Mr Udnam?

Mary asks it in the smallest, sweetest voice she can muster.

Rain has softened into rivulets on the windowpanes.

He takes his head out of his hands.

Archie is staring at him. He is unable to hear anything but he somehow understands it all. He is close to his wife, much closer than she knows. Agnes's mind and heart and soul are totally open to these girls and their heartbreak, she will not stop this seance until they are heard.

— We died on a Wednesday.

— Five of us in one fire.

— The fire was in Leith, I remember. It's you?

Agnes asks this.

All the girls nod.

Archie wipes tears off his cheek. He wrings his hands.

— I am so sorry.

— We don't need pity, Mrs Campbell. We need answers from him.

— You must answer them, Mr Udnam. You will only get one chance. You do know they have come to escort you from here today?

— Escort me where?

The girls smile.

The little ones begin to play a hand-clap game to keep themselves amused while the older ones keep talking.

— Our wrongs always escort us when it is our time to seek judgement, Agnes says.

— I am not ready!

— You are not the one who decides when you are ready, Mr Udnam. Did you think retribution or repentance only occurs in this life? It rarely does. You will be served for all your sins. You are being given one chance to tell the truth and account for your sins while here in human form and I suggest, Mr Udnam, that you try for the sake of these girls to get – at least that right!

Agnes's one blue eye swivels toward him.

The pure white one is swirling.

There is ether in there — the other side. It is present inside her. She is a portal and a gate. Agnes has no fear of what is occurring. But she can feel a darker presence grow near.

— They can ask me, I'll answer.

His shoulders slump.

— Where is our sister?

— Who lit the match?

— Which do I answer first?

— Did you pay a man to burn us to death in our beds as we slept?

— Aye. I did. He was a tenant of mine, on the second floor, he used to shoot the one o'clock gun every day and owed me, for decades, for something only known between me and him. I told him if he didn't want to go to prison he must do just one thing.

— Our little sisters didn't die from smoke inhalation, Mr Udnam.

— They died in the fire.

— In the newspapers it said we all died from smoke inhalation, that we were all dead before flames touched our skin. It wasn't true.

— Where is our sister, Mr Udnam?

— She went to America. She left me!

A heavy tremor goes through each floor of the building.

— We don't believe you.

— That's because you are wicked! Liars! Fantasists! Delusional! How do I know you are not evil lying spirits?

The girls speak together in one voice.

— So says the man who murdered us in our beds.

— It was a long time ago, I cannot remember!

— That's what every evil man says.

— *Can't remember.*

— *It wasn't me.*

— *Don't ask me or you are wicked.*

— *Leave it in the past.*

— What has to be gained from bringing it up, girls?

— We've searched the world and the ether for our sister and she has not appeared yet.

Agnes looks up at the girls.

Each has the bitten lips of an angel — just a step out of the light.

Some of their arms and legs and cheeks are heavily scarred with burn marks.

The two little girls stand up to join the older sisters now and all of them take hands in a row.

Angel wings poke up above their shoulder blades.

Feathers sway down by their thighs.

They hold hands tightly.

— Dear Mary, Mother of God, please forgive me!

— It is not her forgiveness that you are going to need. We will only ask you this one last time, Mr Udnam: where is Elise? What happened to her? You burnt us to death in our beds so we would stop asking questions. Why did you need our silence if she had gone to America? Did she drown on the way? Where is Hope? Where is Jessie? We are sending you to the other side today, Mr Udnam, any minute now. Where is Elise?

Mr Udnam stands up.

Agnes looks from him to the girls.

Her husband is hunched over, crying, catching as much of

this narrative as he can from what his wife says. The parrot is stunned silent and pretending to be dead. Dora is wide awake.

— I don't know where they went!

— What do you mean?

The planchette starts spinning and spells out.

J
E
S
S
I
E
M
A
C
R
A
E
I
S
C
O
M
I
N
G

Agnes looks up at Mr Udnam.

— Jessie MacRae is on her way. I can feel her coming down the levels.

— No.

He shakes his head.

– Is she alone?

Olive asks it sadly and her sisters look at her worried.

– No, there are two others. An adult and a child.

– What did you do to them?

The smallest girl flies down from the beam to scream in Mr Udnam's face – her feathers flutter around her and fall to the ground. The sound of cloven hoofs progresses slowly down the hallway. Mr Udnam begins to shake.

William Burroughs (49)

*take me to your word maker so
I can plead for my pitiful life*

BILL TURNS his head so his ear is pressed against the floor.
It is entirely possible to slip through the decades in between
these floors. Travel forward or back in time. There is the
voice of a woman. A girl child and an older sister maybe, it
is hard to work out. Someone should let that parrot out the
window. A bird is not fit to see these kinds of things. The
past is superimposing itself on the present. He could try to
work out what the great unconscious is trying to convey but
there is no logic in it. His lover is going through all of his
collected futurism images. He throws his fingers out. Still
tripping. He holds them up in front of his naked body. Waves
them back and forward. Selects another image. He holds up
each picture for Bill to inspect. There is a family on a boat.
The mother has an antenna growing out of her head. Then
there is a glass split-level house. His tackle sways as he raises
each image. His lover looks so serious as he inspects a picture of great domed worlds with trees in them. He stares for
a long time at spaceships that look like electric jellyfish in
the great black deep. There is a hospital using centrifugal
force to counter ageing. Spaceships to fly home from the
opera. A self-driving car whose passengers look out the

windows forlornly. There are networks of multiple tube trains under cities, and telephones where you can see the person you are talking to. His favourite is a tall tattooed woman wearing a glass space helmet. He looks at it for a full ten minutes and then lifts it up to the daylight.

— Tomorrow land is going to be so bright, John!

— Skies of fire, space invasions.

— Robots everywhere! We already have those, you know.

— Where?

— Your clock, that was the first robot.

John looks across at the kitchen clock as if seeing it for the first time.

— Or the washing machine, all the gadgets designed to do jobs we don't want to do are robots. They are building cars, fixing brains, they'll be writing all the words for us next, retraining us to be like them — robot poets to replace the real messy imperfect originals like me.

— Bill, do you want to go tae the movies?

— Why are you whispering?

— Am I?

— You are, John, yes. We will go to the cinema but I am too high right now. Is it true?

— What?

— They used to bury cats in these big old walls?

— Aye, they did that.

His lover gestures wildly at the wall.

— Why?

— To ward off evil.

— Funny way to ward off evil if you ask me. Not that I love cats, I really don't.

— I want to take you to the Dominion. It is a nice cinema.

Mr Burroughs, would you like to go to the movies and hold hands with me?

— What's on?

— They are playing a movie version of *To Kill a Mockingbird*.

— The Harper Lee novel?

— That is the very one.

— I do want to hold hands with you, however films of novels make me uneasy. They're trying to steal words and put them into boxes. It's not where the worlds of novels are meant to be. My words exist in here you see, in my mind. Then they exist in your mind. Nobody else gets to see how they pass between us — it is a form of alchemy! Of all the art forms writing is the most intimate and strange. I'll never see how you see the world I've created. You can't ever really see what I see either, no? Still, we somehow meet each other in that world, or recognise in each other that we've both been there.

He lays on top of John, bares his teeth.

— Is that a yes, Bill?

— Films are often just moving adverts for fuckability.

— You have that.

— So does Monroe, but I don't want to watch her mutilate Miller.

— So harsh!

There are cut-out words stuck all over the television.

— Words belong out in the ether — out in the programme. They are the very first virus.

John sits in between his lover's legs and rests his head on his thigh. He strokes his ankle and smokes.

— They infect us. There are ways to go back into that original programme — to experience freedom from all these things we have to do in our bodies each day.

— I like the things we do in your body.

— You are too complimentary.

John watches him pensively.

— Is it true?

— What?

— Ach, it doesnae matter.

— You want to ask me about my wife, don't you, if I really shot her dead?

— Not, if you dinnae want to talk about it.

Bill does not want to go there because whenever he remembers it the words and scene are clear as a snow globe he loved as a child, his wife's voice coming back to him again.

— *Let's do our William Tell.*

— Balance a glass on your head?

— *I'll trust you with my life.*

— Don't be dead on me for so many decades!

— *Why, Bill?*

— It's a dagger to the senses, Joan.

Whenever he is in this building she is on his mind and he doesn't know why.

— What do you want to know, John?

— How did you learn to live with it?

— I didn't.

Bill takes off his Marigolds.

— They're for keeping your hands dry when washing dishes, Bill.

— Not for jerking you off?

— That too, he smiles.

— But humans are waterproof.

— It's so you can increase the temperature.

The poet looks up at the ceiling and his eyes are watery.

The air around them changes. Outside there is a fairground somewhere. Buskers and a band play on the street. All of Edinburgh is alive and pulsing just outside their window. The day has done what it always does — it has passed the humans onto night so it can take a shift. There have been four seasons in one day. This early evening has brought an azure sky.

— I did do it, yes.

— And they put you in prison?

— No.

— Why not?

— Because I come from a wealthy family and they don't punish people like me. What happened was a mistake, that's all. A hideous, and highly regretful mistake.

Bill takes his hat off.

He looks older without it on.

John hands him a perfectly brewed cup of tea.

Tears.

Eyes.

— You are the most precious form of kindness, John.

The words of cut-up running alongside them on the wall begin with 'I am'.

I am Nixon.

I am an industrial robot.

I am the first teacup to orbit Earth in an American.

I am but you're not.

I am a word, but words have birds, birds are the words and I am birdy.

I am the arse snake — you are the idolator.

I am Maker and Melody and Plan.

The younger man traces his older lover's hands and stops

at the lower part of one of his pinkies which has been entirely cut off.

— Where is your fingertip?

— St Louis.

— What's it doing there?

— Just being a fingertip. I don't know, maybe they buried it. Farewell, small digit! They put me in the psych ward for this, you know. I delivered it as a young man to my psychiatrist one day and he did not appreciate it.

— He clearly never had a cat.

— Quite.

— Okay, Bill, how about music instead of the cinema? Shostakovich is playing with the London Symphony Orchestra, he has eight cellos in his ensemble. I think I prefer Vishnevskaya. I used to play Shostakovich when I was preparing bodies at the cemetery – it's meditative.

— All they want to know is what he thinks about Stravinsky and to concoct some story of a rag-and-bone boy done good. Europeans are obsessed with that kind of stuff. He's a nervous man and he's talented, they should leave him alone.

— I wish that parrot would stop screeching. What the hell is going on downstairs?

John thumps on the floor with his foot but the cacophony of bangs and noises and squawking only appears to keep building.

— The media is used to hound and censor free thought.

— I'd agree, Bill.

— The problem with mind control is finding ways to create enough distance so that even for a short time, you can see it quite clearly for what it is. I find putting my brain in the middle of the universe helps immensely.

190

– How do you know it is in the middle?

– Can you hear that parrot?

– I can hear the parrot.

– You know, John, when I was receiving ever more criticism and they wanted to ban more of my work, I decided to go and visit an old friend in the desert. We went up to the top of a volcano. We took something similar to LSD. Not your garden variety girl-next-door kind – this is a special hybrid similar to peyote. It's called DMT – the spirit molecule – I won't go into it right now because your beauty is distracting me, but we were ready. The night was dark and all you can see out there in the desert at night is stars. And you can see the actual curvature of the Earth rolling down the hill – when I laid back I was falling into the sky. It is only ideas that keep us here. Brainwashing from the machine makes us think our bodies are places that house us until we die when in fact they are just a rental space and we could go on vacation from them any time we want – leave for other dimensions without a passport or a permission slip. Do you want to come to other dimensions with me, young man?

– I want to go to the cinema. It's all I could handle right now.

– Where is your sense of adventure?

Bill laughs, kisses his lover on the neck, runs his fingers down his legs.

– To go where, Bill?

– Nearer to our real home, not this here illusion of life.

– I like illusions, especially if they are comforting.

– I like the way you taste.

– I like the way you kiss.

– I like your cock.

– How very delicate of you!

They grin and dance slowly together around the small apartment. They have pulled the futon out so they can lay on it. A lava lamp in the corner gives a warm glow to the room. The parrot downstairs has quieted down. John places one hand very gently on Bill's cheek.

– You want me to be your partner in the cosmos, Bill?

– Yes, I would. If you'd like to do so.

– I could dig that.

– Everybody could dig an astral companion, my friend. If you find the one you truly love above all others then it makes every second so much better, utterly mind-blowing in fact. So just last week, I am out in the universe, having a little time out from the Earth-grounded gravitational axis, and the stars and universe were just flying in through my left ear – see this big one?

John snort laughs.

– Uh-huh.

– All of that universe was flowing in here and right out through the other side – I was totally bodiless – headless even. I experienced sensation but I can't tell you what form I was in out there.

– It sounds terrifying.

– What I do know is the programme was fully aware I had left my body at that point – they could tell that I was infring-ing on territory hitherto unexplored by the two-legged mammalian variety. And not only that but I was open to staying.

– What did the programme make of that?

– It was unnerved.

– Why?

192

– Rules, my friend. Like the rules of this building we are living in.

– The stair cleaning? Nobody does that any more.

– Can't you feel the energy of this place? All those other years are tugging at our coats. Every time you walk in here it pulls at you, frays whatever it can get a hold of – at the edges. This building is a psychic vampire – it drinks human essence. It leans psychic tendrils into your aura and takes a long, hard hit. It's why you are weak! It's what vampires do, they make you think that siphoning off your energy is normal!

– Why don't they take yours?

– Because I'm a time-bending machine – time travel is literally at my fingertips. I exist here in this room with you right now, but I also exist in other rooms right now – with other people, at different times. People who I have not met, who I will never meet – those people are reading my words right now. In their own personal way they make those words come to life, but they have travelled from me right here to them right there.

– You're making my brain hurt, Bill.

– I meet them in some way in other dimensions. My imaginary worlds travel in and out of homes I will never see. They go through minds and cars and buses and boats and planes. They interrupt happy events and broken hearts. I send my worlds to those places. Other people seek them out. I don't go in person but I pass through other souls and leave something of my imprint. But those readers, they are in those worlds too – and they leave something of their imprint. In that way, there is a world created out there that none of us can point at – something invisible but ever-changing. Many of us have been to it and left something of ourselves there and took something for ourselves out of it.

John pulls on shorts, curls under Bill's arm.

The three-bar gas fire burns merrily.

— I love your voice.

— That's kind of you to say, John, but my voice is best in words, in writing. That is where people meet me and I meet them. They bring their memories, tastes, the smell of food in their kitchen as they walk through it reading my book. Or the feeling of sorrow ripping out of them. Or the way their head turns caught by some pretty thing that just flew by their window. There is a me that exists both here in the space I am in with you now — but also in the space where I was writing those words. Then I left a time continuum. Those words end up within the inner dimensions of strangers. They might pick up a world I made. Take it through their own time travel. Get on a plane: attend a funeral: ignore their lover. Flirt with a stranger — my worlds are in their possession for those times. They are not mine any more. In art we can compress the present and the past into a time capsule — pass it forward into the future. It can be done via images but words do more. There is a level to them. There is an imprint within them. We alter compositionally in relation to that interaction. The virus of words is not outside us — it is wholly within us. It holds the key to unlocking our inability to metamorphose. Kafka had it absolutely right. Gregor Samsa awakes one morning without the ability to speak — he is only able to screech like some kind of *ungeziefer*. What kind of a monstrous vermin has all language removed from it? Gregor Samsa has no ability to communicate by blinking, or talking, or writing, or drawing — without that facet he becomes reptilian to others. With no ability to trade our intent or ideas or affiliations, we are atomic meat parcels – flesh-covered skeletons – shit-dripping parasites. Even with the ability to communicate, most of our race struggles to transcend because we have been wholly programmed by language. Think about garbled political speeches – they cause confusion while also exerting some kind of terrible and powerful psychic and material control over billions of people.

— But a silent person is not an *ungeziefer*?

— No, not at all. Society won't have that as a truth though, will it? Society says that we must communicate in mainstream ways only. We must conform to what is expected or we shall be ostracised, or worse. Having our own thoughts to respond to the institutions that raise us is almost impossible. It makes people weary just to think about it. What would we do without the distraction of words ordered into a structure that keeps us behaving in the way the structures want us to? Without such tyranny and obedience to language, would we more clearly see the actual mechanics of the machine out there and inside here? All around us and in every atom. We are trained like Pavlov's dog – to respond to an endless supply of fake and essentially empty reward-based systems. We seek the approval of things that are not even real. How do we ever see the machine clearly for what it is? All structures have been built to manipulate us into believing that they are the powerhouse, that they are the mains supply – so if they get disconnected all the lights go out. As if they are the only word and reason and hope . . . If we ever truly managed to see that monstrous machine – that *ungeziefer* – clearly for what it is, all the structures would fail.

— Every one?

— They are failing already, my friend.

— Society can't continue like this?

— No. You mark my word, all the structures are going to come down, one by one, like this building.

Bill picks up his hat and places it over his eyes to take a nap.

John lays down beside him on the futon, the two of them tucked under a blanket. The poet never makes any attempt to touch him unless he indicates in some slight way that he wants it first.

— Thank you for not . . . expecting anything from me.

— Why would I expect anything from you? I am not one of those predatory older male homosexuals, John. I find them such a bore and to be honest, lately, I'd rather just have company. Sex is not everything — is it?

— No.

John physically drops his shoulders in relief.

— It's not that I hate to do it, Bill.

— It's just that you . . . hate to do it?

— I do.

— It's okay.

— Do you think I'm a freak?

— No, I think you're a divine being of complex and nuanced wonder.

John gets up to make more tea.

— There's biscuits, or Benzedrine?

— A little Benzedrine is always welcome. I do have opiates that are a touch stronger though. I may have to imbibe again soon but not if it bothers you.

— No! My friend will be here in a wee while. He'll bring wine. He's probably been held up by the celebrations, some festival in town, not as good as the book festival that year. I'd never seen anything like it! Me — just an embalmer of the dead – sitting in a bar with all of you. Real writers – I've only ever read or seen in the papers and never thought . . .

– That one of them would be offering to suck your cock at half past ten on a Thursday morning in a rainy city – where bagpipes play alongside trumpets and thinkers demand their platforms – because thought is everywhere and should be spread far and wide for the benefit of those that should be free?

– Aye.

– You are quite beautiful.

– I would have let you suck my cock that morning, you know.

Bill waves his hand dismissively in the air. John bends down to kiss the poet. He cradles the man's face in his hands like an infant. For a long time they are just souls staring into each other's eyes. It is gentle and intimate. More so than touch. More so than the heat or the want or the violence – although there is time yet for that. The face before John changes as he stares into it. He sees Bill as an older man with a much thinner face. He sees him as a Viking. As a fisherman. It's like he can see him in all the other lives he has been incarnated through and he loves him – in every one.

Ivy Proudfoot (17)

the palais

THE BOOTHS on the High Street sell silver jewellery. I gave Morag 4d and she is standing in a queue at the phone box. A man holds the phone down while people shout at him. He is clearly expecting a call. I run my fingers over silver earrings. Stop at the rings. There is one with a heart held in two hands.

— That's a Luckenbooth design. It was gied as a gift tae a fiancée.

— It's pretty.

— Aye. What's lesser known is it was cried a witch-brooch, protects its wearer from the evil eye. A kind ay talisman.

I pick one up. Hand it to the sales assistant. I pay quickly as Morag waves at me through the phone-box window, she's finally got in. I see them on the other side of the road, watching me.

The recruiters.

When I look up again Morag is chatting on the phone across the street and Violet is in front of me.

— I thought I had passed all the tests?

— You have. I just want to make sure you really want to do this tonight?

— Yes.

I must look like I am just standing next to a tourist who is looking at St Giles' Cathedral. Morag waves. I wave back. I remember once I left her in a bar at the bottom of Leith Walk because I had to take my brother home. When I walked past on the way to work the next morning she was still there. She had out-drank everyone and was having a bacon butty and doing a crossword with the cleaner. I turn and Violet is already gone. The night is clear now. I can even see a few faint stars. I touch the cold Luckenbooth ring and get a horrible feeling. Morag opens the red phone-box door. A police car pulls down the street. All things slow. Time is not going to be the same any more. Already it is different. Morag looks left and right. Crosses the cobbles. Presses her cold hand to mine. Takes my arm. She always puts hers inside mine. Same with her hand. Her side of the bed is right, we think in opposite orders to each other.

I must think of ordinary things.

It will keep me calm.

— Look, Ivy, there's Mr Udnam with the Lord Provost.

— I see!

Mr Udnam holds a booklet. *Edinburgh — War Time Guide.* He brandishes it in the air. The men laugh loudly at something. A car waits beside them with its engine running. They are no doubt going out for dinner somewhere fancy.

— You know it was the Lady Provost's Comfort Fund paid for that, Ivy?

— No, I did not.

— Aye, I used it tae find the address ay the Citizens Advice place. It's got a guide to sleeping accommodation for men in the forces. They can go tae the American Red Cross on

Princes Street, the YMCA, the Gunner Club, the Royal Scots Club, lots ay other places, and they can get fed at Church ay Scotland canteens, or the Granton R. N. Trawlers Club. The soldier I went out with last week took me there.

I swallow a fleeting moment of jealousy.

— What else does this fine publication recommend?

Mr Udnam and the Lord Provost show two women into the car. They wear glittery dresses. Faces over-powdered. Mr Udnam makes a great point of his own dignified exit off the street. He slips down into a plush leather interior.

— They have addresses fir cinemas — Garrison Theatre on Clerk Street, New Picture House on Princes Street, the Usher Hall fir music. It mentions the polar bear pool at the Zoological Park. There's a quote fae Walter Scott in it next tae the Scott's Monument, it says — (He) *stood for his country's glory fast, and nailed her colours to the mast.* It recommends the public baths on Infirmary Street, golf courses, Central Library, Fountainbridge library — all the usual.

We walk quickly through the city. Entirely in our bubble, inured from cold. Approaching the Palais, we can see there is no queue.

— Okay, baby girl — let's do it!

Morag wears a silk scarf tied in a bow and twisted to the side. Palais de Danse is best after midnight. We are early.

— D'ye think he'll be here?

— That yin fae the gang?

— Aye.

— Morag, ye can do better than him! It'll be US Air Force and local lads, same old. We should line up with the girls. Let them dance with us.

– No!

– Aye.

I say it firmly.

Hope she doesn't notice.

We turn onto the pavement outside just as a boy who looks like my brother walks by.

– Oh, Ivy!

– I know.

– Just like him!

Shake my head, numb.

– Craig had such a beautiful face.

– Like yours, my lovely Ivy.

– He was the bravest boy I ever knew.

Morag pulls out a wee bottle of gin and hands it to me.

Take a tot.

– Did you ken Craig was born too little?

– No?

– Aye, he weighed the same as a few bags ay sugar. That tiny wee thing grew strong uhn wily uhn fearless.

I will train harder than a girl has ever trained before.

Tonight is my biggest test so far and I am ready for it. My skin feels electric.

I see the boy across the dance floor.

He looks just as young as Craig did when he left for war.

The recruiters got here before us.

They are in the middle, dancing happily.

They do not look at me. I glance over them like everyone else. They say that boy is thirty, I get a jolt when I look at him as if he might be able to tell what I am to do. He's been here for three months. I didn't think it would happen like this. I am meant to be doing this in another country. I am still the me I was before. I am not changed yet. It's okay to see that he is a person and it's okay to discount it. That separates me from them. There are those who are good and do not hurt others and then there are those who do so deliberately because they are full of hate and there are those who will only hurt those who have given up the right to live by taking other lives without reason. My hatred is based only on what is right and what is wrong and I suppose he thinks that his is too. I am to leave a little of the good me behind forever on this dance floor. I prayed hard to God to give me strength. I did not want to let my heart be filled with hate for the bad people of this world but it did not work. I hate them with every fibre of my being.

Does it make me no less good?

— Ivy, you look so serious. What are you thinking about?

— Lilias Adie.

— Who?

— The last Scottish witch pulled out from a church congregation. They tortured her and then drowned her face down in the mudflats ower in Fife. Her head is on display in St Andrews.

— That's horrific!

— Only scientists see it.

— I'm not sure that makes it any better . . .

— I went to see Lilias Adie's resting place.

Morag pulls me onto the dance floor. And then there is him. I feel a need to keep talking and watching every move without appearing to have any concern. I smile and tell her the rest of the story.

— Where is it?

— Torryburn. I went to see where she lay in the mudflats.

They put witches down that way so they could not get back up again and seduce mortal men fir the devil.

— You could seduce the devil himself, Ivy Proudfoot.

She pulls the small of my back in a little closer.

Smells my hair. It is so beautiful to think of us like this, or in the bathrooms when we've locked ourselves in a cubicle. I spin her around. See the man behind her again. Fate has called me here. I watch him. Smile at her. Think of how to progress. I must be as clever as I can be. I will underline all of the things I need to learn. Say them in my head. Then out loud in secret. Then test myself. Plot. Plan. Train. If I do not act – then I am complicit. Who can refuse their own moral obligation when a war like this is going on?

— He's handsome.

Morag spies a young American soldier smiling at her.

— Very.

Two of the big Edinburgh gangs file in and take their walls, away from the US soldiers and the Scottish ones. The dance floor is busy. I have to still watch the boy – he is at Cupid's Corner buying a drink. Just one more minute like this. It feels so good to have her in my arms.

— Do you know what I heard, Ivy?

— No.

— Up and down the country witch covens are gathering en masse to spell-cast against Hitler.

— I'd like to spell-cast him with a bullet and a vat of boiling oil, some poison and a stake. Then an electrified bath for good measure.

I nod and watch the German spy skirting around the dance floor.

His eyes fall on me for a second and my blood runs cold.

The devil hides in mortal men. He does not deserve a clean death. Perhaps we should do to all the Nazis what they used to do to witches in Scotland?

Torture first.

Starve and interrogate.

Humiliate and parade for everyone to see.

Drown them all face down in the mudflats on the Firth of Forth?

Cut their heads off.

Then drop a huge slab of stone onto their back.

— What I don't get, Morag, is how come men can be so evil and ignorant they get like, entire countries to play with? But women — well, we get a fucking wart on our face so they drown us?

— Not totally true!

— Not far off. If you're a woman and you had some kind of disability, or maybe you just smelled weird, then before you know it, you are being hauled out of your lifelong church congregation and put to death in front of everyone in the most inhumane way possible!

— You make me hate men sometimes.

— Not all of them. Not Craig or my dad. Not the good ones, it's those other ones I hate, they can murder millions and get medals. They can commit the most heinous crimes and everyone around them is set on nothing but protecting them and pretending they are good and righteous and not just fucking despicably evil. They get gold bathrooms and private planes. It is not right! It has to stop. When will it be right, tell me?

Morag kisses my cheek gently and grabs my hand.

I follow her over to the wall and she gets cigarettes out the machine. We go back down into the main hall and I go over to the bar where he is.

He is next to us now.

I position us so he is looking at Morag only. She smiles at him. He is not looking at me. Men never look at me when we are together. Now I see the use in it. I point at two fruit cocktail drinks behind Cupid's Corner bar. He has one with an umbrella in. The barman makes two more, identical to the others. I reach into my purse. Put down coins. In my bag, I unscrew the little bottle with one hand. He is talking to Morag now. I don't hear words. I hear the room as if I'm in a swimming pool. The band sound like they are playing underwater. A warble of so many voices and feet tapping and clicking and hearts beating and slipping the liquid down into his drink. He takes his cocktail without looking – he is still spellbound by my girlfriend and he drinks it, fast. I feel panicked – what if I got it wrong? I don't want to drink our drinks any more so I spill them both . . .

– Ivy!

– Sorry!

– Are you okay?

He leans over and I do not want to look back into his grey eyes but I do.

I nod.

Grab her.

– This rotating dance floor is so good! There is never a break between songs!

He says it to her and we walk away. My entire body is shaking. The music comes back in so loud again now. I hear everything crystal clear. Like I just came up from a submarine. One band spins off the stage. The next one comes on playing even faster and wilder. There are girls on the balcony upstairs, feet on the railings, pretty dresses, smells of perfume. I don't look back.

– Bathroom.

– Okay.

We make our way around to it, it is our favourite room in the Palais, so decadent and huge. I throw myself down on a chaise, light a cigarette, pull her down onto me, grinding into her until the whole place shudders.

Floor.

Ceiling. Chandeliers.

As we walk out, there is a fuss in the corner as the man falls to the floor.

Other side of the room.

Someone rushes in.

He is put in the recovery position. Pale. Another member of staff looks frantic. Morag is saying something. I am nodding. The man is carried out of the dance hall. He disappears from sight. Dancers reconvene in the space where he collapsed – as if he was never there. We join them. Morag spins me back out and in.

It was as easy as I hoped it would be.

I dance – as if I won't sit on a tiny, rickety warplane flying out of England tomorrow. The engine so loud as we fly over the French sea. A stranger beside me keeping an eye out for German bombers. Flying low down over an area where I have never been in my life. I dance as if I won't strap on a parachute. Jump into a blue sky. As if there won't be utter panic for a second before I pull the rope. As if I won't be flung back up into the sky, before sailing down into France like a white fluffy dandelion being guided by a warm breeze. I dance as if I won't utter a word again — unless it is in French.

I have a sense of what will come so I dance — as if I won't be shot at one night while walking home from an explosion that was laid by my own bare hands. I will think the bullet only grazed my head but it will in fact be lodged in there — without me even knowing — for years. I dance — as if when I am caught and repeatedly drowned to almost the point of death, when they ask my name again, I still refuse to give them it. I dance — as if I don't already know that they will give no recognition to a woman like me. I am not rich, or middle class, or educated. I don't need that anyway. All I need is to keep seeing my brother's face and that one day he walked into a camp and never came back out again. I am doing what I can for my girlfriend, for my family. I dance — as if I don't know that no matter what I do — when I utter my last words in French, as an old, old lady and when they celebrate so many of the British spies, many, many, many years in the future — the name Ivy Proudfoot will not be mentioned at all. I dance — like when I die, the other Night Witches will come for me in a wooden biplane — and fly me out in formations of three.

1956

Flat 5F5

Agnes Campbell (63)

the devil's daughter, her lover and the child

THUNDER RUMBLES across the Firth of Forth. The sea is black. Whorls throw up seaweed and driftwood. Waves slap off Granton harbour. Masts rattle and shake. There is a whistling sound from boats funnelling wind. All the pubs in the city are closing. Bar staff hunker down for a lock-in. Those still on the streets hurry. Coats over their heads. Umbrellas' torn-back spikes exposed and useless, abandoned on streets and bridges and bus stops. The trams have stopped. Soon they will be stopped for good. No trains will run tonight. Buses swerve on slick wet streets. The Water of Leith has burst its banks. The colonies in Stockbridge are flooded. Residents evacuate lower levels. Fire services are on high alert. The hospital emergency room at the Infirmary is overwhelmed. A man mops the floor continuously so wet shoes don't make someone else slip on it. Under the city the catacombs are still. Down in the belly of the city there is scratching. Rats scurry out of tunnels. From down the street, golden lights at No. 10 Luckenbooth Close go out one by one.

It is the third time in ten minutes that this side of the city has blacked out.

Archie finds his wife's massive box of candles.

His hands shake.

So does the flame.

He strikes match after match. Each nook and cranny of the apartment becomes bathed in light. Shadows flicker. Archie could swear he sees the shadow outline of five angels for a second but he has never been able to see what his wife can. He sits back down, unaware that his wife can hear cloven hoofs walking down through the building.

Agnes steadies her breathing.

Draws on every bit of experience she has from all the seances held before.

The sisters wait on the wooden beam, they are looking towards the door.

Mr Udnam clenches his fists.

Dora is meditating as deeply as she can to hold Agnes in a space of strength for what is coming. The sisters begin to hum a song quietly. It lilts in and out of the footsteps. They hear another set follow behind them and then a third, smaller. They somehow seem to be coming from the belly of the building, from the guts of the basement and from an echoey spiderwebbed attic – all at the same time. Mr Udnam shakes. Agnes nods at her husband to give the man a throw. He cannot pass out yet. Archie awkwardly drapes a woollen shawl around his shoulders. In all the years she has practised. In all her days! It turns out we each only have one true calling! For some it is a love affair, limbs entwined. For others it is their child, or a house that meant more to them than any other, or a job. Saving someone unexpectedly or overcoming fear. For little Agnes Campbell – it was a natural-born skill that made all the other children not want to play with her. It made her afraid in every class she ever sat in – that one day she'd be pointed out and dragged from the classroom and taken to prison or the mudflats. She has practised day in and day out regardless. Let people know through her work – that this world is far from all there is. Energy resides in flesh only as long as the earthly plane ties us to it. Those we love or miss or need or hate or want answers from – they are not gone, they are just not here in physical form. Agnes has played her part. Healing those so weary with grief they cannot go on. She can feel last remnants of thunder rumbling across the dark crags of Arthur's Seat. Little kids unable to sleep, faces pressed to windows or under blankets. She wants badly to hold the two younger sisters. But you can't do that with spirit. What she can do is hear them. Do whatever she has to do to allow this to play out. She feels other spirits coalesce. Those who have looked after her all through her childhood. They too are gathered in this room and worried for her. Archie's ancestors stand behind him. Dora, too, is surrounded by the people of her past. It is how it is – all of the ancestors convene, especially when we need them. A light appears behind the sisters, leading all the way back to the one light.

– Dear God, let these girls finally reach their true home tonight.

– Amen, says Dora.

Archie crosses himself.

He never does!

A peaceful feeling settles over Agnes. Not all who claim to possess her powers are fake. It is indeed worth risking jail, or her husband's disappointment. For decades, his lack of understanding has left her more than lonely but what great thing is achieved in comfort? The littlest sister clutches her elder sister's hand so tight. Her fists and arms are still dimpled. Her tiny feet are so perfect. Two tears slide down Agnes's cheek. The entire sky flashes light pink and then black again. The footsteps are now so close.

– Where has she been, Mr Udnam?

It is the eldest sister, allowing him one last opportunity to save his soul.

He shakes his head.

Archie sits further back in his chair as their living-room door appears to open by itself. Rain rattles the windows. It flows down the gutter outside. A rumble builds so deeply it feels the entire building could split in two.

– Jessie?

The littlest sister, Mary, tries to run forward and is stopped by Olive.

– Wait . . .

Agnes looks up.

Mr Udnam turns toward the door. Right in the middle of it is a young woman with black hair and bright eyes and two perfect horns on top of her beautiful head. She steps into the room. Raises her long skirts. Reveals perfect cloven hoofs – a gift from the ether. She extends a hand into the dark hallway behind her. It is taken by Elise – delicate as ever – still in love with her Jessie – even more now in spirit, it seems. The two women stand in the doorway. Between their legs, emerging from under their skirts, is a tiny little girl. She is no more than three years old, with her own perfect white ivory horns – a contrast to her mother's long dark ones – and she has dimples, much to the delight of the younger angels.

– Hope!

— We never stopped looking for you, not all these years. He wouldn't say where you had gone!

— Olive, Mary, Clementine, Rose, Bessie.

— Elise!

— Did you know what happened to us?

The five red-haired sisters look at their elder mirror image who is wide-eyed with emotion for her younger siblings.

— I know, I couldn't come . . .

— Why not?

— Mother didn't make it in the end. You know that too?

— I know.

— Is she with you?

— She's in the in-between place, for now.

— Is that where he's going?

The twins point at Mr Udnam.

— No.

— I thought I was being escorted by angels?

— Angels don't get to go where you are going, Mr Udnam. Jessie carefully says.

She turns and curtsies to Agnes, at her table, all lit up by candlelight.

— Thank you, ma'am, for having us in your home. We have waited a long time for this opportunity. We've been unable to make contact properly with anyone since we passed, despite trying. It feels like we will never move on from this building . . .

— What did he do? Clementine asks Jessie.

— This is a trick. It's witchcraft, you hear me? I can have you put in prison!

Mr Udnam points at Agnes and Archie stands up, ready to go for the man if he moves toward his wife.

– No, it's not, Agnes states.

– Elise went to New York when she left me. This is not real . . .

Elise turns to him.

– You would lie to my face after what you did?

A dark energy warms the room.

Agnes levitates slightly.

The sisters rise up into the air.

Wings flutter. A breeze lifts papers on the sideboard. The sisters' voices are like bells. Mr Udnam recedes – all of their eyes are on him.

– We can smell blood on your skin.

The sisters say it together. Around the walls, five sets of wings open as shadows.

– You can't feel pity for her – she's the devil's daughter, her father came to me on the day she died and he asked for her head because of what she did to him . . . ask her about that!

– We can't pick our fathers.

– Elise loves a monster!

He points at Jessie.

– My father sold me to him, Jessie says.

– Why?

Agnes asks it quietly.

– To give him a grandchild that would be raised with all privileges possible.

– Why?

– So his descendants could destroy what God made. The world and all good people in it!

Hope clings to her leg, peeping out at Mr Udnam.

– She's scared of me!

– My child is not scared of anyone.

Jessie's horns are even longer and sharper than they were in her mortal life.

— Mr Udnam — you murdered my sisters, because they came looking fir me . . .

Elise does not shrink back in spirit. His heartbeat pounds in his neck and temples. He tries to swallow. Jessie's horns glint in the candlelight. Agnes prays for all of them and the sisters join in as the layers between the worlds peel back.

— Dear God, thou art in heaven, hallowed be thy name. Thy kingdom come, thy will be done, on earth as it is in heaven. Give us this day our daily bread and forgive us our debts as we forgive those who trespassed before us, for thine is the kingdom, the power and the glory, for ever and ever, amen!

The smallest girl, Mary, closes her eyes and extends her arms out. She is feeling something that none of the rest of them can quite see yet. The youngest child is open to visions past and future in a way none of her sisters are.

— There's a big knife . . . and he's running up to Jessie.

She says it in a very quiet voice.

Agnes feels a burning sensation.

Pain like she has never felt.

Wind howls through the floors. She is trying not to panic. It is taking a great deal of energy to let all the spirits through and to let them speak. She looks over at Archie: he is terrified, chain-smoking, not knowing whether to get up and close the door or go near his wife. She feels fearful then, too. Looking at the sisters Agnes realises they remind her of a girl she used to sit next to at school. Their mother. She is sure of it. They played hopscotch. The woman has sent her daughters to her home and it is their right to be allowed, all of them - Jessie, too, and her daughter — to speak freely.

– Tell me what you need to move on.

– We don't get to, Elise snaps.

– The girls can though. If you can help them that will help at least, Jessie says.

– I can see him walking through the rooms. His knife has my sister's blood on it and Jessie's and Hope's. The walls are open. He has a huge saw in the hall. He planned it. It's just him in the building with three bodies. In the hallway to his parlour downstairs there are stains on the wood like tears of blood.

– You killed them!

Clementine lands in front of him and shakes her wings out.

Agnes feels one side of her body go entirely numb.

Mary puts her arms down and opens her eyes. She looks at Mr Udnam with such hatred and confusion. He steels himself against it, his eyes turn black and his reptilian skin is revealed, his deep hatred! Agnes watches as the other side of her body goes numb. She can no longer understand words properly. The light is fading. She grips Dora's hands even tighter and the woman opens her eyes, realising her friend is in danger.

– Send them to the light!

– Who?

– All the younger sisters, I can't do it for Jessie and Elise and Hope but the other sisters can still go – there's a light there, look, see . . .

The sisters turn. A light comes into the room from the storm outside – clouds swirl through it. Mary looks at Elise who nods, emphatically. It is her job as the youngest to go first.

– He took off her head. It is still here! They are all still in this building. She must lead her sisters out of this realm.

– Agnes, you're not breathing properly!

Over at the table, Archie touches his wife. She cannot see anything at all and she is stiff on one side.

– Let the girls go!

These are Agnes Campbell's final words.

Hope runs forward – as her angel cousins all pass – one by one – up into the light.

– Come with us!

They call back to the infant.

– She can't!

Elise is frantic.

As the light begins to dim Mr Udnam hits the floor – his breathing is ragged. Colour drains from his face. Jessie stands over him. Her horns are silhouetted in his black eyes as the light goes out in them.

Jessie and Elise, Hope – they too are fading.

Archie opens the front door wide and shouts down into the stair . . .

– An ambulance, somebody, please, please! My wife! Agnes needs an ambulance.

Dora gets up, knocking the Ouija board to the floor.

There is a blue light flashing on Lauriston Place as an ambulance pulls out from the Royal Infirmary. The Victorian hospital's huge windows watch it go, its windscreen wipers barely able to stop the rain lashing off it. Dora Noyce is stood at the entrance to No. 10 Luckenbooth Close, ready to wave them down and take them upstairs to her friend. Tears pour down her face in the rain. Upstairs, a man's body is inert and gone. Archie holds his wife like he never has.

Knowing he got it wrong and that he should have held her like this every single day, howling at this cursed building for taking his wife away.

Agnes drifts.

Angels above her rise up and up into light.

It's so beautiful.

That moment of freedom – when souls are no longer tied to human pain.

What an awful and terrifying and wondrous mortal coil!

The angel sisters hold their hands out to her – as do all the other spirits she has helped over all these years. They are there too – lines and lines of them – leading up to the place of ancestors. She wants to follow them so badly! Somewhere far away, her husband shouts in the stairwell and footsteps pound up stairs. No. 10 Luckenbooth Close shakes. The fabric of time dissolves and, for a second, she sees exactly what Mr Udnam did. Then, her tiny circle of vision goes out entirely.

William Burroughs (49)

this building is a psychic vampire

AS LATE evening approaches the city's sound softens but it still has its garish bursts. Street lights on Princes Street and Queen Street come on at once – all the way along the Royal Mile and down the hills to Stockbridge, the New Town, Leith and the South Side and over at the West End, Dalry and Gorgie. All the lamp posts create their moon glows for creatures to walk home. All of this while the poet stands at the window never more content than with his lover's arms wrapped around him. Just to hold and be held, this is the only place he wants to be.

– So, if that's how it works then do you think that the very first human who spoke was just the first person infected by the virus of language, as it were, Bill?

– I think the written word came before the oral tradition.

– Surely we spoke in grunts, or noises?

– I'm sure we did but on the walls of caves we carved pictographs and symbols – moving images. Those symbols were telling stories before people were chit-chatting around a fire. They were our first poems – our first way to impart knowledge. To teach. To learn. To comment. To show others what we think and see how they respond. We were writing words before we could walk upright. We used to carve them on the walls – language is an ancient and deadly form.

– And now, it's your trade.

– It's my way of being.

– But ye can't leave it once you've started?

– Some can.

– You can't?

– I can't, no. I couldn't leave it if I wanted to.

– Why?

– For those of us who have fallen – into the affliction of addiction to a virus sent to humans from the origins of time – we don't understand exactly how it simultaneously rewires our hearts, souls and minds – or how it is allowing us to evolve a part of the mind barely understood yet. We can't explain, even to ourselves, why we would steal for the time to do it – but there is no doubt poets and writers have died for this, sacrificed their lives for it. Those few born ones, they will do anything at all for it.

– Would ye get arrested for it?

– Yes. They've banned my work in plenty places.

– What is it that addicts you?

– There is an energetic imprint of the original source that travels via words.

– God?

– I don't like that idea necessarily, but I couldn't refute it, no.

– You think that words are a kind of time traveller of an imprint of the energetic light we originally come from? The light source, the God source as some people would see it?

– Exactly that, you've got it.

— I'm gonnae be having some interesting conversations at the morgue tomorrow.

— I see it like this, my precious man: it is the written word that was the first virus and it made the spoken word possible. Maybe the word virus is wrong, don't quote me on it. Maybe if it is a programme within the wider programme we are all residing in — a code if you like — then maybe this written form is the most ancient of arts. Then think on this: codes are there to be broken. When that happens they lead us to truth — perhaps words are the only thing that can lead us to truth and those willing to go into the programme completely bring truths back out that they barely understand.

The two men hold each other.

Stand at the window watching lights come on all over Edinburgh.

Bill's fedora is sat atop the prongs of the television and all around the walls the words appear to move by the light of the lava lamp.

— If language came to us from the origins of time, then it has travelled space and ocean and air and touched every single heart and mind that ever walked on this planet. It has been more ferocious than the whip on the back of an adulterous woman in a village square in Lebanon. It is passed from father to son so they might loathe and fear what it is they desire — whether that thing carries a uterus or a penis. It labels all things — *other* — as something to be destroyed. The flesh knows its own queer predilection or its lack of normalcy and it denies it — all of our urges and want and knowledge exist in the subconscious first and foremost — so-called reality lies to itself and to everyone else. It is weapon and trap — liberator and monster. We are all at the mercy of and malleable to the programmes that raised us – whether they be religious, or class based, or gender biased. All structures are implemented through an underlying violence and brutality particular to this planet.

– Do you think I'll still understand this when I've straightened up? John asks.

– Aye.

– You tried Scottish!

– Badly! Thing is, John, creatures like us, word travellers – we download transmissions via twenty-six letters of the alphabet, or twenty-four in the Greek alphabet, 3,000 characters of the Chinese alphabet, twenty-eight in Arabic, twenty-three in Latin, eighteen in Gaelic, twenty-seven in Spanish, seventy-one in Japanese including diacritics, thirty-six in the African alphabet that forms the basis for Fula, Ewe, Hausa, thirty-three in Amharic which originated as a consonant-only alphabet so Ethiopians could write in Ge'ez. There are twenty-two in Aramaic, twenty-seven in Spanish, thirty-two in Icelandic. There's Cherokee, Javanese, Mongolian, Ersu Shaba, Nüshu, Ogham, Sinhala, French, Italian, German, Balinese, Burmese, Armenian, Khmer, Thai, Lao, Tibetan, Dravidian, Cyrillic. I could go on for days because we have over 7,000 living languages and about only half of those are written, yet somehow your country persuaded the world that English was the only important one. You publish all your books in it. You are still scared even of accents!

– That was the neighbours more than us to be fair, John says.

– You blame everything on them!

– They've a lot to answer for. So, if all languages come

from an original virus, or programme, the light source, the primordial matriarch as it were – what are they doing to us?

– Altering our chemical composition, our molecules, our energy imprint.

– It gets into our chromosomes?

– Every single one. It gets into absolutely everything, it changes the patterns of the brain. It exists here. See where I *write it on the page* it is simultaneously here and out in the universe where my mind expanded last week.

– I love you.

– I love you too, John.

– Is it crazy to love someone you've only spent seven days with in person?

– No, it's crazy to love someone when you've known them for years.

– So, if scientists are right and every particle has another particle with exactly the same mass but an opposite electric charge – then it's possible two people can fit together like yin and yang, noh?

– My understanding is that when matter and antimatter come into direct contact, they annihilate each other. They just totally disappear in a flash of energy. It's what should have happened directly after the Big Bang spunked its guts out. When matter and antimatter meet they leave nothing behind at all – so really we shouldn't exist.

– Perhaps we dinnae exist.

– What they do know – is there is one extra matter particle for every billion matter and antimatter pairs. Somehow, just that extra one means we aren't totally zapped into the stratosphere.

– One sole particle can change everything, Bill?

– Yes, if one sole particle can change everything then so can a person, no?

– Then one thought could?

– One day the right thought will, my lovely John. Any person walking around this planet today could land upon a thought that would change the evolution of the human race. I mean most of them won't because evolution has been careened through space and time mostly out of religious extremes, right? Our need for gods to give us permission for whom we hold hands with, or how we work or live or lay in our beds. It's all been geared to favour men though, hasn't it? I don't need a fabricated deity to raise me in some archaic programme so I can feel okay about being a moral man in a universe without explanation. However I am free – so many men are diseased and by that I mean they are dis-eased in their own masculinity. In their desires both homosexual and heterosexual, they are so twisted by it the only answer they have is to try and control literally everyone – women, children, dogs, trees, oxygen, space, other men.

– Language?

– You've got it.

Bill and John grin at each other.

– Keep talking to me. I could listen tae your voice forever.

– Some people got hit by good cosmic rays and some by bad ones. Antimatter constantly rains down on Earth. It arrives as cosmic rays, energetic particles descending to Earth. They can be seen more during thunderstorms and sometimes you can get 100 cosmic rays per square metre all containing antimatter. So how does that pan out for the person on the bicycle cycling through the rain? A gram of antimatter could create an explosion as big as a nuclear bomb. We can only produce a tiny amount, it costs too much. They haven't figured out how to do it properly yet – however, someone is walking around with their particular programme of language and science and in their own particular unique imprint, one day, all those things coalesce in their brain and they will find a way to slow antimatter down so they can study it and unlock all it has to teach. And for that they will use the virus, the glorious virus from outer space, language, the territorial tyranny and wonder of words! Antimatter can diagnose cancer and one day treat it, all things will be treatable in the end but we have to discard – many – of the programmes – if we are to evolve to the next level.

– I didn't know poets were so well informed, Mr Burroughs.

– Don't trust poets unless they are scientists.

– I wish I'd studied mair science!

– Poets are by far not the only people trying to unlock and deconstruct and prove the great secrets of the world. All poets write about people. Why are we still so barely evolved in some ways and so utterly astonishing in others? People are like matter and others are antimatter – there are those who want humanity to evolve fully and their opposite is a source that seeks only to keep things the same or turn them back toward the Dark Ages. To stall or deny or destroy progress so they might for that sneakiest of seconds that makes up a human's whole life – they might fool themselves into thinking that by controlling – dominating, torturing, colonising, segregating, raping, murdering – that they managed for a period of history to fix time to them. That they won't die. That antimatter is not destined to destroy them.

That death is not imminent and cares not for power or wealth – that they can't escape it.

— To control their fear ay it?

— Impose themselves on matter and particle. Maybe humans want to make something that can annihilate everything – much in the way death annihilates us all – as a way of denying their own place in the void, their utter core of nothingness.

— So why don't we change it, Bill?

— I blame the God programmes.

— Even Buddhism?

— Yes.

— Wiccans?

— I do like those but yes. We don't need religion – we need reality – a good solid 24/7, 365-day-of-the-year exploration of reality. Poverty, domestic violence, rape, child abuse, intolerance, bigotry, racism, tyranny! All of those religions are just programme structures if you like, so is class, wealth, racism, they are things people in this world just don't need any more – they are holding us all back. What we need is every human fed and educated and told to question their own programme – every single one – to know that the real idea of why humans are here can belong to this generation. That we could explore it on a daily basis until we find a way to replace bad men with good children – to overrule archaic modes of human intervention over the fates of others via totalitarian brutality.

Bill is crying.

John puts his arms around him.

— I think we should have some tea and then we should go and walk all night long, I'm going tae take you on a train tomorrow, out of the city, just fir the afternoon. It won't be like California, it will be cold.

— Good, I loathe the sun, unless it's falling.

— We can walk along North Berwick beach, go for a pint or two. I'll take you to the lobster shack before we come home. You can see where they burnt all the witches then we can get back into town well before your reading starts.

— That sounds perfect. I'll meet Jim beforehand. It was so good at that conference, I'm not sure they'll ever top it again.

— When all those men began jumping up to say they were queer, I felt proud to be from Edinburgh, to have all that energy here and that handsome Dutch guy wanting someone to baptise him!

— We all wanted to baptise him.

— What about the Sikh guy, saying queers are incapable of love and hermaphrodites can't cum? That hair down to his waist – I wanted to chop it off with scissors.

— Quite the conservative you are, John!

— You were getting along well with Miller.

— It was civilised.

— The press had never seen anything like it. It's been reported on everywhere since you left!

— I know.

— You'll be so famous. You know they love it when you talk.

— I can't think of anything more hideous.

— But how will anyone know that language is a virus and how it works if you don't send those words out into the world?

— True.

— Mary McCarthy said how much she loved *Naked Lunch*.

— She clearly has taste.

— Perhaps we should go sailing together, Bill.

— Into the sunset?

— Something like that, John grins.

— I once knew a man who sailed for twenty-three years without an incident and just after he had bragged about it, that very day the ship had an accident and killed him and everyone else on board. That evening I heard another bulletin on the radio of an aeroplane that had gone down over Florida, Flight 23, everyone dead and another captain with the exact same name. By this I mean to say it is like what MacNeice articulates in his poem called 'Snow'.

— Which is what?

— Here we are in a room and it is light and small and warm and we are held by it — despite the carnivorous nature behind this building's facade, however the carnivorous nature behind the building's facade is the same as that in snow — life is so much more than we can manage it to be, it is so much more sudden than we are able to understand.

— I feel that.

— He says how the world is so much more than we think, so much crazier than we think. It is too drunk and too various.

— I need a drink.

— John Glenn circles the world three times in Friendship 7 — he is a man in space. Meantime Polaroids are going to do colour prints that will develop themselves within sixty seconds. The civil rights movement has to see young black men in university and women too! The Cold War is getting worse, they have assassinated Kennedy and they are threatening nuclear arms. All the time we are on the brink of the entire planet's destruction at the hands of crazy, powerful men! They want to put a man on the moon before the decade is done. There is an army of hippies with dogs on strings who will put away their tie-dye trousers into non-recyclable bins, cut off their dreadlocks and burn them. They will scour out their brains with bleach, learn to sit in chairs in square rooms.

– We won't change anything?

– It will need to be changed and challenged again and again! The hippies and thinkers will mostly quit. They will sit on chairs in square rooms and talk to other people in square rooms. They will collect their paycheck from a square box. They will go back to other square rooms. Smaller ones this time, where they will fold clothes and find their fridge without milk or cheese and they will go to another square room where a man with some things to sell them will do so and they will go back home to put their food in square boxes. They will still think about why we all obey these men who have given themselves a catchy covers-all trademark in one single word – government – but they won't keep standing up to shout about it.

– It's so desperately bad! John says.

– The people in charge are not Plato's apostles – they're rich boys on a power trip. I know this because I'm a rich boy who came from rich men. My people have been generationally institutionalised to believe this world and the people in it are theirs and they don't care about cosmic rays and all they do with language is manipulate it so they can get more.

– I hate it!

– More power. More wealth. More war. Those men do not carry the guilt and sorrow of a woman's non-beating

heart. I do, to my great, great shame . . . so what I am trying
to say, my handsome, lovely friend, is I can't think about it
any more. Let's get the train to North Berwick in the morning, let's walk on the beach and hold hands and fall in love
and forget, and may all the cosmic rays be upon us even if
only for one day!

The door is knocked quietly.

— Archie? Are you okay?

— I am, John are you alright? I didn't want to disturb you
so late – it's just, I'm out of milk and my dear wife likes to
sup tea before bed and I don't like to leave her in the flat in
her chair.

— Of course. Do you want biscuits, snacks?

— Hard drugs?

Bill offers the last – appearing behind him as John goes to
get milk.

— No, thank you, good man. Those are not for us. A cup
of tea more than suffices!

Archie looks so much older now and he is clearly tired.
It takes him a minute to just accept the milk in a mug and
smile, balance it and walk slowly down the stairs.

Bill and John stand at the door until he is gone.

— So sweet. His wife had a terrible stroke seven years ago.
You know he looks after her every day, plays her music, cares
for her insane parrot, bathes her, buys her soft cashmere
jumpers so they are kind tae her skin. He dotes on her. She
can't speak, cannae say a word. Often doesn't seem to understand anything but she never wanted to leave this building
so he's caring for her here. She's not been out that door in
seven years and he barely leaves her side.

— The course of true love!

Pad back into the warm flat. All the way down on the street the lights of No. 10 Luckenbooth Close glow warmly in the dark air. Rain begins to spit again on the street. Some of the building's curtains are open. Some are closed. A few have gaps. A lot of the shutters are now nailed back or removed. In No. 5F5 Ovid scratches the bottom of his cage and whispers – *walls. Walls. Walls. Walls.* The only one who knows why he is doing this is Agnes but she can't even blink properly any more. In the window she sits looking out at the city. Her husband combs her hair. In the window above Bill and John have their arms wrapped around each other. They too are staring out at the lights of Edinburgh and even the ones which sparkle away out there across the water – the long dark line underneath the Firth of Forth. They turn toward each other and kiss for the longest time – atoms and particles, words not better than feelings. In their kiss for just a minute there is no yesterday and no tomorrow – no fear, no pain. Cosmic rays shower secondary particles soundlessly all over the world.

Part III

Queen Bee (21)

the red room

COCO CAN'T be more than fifteen years old. She twirls around a pole on the small stage at the end of the bar. She is wearing stiletto sandals, with ribbon snaked around her ankle and tied in a bow at either side of her knee. Her skin is pale and unblemished. She turns back to smile at the small audience of men, undoes her bra, holds it out and lets it drop.

Her older sister has just finished dancing. Ellie has blonde hair and blue eyes too. She sashays toward the toilets, down a narrow hall where there is a small nook for lap dances. A man walks behind her and they disappear into the recess as the double front doors to the Red Room are pushed wide open.

The sisters' mother looks up from behind the bar as four people walk in and stand in a row.

Drinks are poured in silence.

Four whiskies slide across the bar top.

No money changes hands.

The Original Founders are rarely seen.

They are spoken about in whispers across the city. They are said to speak a language entirely of their own — a cross between Romani, Doric, and Manc. The men wear tailored trousers, braces, silk-lined waistcoats and heavy stopwatches of 24-carat gold. Each has a delicate chain with a St Christopher, and sovereign rings on every finger. The look is topped with fine, expensive bowler hats from the milliner at Lock & Co. Hatters in London, and each holds an identical bespoke cane. Bee commissioned them. They are beautiful works of craftsmanship, tailored to the client's instructions. Sometimes it's a family crest or a personal inscription to a loved one. Bee requested cane heads that twist off, each one slides out to reveal a long, thin dagger. She sips her drink. Teardrops are tattooed below large eyes. Shaved head. Fringe. Dr Martens boots. Black tights. Red lips. Black nails. Velvet shorts. Her shirt is white and she wears a tie. There's a lipstick in her bag. It has a Stanley blade inside it. There are wet wipes from looking after her babies, cigarettes, Tampax and a small but solid cosh. On one wrist is a feather tattoo. On the other is a Celtic tattoo from the Iceni tribe. They call her Boadicea. It's not her real name. In close company she is referred to as Bee. Only a few strangers actually know her real name and it is not good for them if they do.

The Red Room is quiet. A cluster of regulars, a few local businessmen, two tourists.

The energy shifts subtly. Men nod at the Original Founders. Look quickly back to the stage. The room is dimly lit. Bathed in a deep red glow. A mahogany bar top. Above the optics is a selection of whisky, brandy, gin. The girls' mother wipes down the counter, then the till and the fridges.

Onstage, the girl dances so slowly the entire bar appears as if it is going almost into reverse to accommodate her moves, a man steps back, puts his pint down. She slides down onto the stage and grinds her hips to 'Hurricane' by Neil

Young. The smell of alcohol, cigarettes and weed softens the dense air as she reaches one strong arm and leg up and grips onto the pole. She is upside down. Coco spins gracefully to the floor. Lays with her elbow out, head resting on her hand, and stretches one leg languorously up. Notes litter her feet like flowers. She twists around. Sits up on her knees. Hips wide, she pushes her legs as far apart as she can. Tips her head back. She is all ribcage. Pink nipples. Long blonde hair shines under the light. The Original Founders nod. Until she comes of age, nobody will touch her while they are here. The infamous Pubic Triangle is made up of three strip bars at a busy junction leading down to Lothian Road. The Red Room's youngest star can dance and make money, but she is not to be disrespected. This only makes every man that frequents the Red Room want her more. Strippers in the Pubic Triangle's two other bars despair at her untouched prettiness. Before long another will take her place. For now, Coco seems like the only girl in the world who can wear such tiny knickers, suspenders and stockings and somehow look wholesome. Her mother keeps one eye on her elder daughter, Ellie has come out from the private dance with a red glow in her cheeks. Coco finishes and steps offstage. She gives a quick smile to Rab, the eldest of the Original Founders.

— Don't even fucking think it.

Bee says it without looking back at her husband.

— I never said a thing, Bee. Is it time?

— Yer fucking right it is.

Bowler hats are laid on the bar in a row.

A cellar hatch behind the bar is opened and the mother goes down a wooden ladder. The smell of damp wafts up – spilled lager and cider and the cold metal of kegs. An electric light bulb sways down in the cellar, it illuminates the upstairs bar briefly until she is back. Closes the floor hatch. Slides four boxes across the bar counter. The Original Founders each open a box and take out what is in it. They walk out leaving empty glasses behind them and the mother quickly tidies away their boxes and bowler hats, ready to be collected later.

The Original Founders push the double wooden doors open onto a street lined with snow.

Flakes cascade down through the sky.

They put on their masks one by one as they come out.

There is a ram with long curled horns.

A zebra.

A wolf.

A fox.

They walk down the middle of the road.

Canes click on the cobbles underneath the snow.

Brightly coloured lanterns are strung along the ancient West Port. They go down by antique bookshops. The fox gazes at one or two covetable titles. They pass the tattoo parlour. Dress shop. No police pass them.

The sky is a heavy, dense white and there is little light in the city.

Snow makes everything sparkle.

Along the West Bow and up onto the High Street. At the top of the Mound, they stop at a bicycle that has been left locked up by the fresh-bread delivery man, he smokes a cigarette and looks the other way as they pick up some weapons from his cart. He gets on his bike and cycles away, the cart disappears around the corner and the Original

Founders look down toward the huge Christmas tree lit up on the Mound.

— What's Santa gonnae bring ye this year, Bee?

— A man's head in each hand.

— Nae body?

— None.

— How many do we kill?

— All of them, if we have to.

Bee wears the fox mask, her husband Rab is the ram. The zebra and the wolf are two broad-shouldered men: Davey and his younger brother Ali, respectively. They walk up the hill and down past the court. A street performer painted entirely silver and wearing a wizard's hat appears to be levitating. He does not blink as the four animals, dressed so fine, walk by him. The Original Founders turn onto Luckenbooth Close. Rab raises his cane as if to knock on the scarred old door of No. 10. The street is hushed. All sounds are softened by snowfall. A light goes on in the second floor. Then it goes dark. The street has chip wrappers on it. Bicycles are tied to railings. Two have had wheels stolen so only the frames remain. Bin bags squat around the door. Rab pushes the door but it has been fixed with a shiny intercom plate. He inspects it, his horns casting a shadow as he tries the service buzzer but it doesn't work. Rab takes one step back and kicks the door in with a hard boot. Wood smashes on stone, the sound reverberates and he takes a bow, gesturing with an elaborate flourish that the entry is now clear.

— Don't kill them all unless there's no choice, Bee.

— Of course, Rab.

— Promise me?

– Cross my heart and swear to die.

She crosses her chest and her husband tries to contain himself because there is always something magical about Bee. Even now in her fox head, with snow falling around her. He thinks of their two babies tucked up at home. All their fights, the angst, the days she hates him . . . despite all of it, he is still as drawn to her as he ever was. It's not because she still has a beautiful body – although even after twins, even with its silver lines and the stomach she hates, to him, she does. What strikes him most is her absolutely unrepentant spirit. Rab has long learnt to accept that his wife is uncontainable, she always has been, and she always will be.

They disappear from the street.

Leave footprints, barely noticeable in the snow.

The stairwell of No. 10 Luckenbooth Close is garishly lit. It smells of poppers. There is a big clunky plastic light on each landing, glaring down on the chipped paint and worn steps. They look at each other, their eyes animal-like behind their masks.

Davey and Ali are the hardest boys around. Ali was born exactly nine months after Davey. In many ways, they are almost like one person. But there are several fundamental – and problematic – differences between them. Davey does not love women but he cannot help but pursue them. They always want to marry him and he has now been down the aisle three times. Ali believes in love for life but he always falls in love with his brother's girlfriends. The brothers have eight children between them. It is uncertain who is the biological father of each child. Ali has been sleeping with Davey's girlfriends, then wives, since they were teenagers. He will pretend to be his brother if it means he can get something he wants. And he can pull off the Davey persona so well even his dad can't tell sometimes who is who – it is almost impossible for anyone to tell them apart. They are easier to differentiate in their masks. Otherwise, they are so identical that nobody believes they are not twins. They are both huge, dark-haired, and Italian-looking.

Don't say that in front of their da.

It won't go well.

There are many things that cannot be said in front of their da. The brothers learnt everything they needed to know about their father when they were six years old. He parked them in a car with lemonade and crisps and went into the pub. When he came out, it was getting dark. Another man stoated out behind him. There was an insult and then a shove, and then their da turned around, shoulders squared.

– Ye fucking hink sae, aye?

The two brothers, six and almost seven, watched in silence. Another man was at the bar door. He made any witnesses go back in. The boys had the dread in them then. Both in the front seat. Crisp wrappers strewn around their feet and the laughter of a minute ago all gone. They had stopped playing with the steering wheel, unable to look away as their father head-butted the man until his face was a bloody purple mush. They could hear the crack of bone on bone but were too scared to wind up their window to block the sound out. Their father stepped back and pulled out his cigarettes, lit one.

Both tiny boys hoped that would be it.

He was walking toward the car when the man said something.

They will never know what.

Their father strode back to the man on the floor and gouged his fingers into one of the pulped sockets.

Pressed down until an eyeball popped.

He then pulled on it slowly and deliberately so the man could watch what he was doing with his other frantic eye, and he kept doing it until the sinew snapped altogether. Making sure the man was still watching, he put it in his mouth. Chewed. Swallowed. The guy is still alive now. Lives three streets away from them. He wears an eyepatch and occasionally helps out in the neighbourhood library. The brothers did not ask their father for a chippie after all that night. They went home in silence. It is not discussed. There is never a good time to comment. There has been no appropriate point for it to turn into one of many humorous myths in the Davey–Ali itinerary of fucked-up-things-to-laugh-about-later. Like their uncle's wake. Someone had put a cigar in their embalmed uncle's mouth and that had been a laugh until their grandmother had taken it out and smoked it whilst telling each grandchild what was utterly pathetic about them. Then there was a fight between Davey's wife and Ali's girlfriend. A barmaid was crying before they'd even ordered a third round. The entire family proceeded to get so wasted on uppers, downers, alcohol and the potent exhilaration and terror of grief, that their auntie forgot her husband was dead. She dry-humped the corpse in front of everyone until her sister pulled her off. She could not remember the wake at all the next day. Nobody said a thing to her. She looked pious at the funeral. It was better that way.

Just another family party that got out of hand.

Or then there are the fights at funerals.

The McBains are notorious for fighting at a funeral. So

much so that their father adopted a rural Chinese tradition: inviting strippers to attend. He claims it's done over there to get more people to come along and bless the deceased. Over here, he thought it could encourage peaceful relations between mourners. The sisters from the Red Room have done six funerals this year. There has not been a fight at a single one. There are other unusual things that happen around their father. He swears he met the devil's daughter in the White Hart twenty-six years ago. He claims she told him that she had lived with a Mr Udnam – a man who used to own half the city and kept the women in his life in check with a constant fear of their potential murder. The city has a big statue of Mr Udnam. It often wears a traffic cone on its head due to the pathetic inability of most students to commit any proper kind of crime. The story goes: the devil's daughter told their father neither son would make it to thirty. He claimed she was the most beautiful woman he had ever seen even in spirit – far more alive than most. He said that she wore a charcoal-coloured dress and a Luckenbooth brooch and she still drinks in the White Hart with her pretty horns on show – even to this day. To be fair, all the pub's cleaners have quit over the decades. They just can't find one who will stay. Nobody talks about it. But what isn't haunted in this city? This city's ghosts haunt babies from the womb. Real Edinburgh people are part otherworldly; it underlines their particular brand of crazy. Their father responded to the woman's premonition. Trained the boys in boxing and weapons from the age of three. Once, an older laddie on their street battered Ali. Their da went mental. Smacked Ali. Put him out the house. Said he would not be allowed in again until he battered that twelve-year-old senseless. He locked the door. Left him on the street in the rain. Ali knocked and knocked. Eventually, he went and found the boy. Battered him until he couldn't speak. Went back home again. He was seven years old.

Ali looks back at Bee and Rab and he does not smile.

The basement door is covered in graffiti.

YLT.

YCD.

JUNGLE.

YNT.

Chinese symbols are carved into it too and there are four long marks which look like a big cat has gouged the door.

— What are you doing for your birthday?

— We'll go for a pint or two, Bee.

— It's your thirtieth, you've got tae do something better than that!

— Are you ready? Ali, Davey?

— Aye, Rab.

Davey pulls out a wide sword. Ali clicks the lock off on a double-barrel rifle.

They walk up the stairs in silence.

They stop at the seventh floor.

All nod.

Open the landing door and go down to the end.

— What did Dora say, Bee?

— She said the girl was still missing.

— Who is she?

— Dora's third cousin, on her mum's side.

— My da still calls Dora by her original name, Georgie, did ye ken they went to school together? Ali asks.

— Aye!

Bee looks over at her husband much in the way she did when they first met at Dora Noyce's three years ago. Rab fell in love with Bee over tea and sandwiches. She had whispered to him later that she thought it was sweet of the madam to call it a *YMCA with extras* and then giggled and covered her mouth. She had been wearing knee-high white socks, high heels and a short black kimono with a flower in her hair. Rab had thought it was just a matter of fate where any man finds his wife.

Since that morning, there has been a ring on Bee's finger.

Dora was mighty pissed off with Rab for taking her most talented girl.

He owes her.

Dora has always had issues with street gangs trying to muscle in, and now shitty new saunas with no class and no rules to protect the girls – which really, really pisses her off. Last week, one of her girls disappeared. It is rumoured that the boss of a recent Triad faction in the city has arrived and has not been adhering to his own people's rules. He has offended the oaths he took in the most serious way. In fact, he is said to have a rogue unit that is in no way endorsed by Triad factions in Hong Kong (or anywhere else). This boss was the last person to be seen with Dora's third cousin. None of the true syndicates will tolerate trouble returning to them because of someone who no longer has the right to operate under their protection. Boadicea has her own personal vendetta against traffickers. Ali and Davey do not tolerate frauds of any kind. Rab knows what such men have done to his wife in the past. He is also against the recently growing drug trade. There's a lot of unspoken heat between the Original Founders as they walk down the seventh-floor corridor. The door opens to flat 7F7 and two men step out onto the landing.

— We didn't expect a welcoming committee, Ali says.

— Gentlemen!

Bee smiles sweetly at them both.

There is a tall, handsome Chinese man. He wears a black leather bomber coat and expensive leather Chelsea boots. It is certain there will be a gun stuffed into the back of his trousers. Behind him, a younger man wearing black flare corduroy trousers, a plain T-shirt, and a tailored brown jacket with long lapels, tattoos are on show around his collarbone and trailing up his neck, and he holds a small crossbow casually by his side.

— We heard that the Original Founders may give us a Christmas Eve visit. How very kind. You must forgive us, we did not have time to bake any mince pies.

The man laughs to himself and gestures through the open door and they all walk in, in silence.

Ivor (37)

deathwatch beetles

IF THE tenant in 9F9 opened her front door right now, she would see two legs dangling from the hatch on her landing. Then, she would see the legs disappearing, as the attic hatch on the top floor of No. 10 Luckenbooth Close thuds shut. Only footprints would be left on the walls. Size eleven. Ivor is not a small man. He hauls himself up onto the attic floor. His eyes are bloodshot, his hangover is giving him the heebie-jeebies and his stomach muscles burn from the effort of pulling himself up.

It's been a bad day.

Ivor lays back, breathing hard.

The cavernous attic is covered in tall grass.

He stands up.

It grows almost up to his chest. A cold breeze ripples through it, reminding him of hayfields swaying in the wind when he was a child. On the far wall there is a huge, old, open fireplace. Next to it there is an armchair with burst foam and rusted springs exposed. An old suitcase acts as a makeshift table. On top of it are the indecipherable remains of what might have been a squatter's lunch. On a dirty windowpane, someone has drawn an outline of a monkey.

There is a single small gas-cooking hob. It's the kind that would be used for camping. It has rusted too. Ivor tramples down grass. Flattens a route through to the chair and fireplace. He looks down. The woman in 9F9's water cupboard must be just below here. A wee bit of light filters up where she has left the cupboard door open. He could drop right down into her flat from the attic. Ivor has heard about that. People living in other people's flats in cupboards or other unused nooks, eating their food while they sleep, watching their telly, taking a bath, sneaking down their hallway past them in the night — sometimes for decades. Ivor read about a woman who was found sleeping in someone's airing cupboard. The woman claimed she'd lived there for over thirty years and therefore could not be evicted. She had wired into the mains and had a wee telly in there and everything. Ivor feels lucky that he would never have to do that at least, or sleep rough. His sister has taken him in without question. Where would he have gone otherwise?

This morning, Ivor left his wife. She was making breakfast when he left and did not even look up. She just cracked eggs. Jaw set tight as it ever had been. This afternoon, the doctor gave him a diagnosis he never wanted. He verified why Ivor cannot work in daylight. Meanwhile, the coal mine he has worked in all his life is closing down so he is doing anything he can to feel useful to anybody at all right now. Two floors down, his sister and Esme are waiting for him to come back and report on noises they've been hearing from the attic.

— You've no fear, have you, Uncle Ivor?

— None, Esme.

– It's a tapping, every night. It's driving Mum crazy, isn't it, Mum?

A nod from Rhona as she popped two tramadol and lay down on the couch again.

– I'll go find out what it is.

– Okay, and if you see my wee pal, will ye give her this?

Esme held out a teddy.

It's in his back pocket – he places it on the broken armchair.

His niece's wee imaginary pal is becoming a bit of a permanent fixture. He won't question it. It's her room he's sleeping in, on the bottom bunk. He's brought his records with him – they were the only thing he took. He's got his clothes folded in the hall cupboard and nothing else of his is in her room; it's Esme's manor. She's the coolest person he knows: eight years old, tenacious as hell and wise as a fucking owl! He does not want to infringe on her space any more than he has to.

The air is cold up here.

Ivor is glad to be wearing layers, as he always does.

It's a habit from twenty-six years working down the pit.

The doctor said he should show his workmates the note, to prove why he can't strike . . .

Funny fucker, his doctor.

His workmates are boys he was born and raised with – kids he played with his whole life, went to school with, watched get married and have kids of their own. Men he's spent much of his life more than six feet under with. He would rather they think he is a scab than know the truth, which is that he is completely fucking mental.

The doctor asked him, didn't he?

– What do you do?

– Coal miner.

– How many years?

– Since I left school.

– No other trade?

– I helped my uncle out at weekends renovating houses but noh. My da was a miner, my da's da was a miner, my da's da's da was a miner, his da was a butcher, everyone before him wiz a miner, ma uncles are miners, cousins, ma brother, ma pals. Every man on ma street is a miner and in a few weeks, every one of us is out of work fir good.

– The Iron Lady has much to answer for.

The doctor listened to his heartbeat.

– Community is going already, doctor.

– Aye.

– The young laddies who would ay been working wi the rest ay us down the pit by now – are sniffing glue in the park!

– So I've heard!

– Next it'll be AIDS in Midlothian.

– Uh-huh.

– I dinnae think anyone's got it there yet.

– No.

– What do you think, doctor? Do you think AIDS is more of an Edinburgh thing?

– It doesn't discriminate, Ivor. Most illnesses don't.

– They're eradicating an entire generation ay young men, nae jobs, nae community, our infrastructure ripped apart and so many people are taking heroin now they are calling Edinburgh the HIV capital of Europe, ye ken that?

– I do.

The doctor nodded sadly.

– This panic that you are experiencing, Ivor, how long has it gone on for?

– Since I was wee.

– What age?

– Always. My earliest memory is sitting on Porty beach with a box on ma head.

– A box?

– A cardboard yin, it was the only way for my ma to stop me greeting.

– I see.

– I could hear the sea. She would hold ma hand to go paddling. I was the only laddie on that beach with a box on his head. I tell ye, everyone knows ye at Porty, the whole ay Bilston was there when it was sunny fir the day. I felt like a total fud.

– A what?

– It means vagina.

A smile, a nod, the doctor checking over his arms and back, tense then.

– What are these marks from?

– Ma work, it gets nuts down the mine, doctor.

A blank stare.

The man did not believe him.

What's the point of saying fuck all? He's never going to let Joanne take another dig at him anyway.

Ivor sits down on the bust armchair.

He does not want to think about the doctor's final diagnosis.

It's still too hard.

This grass is dry at least.

All the attic eaves are dusty and dirty and they crumble to touch.

The roof is punctuated by toothy gaps.

Missing tiles and slates – expose insipid city stars overhead.

Hope Housing Association doesn't give a flying fuck what happens in their buildings any more. The tenants are getting wilder and more feral and the housing association don't come out to check on anything. It's all new builds they are investing in now, whilst the tenements slowly decay. Then they'll sell them back on the private market. This attic is not what he expected though. It's a mystery. How did grass even get up here? It's so tall and green at the shoots but yellow at the top. Something crawls over his wrist. He slaps it off his skin. Ivor is a broad-shouldered man. Bugs do not bother him and darkness is his sunny day. He went to Woods the Barbers after his appointment at the doctor. Ivor got a shave and his hair down to a no. 1. It feels clean. He looks like a monk. A punk monk who is still more into the Dead Kennedys and Black Flag, and Hüsker Dü and the Slits and the Exploited and X-Ray Spex and NOFX and Nirvana and Minutemen and Sonic Youth and Lydia Lunch and Joy Division than he has ever been into anything else. He will let Esme listen to all his records. Teach her a few chords on bass guitar. He can educate her on the difference between punk and no wave and new wave and grunge and metal. Maybe she'll start a decent band one day. It wouldn't surprise him. Ivor stands in the corner on his tiptoes and looks out the first broken slates. He can see all the way across the city of Edinburgh – over Princes Street Gardens and the outline of the New Town and a hulk of Calton Hill, the Balmoral, all the way down the city until a navy belt divides it from the Kingdom of Fife. A sea view is a coveted thing in this city!

At some point a long, long time ago, someone was squatting up here.

It could have been fifty years ago or a hundred.

Time is passing everyone by; that's what it is doing.

All over the world clocks tick, both in and out of time with each other. Ivor's favourite is an astronomy clock. It is in Bohemia. It's 10 p.m. here. It will strike midnight over there soon. Death will appear. It will beckon to a Turkish entertainer. The figures of Vanity and Greed will glide out. Spin on the dance floor. Twelve Apostles will flash from their windows. The Earth is centre. Sky is blue or black. There is Ortis (sunrise), Occasvs (sunset) and Crevscvlvm (twilight). There is the Tropic of Cancer. It has all the signs of the zodiac. Three arms rotate their way through existence. One holds a moon, one holds a star. There is a sun. A golden hand.

It has been eighteen hours. He has left his wife for good. Time is behind them and before them. They are sat on the hands of time, going around and around in opposite directions. The astronomical dial on his favourite clock was built in 1410. The sun passes over Arabic numbers to indicate Babylonian time. The moon hand tells lunar time. Star hand indicates sidereal days, shorter than regular ones by nearly four minutes. He proposed to his wife in front of that clock. When she dies, he will go there and get drunk to celebrate. He will see her six feet under one day. Ivor will recommend another three feet minimum, possibly another nine – if he can bribe the gravediggers. Just in case. It's best not to take any chances with his wife. Pure bile in the woman's veins – but she'd swear on their kids' lives it's fucking honey. She did three sessions of therapy and now insists she's enlightened.

All she has really learnt is a few key terms to bolster her own deluded sense of victimhood. Ivor's wife believes – she is the most caring person on the planet.

He can say whatever he wants.

She doesn't hear it.

Joanne has systematically taken him apart for so fucking long – so why is he missing her, like some idiotic puppy who has run away from the fur traders but is pining to go back and get petted for a few minutes before it is totally skinned? That's what she'd do in the end. That's what people like her have in them. They can't help themselves.

He can hear it . . .

Tap, tap, tap, in the walls.

The roof has rotten beams.

He sticks a finger into the wood and it falls away. The building is sick.

– Terminally ill, doctor – it's not going to make it!

He's seen this kind of thing before when he was working with his uncle on house renovations at the weekends, but this is far worse than anything he saw on those jobs.

Tap, tap, tap.

In the beam above Ivor's head – one tiny deathwatch bee-tle head-butts the wood.

Tap. Tap. Tap. Tap. Tap. Tap. Tap.

He knows what it is now!

It's a mating call.

To lure a fuck from the darkness.

An efficient system – in a heartbeat, hundreds of thousands tap, tap, tap, tap, tap, tap, tap. In all the building's limbs, deathwatch beetles mate, wriggle – scurry. Do they suck – fuck – clatter – spit? Each insect flies along wood on furious, tiny, spiky legs. Ivor has worked on houses with deathwatch beetles. Untreated, the whole fucking building will get eaten. The beams are well tattooed with boreholes from xylopha-gous larvae which is still an earlier stage in their lifespan. The deathwatch beetles will eventually emerge on graduation (thirteen years later) as fully grown *Xestobium rufovillosum*. The deathwatch beetle itself is seven millimetres long but working together there is no wooden structure they could not destroy.

That tap, tap, tap, tap reminds him of being down the mine shafts.

Overalls on, hard hat in hand, whistling.

His place.

Torch switched off.

Eyes like a cat – the boys always say that about him.

Descending down into layers of the pit, further down into the earth, the smell of it, coal underfoot, wooden joists hold-ing up the tunnels, a feeling that something was disappearing just out of vision. In the corner of his eye, a disappearing motion. Just like in this building. On every floor, something is just out of sight. Esme knows. It's why she's having night-mares. It's nothing! He needs to tell her that. Men get it down the mine. Hear songs being sung. See wee kids running away. A bright yellow canary flies by. Things are stranger the fur-ther into the earth you go. Ivor has a feeling that right at the core of the Earth – there is a heart – withered as a walnut. It is the Earth's heart. A tiny eternal thing – sending out its own faint beat toward everything. Ivor touches a beam and it is already rotten. The rest of them will go in time. If he had money, he'd move Esme and his sister right out of this build-ing. It's only going to get worse.

This building is too many things.

Too tall, too run-down, too many floors. It's so high — it is rare, even for an Edinburgh tenement. Ivor peers across the attic eaves. Can see all the way through this eave into the next building. The attic eaves lead into every other tenement for three streets. Sometimes they are used as a route for burglars. Or a penthouse for rats. Burglars get into eaves via the attic hatch in a stairwell, or they climb onto the Chinese takeaway roof and shimmy up a drainpipe. If you don't know how many floors a burglar can shag his way up (via drainpipe) to sniff your knicker-knackers or pawn yer paltry diamonds for porn and cocaine — it is twelve. There are many reasons to never leave dirty knickers on the bathroom floor. Encouragement of knicker-sniffing burglars is just one of them!

After the doctor had diagnosed him yesterday afternoon, Ivor bought a dictionary from James Thin's and went to Rutherford's for a pint. He put the dictionary inside a newspaper so nobody could see what he was reading. Then he sat in a corner and went through as many phobias as he could. First he looked for natural deterrents to a vocation in burglary. These included achluophobia (fear of darkness), domatophobia (fear of houses), anthrophobia (fear of people), leukophobia (fear of the colour white), galeophobia (fear of cats) and koinoniphobia (fear of rooms). Rarely does medorthophobia (fear of an erect penis) or hadephobia (fear of hell) or lutraphobia (fear of otters) hold back a robber — unless they do country estates.

Otters (incidentally) are related to wolverines.

Ivor would still rather be a werewolf than a vampire.

What kind of a grown-up is he?

Maybe fear is a punishment he must carry for the sins of some other life?

He goes over to the hatch quickly, lowers himself down. Outwith a multitude of phobic afflictions robbers right-eously raid the homes of capitalist children, known (in slang terms) as apathy's muse. Burglars adore apathy. That's the thing to think about. Ivor has been considering this when he thinks about how they approach that kind of job. Ivor has absolutely no skillset whatsoever, other than being a coal miner. And now he also has a firm diagnosis from his doc-tor, assuring him that his lifelong phobia of light is not going anywhere – that trying to live his life in darkness while nobody else notices is still the main goal of his existence. What the fuck *is* he going to do for money when they close down the pit? Every man he knows will be out of work. It's been bad enough getting through the strikes. He wouldn't rob from those who go without of course. Ivor would only rob from those who don't go without. He's not a total cunt. He would, in fact, only rob from those who will never go without, even after he fucking robs them. As his feet hit the ninth-floor landing, he hears Esme scream.

Pounds down the stairs.

– What is it, Esme!

In the living room his niece is howling and his sister is passed out.

– It's ma pal, Uncle Ivor, she's gonnae be stuck in this building forever!

– Come here, come on! It's not real, Esme, it's just your imagination. It happens to boys down the pit all the time. Just ignore it! There's nobody trapped in this building but us and that's just cos we're poor, Esme. Do you know what

Granny used to call me? A Brollachan, a brilliant shapeless creature of the night, and I used to think of that down the mine. I'd hear a cockerel crow down there! Once I heard kids playing hopscotch fifty feet below the ground! You feel something in this building like I used to do in the mine.

— I'm not a Brollachan, though!

— No, yer not.

— I'm a wee girl and I see things that you won't ivvir see at all and when I say so ye think it's a lie!

— I don't, darlin, I promise. I don't think it's a lie!

She sniffs.

Ivor lets her climb up on him.

Esme is like a wee monkey, she is. She clings on and he hushes and rocks her until she falls asleep and his big sister is comatose beside him and the deathwatch beetles are tapping like crazy all through the limbs of the building now.

It is the illest of omens.

1999

Flat 9F9

Dot (27)

the death of all the secrets

ALL ACROSS Edinburgh, tourists party. Local pubs are jammed. Nightclubs are heaving. Thousands walked these streets with torches burning just a few days ago for the fire festival. It's enough to give a girl a complex. Police sealed off the city centre for Hogmanay earlier today. To try and get home Dot has to get past barriers without a pass. She uses her – *lady with a baby* – routine. Pushes her stomach right out. It is enough. People's niceness is so exploitable. There are skaters at Winter Wonderland. A brightly lit wheel. Fairground rides cast brightly coloured tracers of light across the sky behind them. The German market wants an arm and a leg for a fucking doughnut. Smells good though. She'd consider it. Here is my arm. Here is my leg. Please can you feed me your doughnut? There is a maze of Christmas trees and when she looks down, all she can see is the top of bobbled hats making their way through pines. There will be kissing at the bells. All the uglies are out and hopeful. Norway donated an extra-large Christmas tree to the Mound. There's not an empty hotel room in town. A choir sings Bach and Handel up at St Giles'. There is cheering out on the street. There is dancing. People meet and fall in love.

257

Scuffles break out. They drink far too much. All of life is happening. A girl holds onto her friend's hands and the two of them spin around. A fairground trails all the way along East End of Princes Street Gardens. There is a fairground ride called the Hammer lit up and swinging with people screaming on it and her favourite is a gravity wheel that tilts onto its side – there are swings high up above the buildings that spin out like a skirt and there is a smell of perfume and candyfloss. The big bands are setting up in the next section of gardens where there is a bandstand and fans wait for the music to start. Fireworks are being safety-checked one last time before they are lit up and send a cascade of light over the Castle Rock.

Silent drums ripple through city catacombs.

Revellers interrupting the murdered, the lost and the damned, the homeless or the cold and hungry, the addicted – those weary of living this life. These are Dot's people – if there have ever been any to call her own. It's where she comes from. Still is. Always will be. It's no wonder she has never fitted in.

Dot slips off the High Street.

Down the close.

Losing noise and wanting the fuck away from it all as quick as she can. The building is bent over, looking down at her – it's as giant as she is tiny. Around this part of the High Street, all the other buildings stand proud while No. 10 Luckenbooth Close bows to the city – ingratiates itself. What self-respecting building would ever do that? Dot understands how tiring it is to straighten a spine. Hers is twisted. The building does not stand up like a time-lord that houses the souls of humans. It is curving over. Subordinance is not for architecture. It's not remotely safe. The housing association have put scaffolding halfway to the sixth floor. A sign reading 'JMB Scaffold' flaps.

It sounds like someone clapping sarcastically.

Dot glances back up the street just as the wood gives under the weight of her shoulder and allows her several inches to slip into the dim. So grateful they've not put a metal door on the front yet. She has been squatting here peacefully for five months and she cannot leave. Dot pulls the door shut behind her. She stands listening. Lights flicker. The building's batteries are almost fully drained. No. 10 Luckenbooth Close is breathing its last shallow breaths.

It might not make morning.

Pulls her beanie further down. She takes out a long kitchen knife. Begins the ascent. This building has the feeling of Penrose stairs. Walking up could just as easily be walking down. After a while it is hard to tell. It's a long climb to the ninth floor. Someone has spray-painted an alien on the second floor. There are notices everywhere. For the housing association tenants. About when they would be evicted. No attention paid to health and safety. Hope Housing Association is run by psychopaths. Much like the city council. Somehow, in amongst all of that, the building has been calling out to her.

Dot stops and pulls out a roll-up.

Liquorice papers.

Her hair is on top of her head in a bun.

Her nails are painted black.

Polo neck.

Jeans.

Hi-top sneakers.

Touch of mascara, lip gloss – it is Hogmanay after all.

Eyes bleary – she is still coming down from clubbing in the Vaults yesterday. There was an amazing guest DJ over from Berlin. Techno and proper MDMA – like the early nineties. All the Sativa Drummers were battering skins. Those drummers push back at the demons. A fleeting sense of intense belonging – that she has never once felt on the street. A pure touch of love in that room.

This building is fucking freezing. She will apply for actual housing again in the New Year. It's just a few more days until the council open their offices. No. 10 Luckenbooth has given her something nobody else has these last months: a home. Dot sings as she goes up the stairwell. Notes rise up ahead of her – a lullaby she sings every day – to a derelict building from a broken soul. A cold wind runs up towards her from the bottom of the building. Hairs on her arms rise. It can hear her and it has been waiting – this building has been sending out smoke signals for a long time, has it not?

Just one puff – to wisp ineffectually out at first.

Then another smoke ring curls up from one of its many chimneys.

For how long?

It has been calling out to her since before she was born – that's what it feels like. As if she could hear it before all the things happened that led her here. She put it all down last time she was at the job centre and they stopped her benefits for the hundredth time because of an error in the system that will take twelve weeks for them to reassess. To detract from their own incompetency and obvious contempt for benefit recipients they demanded that she update her job skills and under Life Experience, she put — astral travel.

— Any vacancies?

— No.

If they make her go for a disability benefits interview, she will tell them she is a key in the cosmos. A being of light. Just another cosmic agent, thanks. They will keep refusing her money. She will come back to this building and shoplift for food and not tell anyone she used to know that her life has come to this.

The trick is to accept things.

It is just how it is right now — the smells, dust, cracks on ceilings and windows.

Going up past the sixth floor.

A light sound of cloven hoofs begins, many floors behind her.

No. 10 Luckenbooth Close pulls close.

It inspects the purity of her want.

Evaluates the depth of her longing.

It's lonelier than she is.

No. 10 Luckenbooth Close is arthritic. It creaks often. Groans wretchedly when it rains. Its elbows are knobby. Knees buckled. It is old. How old, nobody on the street seems to know for sure. It's not as old as Moubray House (1477). St Margaret's Chapel up at the castle sashays by at 1130. John Knox sniffs at them all regardless (1490). St Giles' Cathedral (central pillars, 1124 — the rest of it is — complicated). The dark wee close leading down to No. 10 Luckenbooth — has been here as long as any of them. Nobody sees it. No matter how many times they walk by. It's unseen. As she is. It doesn't belong either. It's an ootlin. Dot has been an outsider in every scene she's found herself in. It's not like she hasn't tried at times to reach out to those who seemed like her own. Artists and writers are everywhere in this city, though. So confident! Most of them have totally different backgrounds from her. Although they all shout loud and some pretend to be from rougher places – they are not. Big personalities! All style, no content. Clanging their own fucking bells all day long, all year long, all their lives. It's tiring. There is little art in endless self-promotion. Every stage is their place to shine. They'd steal your heart, soul or story and pretend it was theirs to begin with and they won't even see how wrong it is to do so. They gossip that anyone who isn't like them is just – mean. Dot spent an unpleasant year around people like that at art school – and dropped out as soon as she possibly could.

It was a vile place.

It made her feel even more dot-like than ever.

The arts! Middle-class kids are raised to own a space. Keep others from infringing on it. And they are very successful at it. Edinburgh – makes a show of herself on that point – at every possible opportunity. Siphons money from punters. Keeps her truth-tellers under the vaults. As if they are diseased. There are gatekeepers who hold the arts hostage. They bang their drums and say: this is our space – we own all of it! They say – culture belongs to people like me. I let people like me through and they have to thank me for it. They say don't you dare make us uncomfortable or we will close ranks like flying monkeys.

Dot is not about owning anything at all.

Not a moment.

Seconds come and then you let them go like pretty balloons – that's how it is meant to be.

Dot puts her hand through her letter box and turns the latch.

Goes into her hall.

Hangs up her coat, glad to be home.

No. 10 Luckenbooth Close has an outsider status as true and fucking righteous as her own. Neither of them have anywhere else to call home. Nobody is coming to save them. Dot is into the weirdly romantic splendour of its faded curtains. Stories tucked away on every floor. She goes looking for them. There are signs to be found everywhere. How many people have lived here? Been housed here? Lost their minds, or hearts, or if they were lucky – found a time in their life to be safe! Ah, for such a thing! Dot goes through to her room. She has drawn the entire building out on the wall. She sleeps next to it. Adds notes. Wakes in the morning and stares at it while smoking. She is not certain what she is doing. It's instinctual. What is she looking for? She doesn't entirely know.

It's something.

No. 10 Luckenbooth Close has a spiritual lock and she is in some way – a key.

Happy to be it.

Dot pours herself a brandy coffee.

Life is now.

It is so much stranger than anybody says.

They are always trying to normalise it! Make it normal. Make it normal. Make it normal. It's like a mantra for the mad. Making things normal seems the goal of modern society and it is so tedious. As if spinning on a ball in the middle of an unexplainable universe is just so – ordinary. Like being made of stardust and having no fucking idea about what happens when you die, is not worth discussing! Life is distraction. Talking online to strangers all the time and living in boxes, paying money to unseen others. Trying not to stand up and shout on a crowded train – nobody loves me! Stay busy. Die quietly. Don't ask fucking questions. Please. It will be better for you if you don't. A world where we poison nature and wait until one day it turns around and poisons us back and it will – that is certain – if we keep poking sticks into the planet or taking its oil or polluting its skies or slaughtering its animals in needless ways then one day it will release a pathogen to take us all out. If the first pathogen does not work entirely, it will at least be a warning to quit what we are doing or next time it will take us out for good. It is a waste of human life to not change everything and even more so be walled into the yellow silence of mediocrity. The planet dies whilst humans despair or deny the truth. No. 10 Luckenbooth has a sickness in it that will take all its structures down soon enough and it is only a harbinger of something that will come on a far, far bigger scale one day. She can feel it in her soul as true as a true thing can be. While all these heart-beaters go around experiencing the miracle of existence they are all living on a planet where dots don't stand up.

Dot wants to stand up!

She is in love with this building.

Japanese Kintsugi is based on the notion that an item is only truly unique when it has broken and been rebuilt. It is then far more beautiful because of its cracks, not despite them – which is why they fill those cracks with gold! Eastern philosophy of aesthetics could better the West. They keep old earthen bowls holding years of oil from fingertips in its grain, memories of time – put them on little dark altars and when candles are lit, gold cracks reveal their truth. If Dot were to pick an ideology, hers would be wabi-sabi. Her life is full of decay and beauty in imperfection. The building called out for a Dot who has also been broken. Perhaps she is the gold it needs. It is ancient as a child. She goes from floor to floor. Room to room, touching all the left things. Dot picks up a mug. She needs another drink right away so she goes through to the kitchen.

In the entire nine-floor tenement, there is only one human heartbeat.

She puts the kettle on.

Walks through her hallway.

Painted ancient symbols adorn the floor and walls.

A black moon with a cross below it.

There are three protection sigils by the front door in red, blue and gold.

Aramaic incantations inscribed around the hallway – trail towards the bedroom.

Babylonian spells stand like sentries on either side of the bathroom door.

Hebrew talismans guard the Hoover cupboard.

There is a painting of Lilith in the hallway.

Dot looks at her every time she goes by.

Lilith was Adam's first wife. She left him in the Garden of Eden to have an affair with the archangel Samael. Her husband followed her. He told her that if she did not come back to Eden, he would curse her for all of history, he would kill 400 babies in her name each day, and he would have her vilified in all religious texts and then written out of history entirely. She was unfazed. She did not go back. Lilith was rumoured to have a tribe of lilitu – female demons – and it was said that she could seduce any man or cause his death with mere thoughts. In Dot's drawings of her, Lilith's thighs are wide and strong. Legs taper down toward three-pronged talons, long and yellow. No shoes required or available for such a design. Her ears are lightly feathered and peaked. She has thick dark eyebrows. Two three-foot-tall owls (companions to travel every realm) stand on either side, blinking long and slow. If Lilith was sat at a bar, they'd rotate their heads all the way around – ensuring all but the truest of heart stay the fuck away.

An icon to aspire to.

Dot likes knowing that on all the floors below her, there is nothing but empty rooms. She puts the radio on. Lights a joint she left in the ashtray. Thinks of the signs of people's lives left on other floors. Dirty marks where pictures hung on walls. Smudges of handprints. Fingerprints. Single-pane windows. So much unopened mail. Straw remnants of a spider plant. A plastic Yoda alarm clock. It goes off every morning in 1F1. Half-empty shampoo bottles. Bathtubs with tide marks. A huge parrot cage in 5F5 and seeds all over the carpet. A piano with no song left in it. Damp socks in the bottom of a chest of drawers. A small box of unused sex toys. A teddy dropped in a hallway. Fridges switched off. Airless plastic cavities breed a multiverse of bacterium. In a flat on the eighth floor, there is a neatly made bed as if the owner might return any night now to sleep here. Mould spores congregate in bathrooms. Books have nobody to tell their stories to. A radio is switched ON but its batteries are rusted. Orange-brown stains seep out. In the basement, there are used needles with traces of blood and heroin. There are roaches, condoms, burnt spoons. An old jukebox is plugged in – its arm extended, record poised – ready to drop down forever.

Even junkies don't break in here any more.

The others are all gone.

Dot feels like she is living in a tall cupboard.

Her flat's saving grace is its huge sash windows, even if they do only look out on brick.

Twelve-foot-high ceilings – all the better to think!

Ornate cornices and ceiling rose.

It's taller than it is wide, to be fair. Each night the walls inch forward imperceptibly as she sleeps. One day, she will wake to find the entire building has become a coffin. Dot goes through to her bedroom and ignores her unmade bed, grabs a lighter and goes back to her living room. It doesn't work. The spark ignites nothing. She pulls out matches. The smell of burnt sulphur soothes. It flares. She drops it into the fireplace. It's why she picked this flat – it still has a working fireplace. Whoever was here didn't let them put central heating in. No three-bar gas fire like on most of the other floors. Dot burns things she's found. Other people's bills, mostly. It's satisfying. Red light flickers. It warms her skin only a tiny bit.

Dot opens the shutters to look up at big old gargoyles – they keep her company.

What if workmen don't come for a bit longer?

She could heat only this one room and stay here until spring arrives or the building falls. It's uncertain which will happen first. If they were able to bury the building whole, it would do everyone (but her) a favour. A graveyard for buildings would be amazing! The gravediggers would have to be giants. The tombstones, vast graffitied walls. No. 10 Luckenbooth Close has been eaten by some kind of bug that taps at night – and now throughout most of the day too. It's not just that No. 10 Luckenbooth Close is about to die and be reborn – nor that it will be wholly gutted and rebuilt from the bones up – it is the death of all its secrets. The longer she stays here, the more she thinks about it.

Washes her hands in a cold sink.

Brushes out her long hair.

Stares at gouges on the wall in her bathroom.

They were not there before. She traces them with her fingertips – they are rough and deep. Like somebody dragged a knife down there. Or something else sharp. It has to have been when she was out. There is a clatter somewhere in the building and she jumps – heart racing.

Candles burn.

Flames lilt this way and that.

Shadows reach out for her from the bathroom walls. They chase each other around the roof and nudge along the side of the bathtub. Long shadow noses peer. City streets snake around the building like a noose. Spirits will be awake all night. One perched on the loo. Another is in the hallway chain-smoking. Two are in the lounge, playing chess in the ether. The spirits hate her, they love her, they ignore her, they are obsessed with her. She is fixated on them too. Dot is not about to be dead again. It was bad enough last time. Next time she goes through the veil, it will be to stay gone. The spirits of the netherworld feel as deprived of love as she has always been.

It's why they come to her and it's why she goes to them.

It's always been that way.

She has no judgement.

Dot pours a whisky into her coffee. She'll be down to the Buckfast soon.

The hoofs . . . they're back.

Clear steps move up toward her from the floors below.

Her fire crackles and spits.

Dot finishes the whisky quickly.

She goes down the little hallway as the stairwell door to her landing creaks open. The steps toward her door are precise and determined. There are sometimes smaller ones behind them, but not tonight. Dot prays that she will finally be able to see who it is. They have done this every night for a month. Dot waits. The footsteps halt just on the other side of her front door. She puts her eye up to the peephole. The lights flicker off. All she can see is black. On the other side of the door she feels a hand up at chest height – where her heart is. Dot breathes slowly. Enough to steady her heartbeat. The lights flicker on. On the other side of the door, there is a young woman with red lips and dark hair, two huge, ornate, curved horns on top of her head. As striking as anyone Dot has ever seen. The woman looks directly at her – as the lights go out again.

Queen Bee (21)

triads vs rebels

THE HALLWAY is black. There are little gold-fringed lights on the wall. The living room has an emerald velvet corner sofa. There is a Formica kitchen with a coffee machine still gurgling. Across one wall, a large tropical fish tank lights the room. Ali peers in. A swarm of thin neon tetra with red bellies and bright blue backs flash by. A large catfish emerges. Long whiskers unfurl on glass like strands of black spaghetti. Two women are standing completely still at either side of the window. They both have long shiny black hair and are wearing bell-bottom jeans, black polo necks, rings and sneakers. One of the women has a tiny monkey on her shoulder. The Triads clear their throats. Stand with legs wide. Looking relaxed, they face the Original Founders. A giant ceiling mirror reflects the two groups surveying each other – over a shaggy purple rug. Davey picks up a copy of *The Joy of Sex* from a sideboard, turns it over, puts it back down.

– Could I possibly use your bathroom?

One of the women nods affirmatively to Bee, who then lights a cigarette and strolls down the hall. They all listen in respectful silence as she begins to sing 'Rip Her to Shreds';

it is her favourite tune lately and one she often sings just before people die. Ali and Davey glance at Rab. There is the sound of a loo being flushed. Taps turned on. Bee noisily hauls a towel down to dry her hands. Then silence. Still no sight of her. She is reapplying lipstick, touching up mascara, putting her fox mask back on. Once back in the living room, Bee stops – feigning surprise to see them all waiting so nicely for her. Rab can tell she is hiding yet another head-ache but nobody else can.

She grinds out her cigarette on a tall ashtray.

– Nice spa bath – whirlpool?

– Yes.

– The pump is prone to problems, the older Triad adds.

– Ah, not so good, but it's fun, right? You got the 1968 water jets?

Rab looks to the Triads who appear a touch confused – then back to his wife in approval.

– Yes, the water jets – it's fibreglass, top of the range, best money can buy.

The younger man steps forward.

– Easy! I was just saying, it's nice what you've done with the place. Also, someone's left a bubble bath through there. Please do not interrupt your plans for us, ladies – I presume it's for one of you?

The older man assesses Bee with a sneer, which annoys Davey.

– Dinnae gie it the big yin, fuckpus, she's just making conversation.

The older Triad looks at him.

– Can you not speak English, Mr Zebra?

– I uhmnay English, pal.

The taller man smiles. Davey keeps his hand close enough to take out the gun stuffed down the back of his own trousers.

— No, please! Gentlemen. We know! I'm just fucking with you, Mr Wolf, Mr Zebra . . . We love yer radge gadge, uhm urnay, ye urr, it's – expressive!

He fist-pumps the air like an excitable amateur-dramatics student.

Ali's eyes blaze under his wolf mask.

— A sense of humour costs nothing, gentlemen. It is just a joke.

— Ma language isnae a fucking joke, Davey says.

— No.

— It's one ay the auldest in the world, Ali adds.

— Quite.

— We're no in the casual witty-banter trade, it's true, Rab states.

— What trade are you in then, Mr Ram?

— Lately it's been murder mostly. What can you do, trends change, we must move with the times.

— I see.

— We like to keep it simple.

— Always a good business plan.

The smaller man folds his hands and waits.

— We want Dora Noyce's girl back, alive and walking, talking, in fair fettle, Ali says.

— Ah.

— Is that gonnae be a problem?

— Yes.

— Why?

– We don't know where she is and to be fair even if we did, this is not your part of town, Mr Wolf.

Bee steps forward. There is only one indication that her temper is rising: when her speech takes on an exceptionally – steady, posher tone.

– It's all – our part of town.

– That's a load ay shite – as you would say – in yer non-English chit-chat.

– We dinnae speak non-anyhin uhn you boys huv only been here fir two months, so dinnaespraff shite. We know the history of every Triad gang in this city going all the way back to 1952 and you urnay part of any of the Triads who came before you. In fact, it's proving to be a bit of a mystery tae everyone in town why you are still claiming that title as yer privilege and protection . . . no?

– Go home, Mrs Fox.

– That is not very polite.

– Nobody wants to see a lady get hurt.

– Oh? D'ye think I might – break a fingernail?

Bee speaks in her best little-girl voice of fey horror. She is as coy and concerned as a psychopath in a fox mask can feign to be. She scuffs one boot behind her other foot and it raises her skirt another inch, exposing slim thighs. Her shirt is open a touch too low.

The Triads grin at her.

– You have spirit.

– I wouldn't even shed an eyelash.

– You have quite a mouth for a woman.

– That's why my husband proposed the very first day he met me, at Dora Noyce's.

The two men glance at each other.

– We have no issue with you, Mrs Fox. Or Dora Noyce.

– There's always a fucking issue. Since Triads got here in '52, there have been issues, no?

– Yes, a few . . . Nothing to worry about in the long run, no?

– My dad was in the first organised gangs in Edinburgh, you know, his dad before him. He'd tell me about those battles in graphic detail – over hot milk and digestive biscuits – just before bed every night. He never really rated Roald Dahl or Enid Blyton or that, my dad. Then he'd tell me about those exact same battles, all over again, while he braided my hair in the morning. And then he'd kiss me bye at the school gates. One day he got killed for what he did to protect another member of his gang. My mother was never the same after. That's how I ended up doing the job I did.

– Okay, so it goes back.

– But you don't go back, gentlemen. You are a lone faction.

– We are connected! Look, how about we don't hire any more of Dora's cousins, would that help relations?

– Give us back the first one.

– We can't do that.

– Why not?

– Our boss – has got attached to her. It's become personal.

– She's dead, isn't she? Bee says.

– No!

– You have no idea why we are really here, do you, gents? Rab asks.

– You want Dora's cousin.

— It would have been advisable for you to never go near any of Dora's family — not for business purposes, or fir personal purposes. That was a mistake.

— You are beginning to test my patience, Mrs Fox. You don't know anything about us.

Ali holds up his shotgun.

Davey grips his sword.

Rab rests his hand lightly on the top of his cane.

Bee is agitated but trying to control it.

She begins to talk in a low, seductive voice — easy — like a long morning in bed with nothing but rain outside the window and clean sheets.

— I know one or two things, Bee purrs.

— What?

— You used to be a Red Pole.

Bee holds up one finger for a first point noted.

— Conjecture!

— I know you think you are a right hard cunt.

She holds up two fingers.

— That's not how I would phrase it.

— I know you and your boss only sleep with white prostitutes, and that you only like three positions — and none of those are nice ones fir the girls. Am I right? Don't answer — I am right!

She raises a third digit.

Both of the Triad men begin to look uneasy.

— I know you and Peter there, used to work fir a man who cut the throats of more than forty victims and he was set to kill another thirty-seven and every one of those was for good reason and you were on the second list, weren't you?

— Excuse me?

— Rumour is you killed him, Bee states.

— Who have you been talking to? The older Triad has pulled out his gun.

— The actual story goes — that you and yer wee pal Raymond over there both have a very pretty price offered for anyone who can deliver your head. Have you heard those stories, ladies?

She looks over at the two women and holds up seven fingers, one for each point.

Closes her fist.

Bee has the room's full attention.

Her fox whiskers are long and they can see her red mouth move below them. Her eyes flash intermittently from grey to black when she becomes angry.

— I know your money goes into movies, Bee says.

— We like to support the arts.

— Snuff films.

— No, Mr Ram!

— Yes, and some commercial films. That's where your passion is, no? You like to see Triads looking good onscreen. We do too! My husband and I have watched each brilliant film over and over. We understand you really invest in the films. You enjoy watching the fights, the clothes, the music, the girls, the bars . . . the whole swagger of it! I understand it! It's a part of your — more romantic side?

— You think that's us being romantic?

— If ye've seen as much death as I have, Raymond, then aye. I'd say it's quite sweet.

— Thank you, I think.

— You don't show films of you taking girls out of clubs who aren't ever seen again and who are certainly not acting in your commercial films and what we've also heard is that you've been up at the Red Room — looking around?

— We were just taking in the view!

— Don't, Rab says.

Bee nods, agreeing with her husband.

— You know in yer wee Triad initiation ceremony, when ye sacrifice a fucking goat or a chicken or whatever, then ye drink some ay its blood with the wine — then yer altar is cleansed with incense and after ye say yer wee oath — and then that gets burnt . . . disappears into ash, doesn't it, but it doesn't mean even one part of that oath is allowed to be forgotten, right?

— No.

— No, it's not!

Bee clicks her fingers as testosterone begins to heat up the room.

— You won't kill us, Mrs Fox.

— Ooh — d'ye double-dare me? Bee whispers.

— If there is nothing more, we must ask you to leave.

— What if we kill every fucking one of you? Even the fish — even that fucking monkey!

Bee points at the tiny primate and it scrunches up its face and runs up the curtain to sit on the long wooden pole above them.

— We have taken your questions.

— Peter, I was really beginning to think you were just the strong silent type, how about you give us back Dora's cousin.

— We can't.

— Is she in a snuff movie?

Raymond raises his hand to silence his younger partner again.

– No. You don't know who we are. This is all conjecture . . .

– Ah, but we do, Raymond. We know everything. While you assume we are just working-class Scottish radges who are not only ignorant but also stupid as fuck – as is always so readily assumed of our kind – we actually happen to be as thorough in our business endeavours as any other organised syndicate!

Bee runs her fingers over her fox ears.

The ram stamps his cane on the floor twice. They all straighten up and get back to the task at hand. Bee begins to talk quietly and calmly, with no expression at all.

– You, Raymond, are thirty-three years old. A Gemini. Your mother still lives in Macau where you grew up – it's the most densely populated place in the world!

The older man pales.

He indicates to his partner not to raise his gun.

– Your mother, Chen, is very sweet. I met her a few weeks ago. I was only in China briefly – for business.

Bee nods.

– What business?

– Well, first I went to Zhuxian Park. I visited the temple and the caves. Then over to Nanping Zhen for some lunch. I had delicious street food – *jiaozi, bing tanghulu* . . . I found the donkey-meat sandwich particularly delicious!

Bee pats her ears as if to tell the women in the corner to cover the monkey's ears and the tiny primate looks down at her with furious little eyes.

– Who are you working for really, Bee?

– I met your mother after that. She made me white tea. It has a very delicate flavour.

— It does.

— You should get her an apartment lower down the building, Raymond. Fourteenth-floor D — it's a lot of stairs to climb. Also, your mother does not have a bathroom as nice as this, does she? Or a decent couch? I might send her a postcard. She has such a pretty address — Rua De nam Keng 444, EDF Flower City-Lei Fung, 25-A N D -M Taipa.

— I know my home address.

— Did you know the landline has been cut?

— No, it hasn't.

— Ah, but it has, Raymond. She can't phone out right now.

The man is visibly beginning to panic and the ammonic, metallic scent of sweat and fear begins to permeate the room. Bee nods her fox head gravely.

— My husband came with me on the trip.

Rab nods.

— What did you do there? Raymond asks.

— 租一个白人外国人, 相当交易!

Bee answers for him.

— And exactly — what was your husband rented to do — as a white foreigner?

Raymond is shaky.

— Well!

— Well!

Husband and wife smile at each other affectionately.

Bee continues.

— You, brooding young Peter, so dashing aren't you, I found enough time to visit your sister, Rose, as well, in Hong Kong. I heard all the news about her boyfriend, about your father's disappointment in you — so sad — your early training . . . the thirty-six oaths you took to help free a fellow gang member if you inadvertently got them arrested . . .

Peter pulls out his gun and unlocks the barrel.

– Except you got a lot more than one prior gang member arrested, didn't you, Peter?

– No!

– They are very annoyed. In fact, they said you are a really naughty boy. I only have two good methods for dealing with those. Do you want to hear what they are?

Peter shakes his head and nods at the same time.

– Well, my dear husband here – the ram as he is for tonight . . . and actually that's often how I think of him – if he has been a naughty boy, if he, for example, has been down to the brothel and had a little threesome and come home without any money for me – well – I bullwhip him . . .

– With a bullwhip?

– Big one. Six feet long. I have to wear heels to really crack it – I'm not so tall!

– She's an expert, Rab verifies.

– Really?

– Yes, Peter, that's the first thing that I do to punish naughty boys. The problem is – my darling husband likes it far too much. But after a proper whipping and all the other accoutrements – he doesn't look at any other girls for a good, long while, he just comes home, hands over his money, pours me a bath, whilst I go for a long soak to soothe away sad memories.

Rab refuses to meet the amused glances of Ali and Davey.

The two women laugh under their hands.

– What you actually want to know, Peter, is what I do to *really* naughty boys, right?

With the fox mask and with her tight clothes and boots – and her soft voice – Bee is hypnotising the entire room. She whispers so they all have to strain to hear what she is going to say next.

– I put on this – latex catsuit.

– You do?

– I do.

– And then . . .

– Well, then I have them oil me up in it – I keep them naked in a collar and leash – and I make them rub oil into every crevice. Do you know how nipples feel through the finest, thinnest oiled latex?

– No, I mean, no.

– Hard, slippery and smooth, all at the same time.

– Then?

– They often beg me at that point . . .

– For what?

Both young women are listening.

One has poured herself a gin and tonic.

The other one smokes a small joint.

The monkey tips his head.

Rab is trying to contain his erection but he has never been able to hold it together around Bee. The woman unravels him – she can do it to almost anyone. Peter gazes at the fox adoringly.

– To touch them.

– They do?

– They beg me for all kinds of things at that point.

– Like what?

– I don't know . . . a cock that I wear, you know, hard up inside them, or they like me to slap their face while I sit on

281

them, punch it even, or place their face between my tits, or their dick. Sometimes they want a hard ball gag in their mouth so they can suffocate to the point of passing out just as they cum, or they want me to spit on their balls and drag them around and humiliate them – it's disgusting.

– That's no way to be with a lady, Peter says.

– That's right. I don't like it. In fact, I have a very low tolerance for men other than my husband. Dora Noyce's cousin did too – she only ever punished them, which is why we know she didn't come to make films with you willingly. Also, to go back to your initiation ceremony – they say – correct me if I am wrong – if you ever break one of your thirty-six oaths – or worse, let one of your blood brothers go to prison for one of your crimes – you would be struck by five thunderbolts, do they not?

– They do.

– Well, Peter, sweet man – today you can call me Zeus!

Bee's last whisper is replaced with the sound of a blade as she glides the head out of her cane and stabs Peter in the throat, five times rapidly – two blood tears slide down his face. She spins and sticks another blade between Raymond's eyes. As both men sink to the floor, she grabs them by the hair – stands with one head – in either hand.

Ivor (37)

after all these years

ESME IS still asleep on him. Four huge tanks appear on the telly. The newsreel reads: Tiananmen Square, Beijing. The footage is unbelievable. One solitary man stands in front of the tanks. They face him. Guns up. The man refuses to move. The rolling bar at the bottom of the screen estimates – over 100,000 students are taking part in protests. Hunger strikes. Mass gatherings. The man in front of the tanks has a bag in each hand. He was on his way home, maybe. He'd had enough. Of watching ordinary people suffer. The newsreel states that protestors are demanding economic liberalisation, democracy, and rule of law. They want to be treated respectfully. That's what they want. Hu Yaobang – who stood for freedom and democracy – was forced to resign, and died. The protestors, many of them students – protest twice as hard in his name. Seven demands are made.

1. Publish the income of state leaders.
2. Recognise that campaigns against spiritual pollution are wrong.
3. Stop press censorship.

4. Affirm that Hu Yaobang's views on democracy and freedom are correct.
5. End the restriction on demonstrations.
6. Provide objective coverage of demonstrations in the media.
7. Increase funding for education.

Hu Yaobang's funeral took place in April. A hundred thousand students came to protest at Tiananmen Square. During the funeral inside the Great Hall, students called for an official to address them.

None came out.

Two days later, rioting broke out in Changsha and Xian.

A few days after that, another 100,000 students marched to Tiananmen Square. A million Beijing residents demonstrated in solidarity. They brought troops in. Armies came from every direction into Beijing. They shot expanding bullets. They expand inside the body to create a bigger wound.

Tank man stands in front of the tanks – now.

One tries to go around him and he stands in its way again.

He climbs up onto the tank to talk to the man driving it – human to human.

Ivor sits in silence.

Telly on mute.

Tears.

It is all wrong, what is going on in this world, what people do to other people.

He pulls a blanket up over Rhona. Her face is too thin. They stopped her benefits again and he can't get any if he's not attending job interviews in daylight. It'll be bar work he'll have to do probably. What else? Esme is existing mostly on shoplifted Pop Tarts and Ovaltine. Gas will be off soon. They've had to jack the leccy meter. Meter man came to read it and they had to run the hairdryer, Hoover and all the lights for three days to try and bring the figures down or he would have known they'd been jacking in to put lots of free electricity on their box.

His heart feels faint.

Sun is coming.

The same dread he feels every day. He knows it is on its way.

He carries the bairn through to her bed and tucks her in. She is wearing her reversible Mickey Mouse pyjamas from Ingliston Market. Rhona took her there last week. She said the bairn all but died and went to heaven when they did the one o'clock fashion show next to the burger van!

He wants to go down to the Scotsman for a pint before dawn but he can't even afford that.

Switch off the telly.

He hates all of it!

The strikes, when the miners are marching, the men he's grown up with – police batons on their backs. They even had gay protestors come out in Wales to support them – Ivor heard the wives were all making them tea and warning the boys not to say the wrong thing. Five thousand miners fought about the same in police in Rotherham. They arrested over 11,000 miners up and down the country, there's hundreds ended up in prison and it was just the state flexing their muscles. Letting them know. They could take the very infrastructure and living out from under them and that protest or even solidarity of any kind against the government will be met with annihilation. Everywhere, it's all unrest!

Brixton riots. Marches against the National Front since the seventies. Racist cunts marching for their right to hatred. Poll tax. Nuclear disarmament. Women's rights over their bodies, their right to equal pay, their right to not be raped by their husband which is still legal in the UK. The Irish hunger strike, going all the way back to the fucking Radical War in Scotland. The policymakers have much to answer for, deaths and ruin all on their soft pink fingers and Britain claims after all of it that there is freedom of the press! What a fucking joke! Rich people own papers and they work fir their other rich pals who run the whole fucking joint. They have systematically shut down mines across every town that has had them for hundreds of years — it is a deliberate attack. Thatcher is after the enemy within: trade unions. Moonlight casts a blue glow on the living room. Ivor picks up Rhona's tramadol. Sits holding them. It's so tempting. So, so, so fucking tempting. Fucking Thatcher! Those who have inherited take all they can from those who will never inherit. They can't take enough! Austerity! She described the miners as a danger to liberty. Refused any concessions through the strikes. Privatised the few pits that are left. Let the Irish go on hunger strike in the Maze and didn't change tack until ten were dead. Even then, she did it solely to save face. All they wanted was for their rights as paramilitary prisoners to be restored. Rights! There's nae rights for most humans. There's only rights for the rich. Thatcher wants capital punishment. Archaic divorce laws. She objects to immigrants. Saw the National Front lose their voters to her they were so convinced by her racism. Makes endless cuts to education as a deliberate way to keep opportunity among the elite or middle classes as much as possible. Allow those you oppress to think? No, sorry, not happening! Or even worse – challenge you in your own arenas? Fuck off. He runs his finger over the packet and picks up his sister's vodka. Taps the painkillers on his leg. Rhona opens her eyes and stares at him. Ivor does nothing. Just stares back until she goes to sleep. She will think it was just a weird, barbiturate dream. He is shaking. What is he thinking? He puts the tablets up high in the kitchen cabinet. Ivor sits there for hours next to his sister just like he used to do when they were kids. Back then he was watching out for her. Now he needs to watch out for Esme and Rhona and he just feels fucking useless. His shoulders shake. Tears burn at the back of his eyes. If he didn't know better he'd be away down the miners' club tomorrow night to batter someone, anyone – get the pain out via his fists, but he's too old now to play that game.

The doctor told him the word for what's wrong with him.

– You are phengophobic, Ivor.

– I'm what?

– It's an acute fear of light, daylight in particular – that's your phobia.

– Aw ma life, that's it?

– Aye, your job and your lifestyle have supported you so you can hide it mostly, Ivor. You avoid daylight most of the time. But now you've lost the job, your relationship has broken down . . . I think you are having an episode of depression.

– I dinnae get that, doctor, noh, I dinnae get depression, never had it, never will.

– Have you had any thoughts of suicide, Ivor?

– Nut.

– Depression is not unusual among young men especially

when they are under financial and family pressure, Ivor . . . I lost my nephew that way and too many men refuse to talk about it – well, we just need to ask.

Ivor did not tell him that he thinks of ten ways to die each day.

He's not an idiot! He told the doctor absolutely jack shit about that. Aye! They'd have him locked up in the Royal Ed, being fed mush and pissing himself, before he could say – fuck it.

He goes into Esme's room and she is up already. Before light comes. She takes his hand. Doesn't comment on his tear-stained face. It probably doesn't show in her wee starlit room. She has set up a tea party with all the Care Bears except Love-a-Lot. She pours tea. Hands him a tiny pink plastic cup.

– Sit!

Ivor struggles to cross his legs.

They stick out awkwardly in front of him like they belong to some other cunt.

She picks up a hanky from her dolly and casual as anything – leans over and wipes the tears from his face.

– I uhmnay gonna lie, it's really no gonnae be okay, Uncle Ivor.

– It won't?

– No, I don't think it's gonnae be guid. No fir the trees. Or the people. It's not going to be okay for anything in the end.

She looks up at him.

A tiny sage with ribbons in her hair.

– It might get better, Esme?

– Noh, it winnae.

He laughs.

— It's no funny, Uncle Ivor, no fir Jessie, or her wee girl Hope, or Elise. They urnay ever gonnae be okay.

— Are they . . . invisible friends?

— Invisible to you!

She smacks her hand off her forehead and shakes her head, admonishing his great unseeing.

— I believe you, Esme, I know there's things other people cannae see that are real.

— They urnay invisible, Uncle Ivor. Jessie is sat right there where you sleep. There's Elise playing make-up with ma powder puff and the bairn — she's always toddling about eftir me. I keep growing but she stays the same size all the time and she's had three birthdays since I met her.

Esme puts her hand down to indicate a child only up to her waist. She holds out a teddy for a little girl that he can't see.

— Why is Love-a-Lot not at the tea party, Esme?

The little girl pouts and frowns. She glances towards the living room next door.

— Because not everybody Loves-a-Lot, do they?

— You are very wise now that you're eight.

She nods gravely. Goes over to her ghetto blaster and fiddles with a tape cassette.

— Why has Mummy never loved anybody?

— Like who?

— Like my dad. The other kids at school have dads.

— Not all of them and between you and me, Esme, and don't repeat this, I ken a fair few of their da's and they are useless wankers.

— They dinnae have a mummy who's been asleep since they were born though.

Ivor wants to scoop her up in his arms. She won't take hugs easy though, unless she's tired. It's a thing in his family. They learn things by memory super-easy, can recite facts and figures and maths and obscure facts. They are aw a wee bit too clever, but when it comes to simple things – like hugs, just, you know, loving someone, being understood in a conversation or knowing even remotely what other people need – it's not something they do well.

– Why urr ye no at home any mair, Uncle Ivor?

– Well, I'm just not.

– Did someone hit you?

– What?

– Jessie saw you get undressed in the bathroom and she says you have bruises aw over yer back and arms.

– Ghosts should not watch people undress!

A big smile.

Curly hair and lots of it, wide eyes – like in a cartoon.

The tap, tap, tap of the deathwatch beetles is fading.

Sun drawing close.

– It's time to go back to sleep, Esme, and stop making up stories. They are why you are having nightmares!

Esme makes a face to the invisible guests.

He'd like to say he does not hear the faintest peal of laughter – female, high, more than one.

He looks to the bunk where she says Jessie is sitting.

This must be how a phengophobic finally loses his mind entirely.

– Scat!

Goes to lift her onto the bunk. She shakes her head. Pushes his hand away. Climbs up the wee ladder in a huff. Stares at him with her Goonies poster behind her. He'll no be a burglar, no end up in Saughton like her da. He'll forget the pit. Stack shelves in Tesco. Work in bars. Whatever it is, he'll do it.

Esme peeps at him.

— Sleep tight, Esme, dinnae let the bedbugs bite.

— Nobody will bite me, Uncle Ivor, don't be daft. Ma best friend's mum is the devil's daughter – she's got horns so long they could stake a burglar through a letter box.

She stretches out her hands to emphasise – with envious glee.

— Sleep!

Esme checks under her duvet. Hot-water bottle is still warm. She watches him for a moment and then the next, her eyes fall. Asleep within seconds. So peaceful – he envies it. It must be his presence that is making her feel safe. Not some imaginary fucking horned cunt. There is a tap at the front door. Who and what the fuck? If it's some cunting junkies, they're going to get a rapid punch tae the fucking pus. Wearing nothing but his Calvin Klein shorts, Ivor yanks opens the door. His best mate is stood there.

— What the fuck do you want?

— Don't shut the door, Ivor. I'm sorry!

He holds his hands up.

— I am warning you, Jake – get the fuck away fae this door or I'm gonna come out and leather ye in the fucking stair-well. I mean it!

The vein on Ivor's forehead throbs.

It's hard not to close his fist and put it through Jake's face. So hard!

— If you want tae hit me, Ivor, go fir it. I know, though – about Joanne.

His pal wrinkles his nose like he has done since they were little kids. Ivor knows what Joanne is like. A few drinks, a high mood . . . hard to resist for anyone. His wife is the kind of woman who lights up a room, no matter how fucked up she is — he will give her that, at least.

— I am begging you, Ivor, you are my auldest pal, please let me explain.

— You've got five minutes and you'll have tae whisper.

They go into the wee bedroom, lit only by Esme's glow-in-the-dark stars stuck all over the ceiling. Ivor sits on the bunk, Care Bears all around him. The wee troll things Esme collects too, and all the My Little Ponyies with their smug pus's. Despite himself, he smiles. So does Jake. They are the hardest men from their town.

Jake sits on the floor, offers him a tin.

— Can I smoke in here?

— Aye.

Ivor pushes a red Tennent's ashtray over to him.

— Alright, Jake, what have you got tae say for yourself then?

The anger is back in his voice then, just looking at him — thinking of him touching her.

— Joanne stabbed me.

— What?

— With a biro, in the leg. It's fucking sair!

He pulls up his jeans and there is a bandage with blood seeping out.

— Fucks sake!

— Is that Hubba Bubba the bairn's, Ivor? Can I have a piece? What kind is it?

— It's Awesome Original Bubble Tape.

— I prefer Groovy Grape.

Jake unwraps the gum and chews it and looks at him seriously.

— Joanne confessed to me what's been going on, ay, it was a sair yin for her to admit to it but I made her, I could tell, I think I've ken't for years really if I think about it now.

Ivor's heart really races then, a roar in his ears. Not wanting the words to come out his friend's mouth. Thinking of how you can know someone your entire life and never even think of telling them your worst secrets or what has been done to you or by whom. And how if he'd taken those tablets, no one really would have had any idea why he'd done it.

— Joanne's been battering ye, Ivor, fir decades, since we were teenagers.

— Get the fuck out of here, Jake!

— She says yer allergic tae light like, that aw the boys calling ye a scab dinnae ken what they are talking about — ye only kept going down the pit cos ye hink yer gonnae die in fucking daylight.

— What a load ay shite!

— For once in your entire fucking life, Ivor, let me in!

The emotion rising up in him, if Ivor had to name it, would be shame and it feels like it goes all the way down inside him, deeper than the coal mine, that he had it even earlier than lifting up a cardboard box to put on his head and feeling like a freak, earlier than when he got married thinking it was better him taking the blame than Joanne.

— I hate you, Jake.

— I know, man. I fucking hate me too and I deserve it. Just dinnae shut me out! I'm not having them say yer a scab any more, Ivor, and I'm not having yer kids think it is you lifting yer hands when it is her! I uhmnay! You are the nicest guy in the whole fucking world and it's not fair! It's time, mate.

    — Time to what?

    — Tell the truth!

    — Get fucked.

Ivor reaches into his pal's top front pocket, where his fags always are. He takes out a Regal King Size. Sparks it. Offers the pack to Jake and he takes one out and lights it, too. Ivor feels as sick as he has done every morning. He doesn't know how to explain that getting up every morning feels like facing a dinosaur — one that is pounding down the streets looking only for him. The two men lay beside each other, awkwardly silent on a single bunk. The tips of their fags glow red — like a sun on the horizon.

Dot (27)

the long walk home

DOT OPENS the door. There is a small hammer on her mat. It looks like an antique. She's reluctant to leave the little warmth there is in the flat. Pulls her beanie down. If she is to spend the bells following spirits – she's glad to have had a drink already. The hammer is in her hand. It works by itself. With a feeling of being a conduit, willingly, she goes into her bathroom and raises it above her head. Claws into plasterboard. She gouges a hole into the bathroom wall. Musty air wafts up from inside the building. Her hand fits inside the cold cavity. Just cobwebs and dust. She tries to be gentle. This building has endured enough. It is a sickly patient! Dot: some kind of mad psychic doctor come to cure its rickets! That's one to put on her CV. Dot – whose cracks are lined only with gold – feted Doctor of the Underworld: references – solely from the spirit realm.

The interviewer described her as non-able-bodied last time.

Dot isn't a non-anything.

Fucking non-entity, that woman was. Her own mum was, too, when she thinks about it. Dot's mother was always disgusted by her faulty child. Not arriving exactly as she should! Not doing what was expected at every single moment! Her mother always said, in her terse tone, that she wouldn't let Dot ruin her life – oh no – she was far too strong for that. She wouldn't let anyone ruin her life! The woman endured, piously, the terrible hardship of her daughter's presence.

Fuck them all!

Tap. Tap.

Tap. Tap. Tap, tap, tap, tap, tap.

In the attic (her temple), thousands of deathwatch beetles stop what they are doing.

She knows who her disciples are!

Dot has looked them up.

Hacking into the Wi-Fi from the Witchery up the street – it is very satisfying.

There is nothing Dot can't do with technology.

It's like she was bred for it.

One day they will use technology to open up communication between this world and the rest of the universe and Dot will have no difficulty in gaining employment then. Her disciples of the attic are many and interesting. After conducting much research and finding various dead specimens to inspect more closely – she's learnt that her only other living companions in this building come from the order Coleoptera, in the superorder Endopterygota. If that doesn't make her Head of an Underworld, she doesn't know what would.

Down below her, wooden joists throughout the whole building creak.

Metal echoes somewhere.

There is a shudder.

Dot stops – hammer in hand – guilty as charged – is her investigative surgery on the building going to be the final thing to make it fall?

With her in it?

No. 10 Luckenbooth Close is a very fragile fucking building.

There is nothing to say she will not be buried alive by tomorrow.

It's a risk.

Dot steps back and gouges another, bigger hole out of the wall. In the attic above her all the insects pause. Hundreds of thousands of deathwatch beetles take a collective breath. She taps. The beetles tap back. Dot stops. They await instruction. The beetles clearly consider her tapping – to be that of a new and great mother. She is the giant Death-watch Beetle Princess. They rejoice! The eternal mother has come back to them. They have eaten the structures (almost) away but she has come to them in the end. What good fortune to live in an entire tenement of oak-rot-donkiopora! The beetles' most favourable conditions have been cultivated by endless gutter leaks, abject building neglect and hundreds of years of damp Edinburgh weather. Mass colonisation wins. Dot taps again. The spirits don't want her to stop looking. They don't want her to leave them. They need her. They would compete with the living for her loyalty, except there is nobody alive who wants her. The other world is fighting for her presence – hard.

– You want me?

Wind echoes up the building's cavities.

– For good?

Why do the living hold on so hard to this life?

— Take the tablets, Dot.

Her friends would say that if she had any. The doctor gives people like her tablets to stop them thinking and friends find it too tiring in the end often too, Dot does not know how to think small or chit-chat idly, time is short and there are things to do before the end. Those other friends in her head, the ones that never leave and have nothing good to say to her, the words that come unbidden as thoughts, they would ally with those who know her but they'd tell her to take all the tablets and give in to the great quiet time of far-away. If this world wants rid of her it can carry her out questioning and fighting. She won't aid its inertia, not one fucking bit. Like when she moved in here, she has friends that would be shocked, that would say she should have gone to them in her moment of need, but everyone knows that is what people say yet rarely what they mean.

Bloody useless things, other people!

Dot lights a joint.

Exhales a small row of smoke rings.

She decides to stop and take a break and drink the remaining half bottle of wine before doing anything else.

— Come on, little Dot, take all the tablets.

No. 10 Luckenbooth Close used to draw itself up to its greatest height on this hill. A tall observer of the city way down below it. It has watched everything happen in Edinburgh. The fairground being assembled in winter. A child falling and skinning its knee and crying, his blood soaking into soil in the Gardens. A couple breaking up. Stages going up and down. Someone being chased by police. A fox walking down the middle of Princes Street at night. The homeless bird man feeding all the birds at 5 a.m. each day – people shirking away from him when all the commuters come out to claim the city as their own. All the roads running down into the New Town in neat lines, exposing views from city to sea – looking all the way across the water. In summer, sometimes golden fields of hay over in Fife catch the light. Luckenbooth has seen all the hearts break. All the people who started new jobs. Everyone who got back up again and walked these roads. Or there is a soft haze of green hills to seduce the eye on an icy morning. At night, on the other side of the Firth of Forth, a glowing dash of red lights up as Mossmorran bolts fire up into the sky from the ethylene plant, way over in the Kingdom of Fife – a place often ignored (or derided) by the many snobs of Edinburgh. It's so pretty there. Seals swim out from Inchcolm Island. Fat white or grey seal cubs pop up every year, all black eyes and whiskers. In winter, the hills across the water are snow-peaked and majestic.

Coolly noted by Edinburgh.

All of the middle-to-top-floor residents of No. 10 Luckenbooth Close would have been witness to even more. They would have seen a changing vista all year round. Pink skies. Yellow dawns. Snow rolling in to drown the city white. Drunken women out on hen do's singing away over on George Street. Street performers trying to make money. Comedians seeking fame. Bin lorries trundling down cobbles, all grim in the wee hours. Protestors marching. Dark cars driving politicians to places where they can't be seen. Steamy buses. Folks from all over the Lothians coming to work in town, or go out to dinner, or do business, or drink, or shoplift, or visit the council, or take buses to the airport so they can fly the fuck out of here. Bodies found. Knifes in hands. Fists raised. Deals done. The sound of a woman crying on empty streets. A front bell ringing at the massage parlour. The upstairs and downstairs, the rich and the poor – they won't ever stop its darkness. It's a city of duality. Lack of investment in communities perpetuates it. Edinburgh is all seasons and movement – space, breadth – modern, ancient – experiment, tradition – conservatives, crooks, academics, bakers, curators, beggars, all the many graves seen and unseen. It is a most uncompromising city. And Dot is entirely alone in it and nobody wants her.

Dot smiles to herself sadly.

She has love in her heart for this city.

No matter how many bad things have happened to her here.

It is her home.

She is an errant daughter who always returns.

On the outside of the tenement, two stone faces on the belfry sneer at all of it – stone features all bashed-in by the north wind. Dot has a feeling she might be the last to see them. Those gargoyles have held that pose fir hundreds of years. Up on rooftops all over this city there are angels and cherubs and saints and sinners and gargoyles and little stone creatures. Dot is more fir them than the humans. Get rid of the humans. Planet – take yersel back – let all this shit decay! Dot picks up a marble. Sits it on the floor. It rolls quickly away from her. The building is sliding forward too quickly. Fireworks bang outside. The bells will be here soon. Tomorrow will be cold. There will be no bright sky. She can feel it in her bones. Even the cars appear forlorn in that kind of grey. Every year around March, or sometimes April, there is a fear that spring may not come at all.

Often she arrives – late and unrepentant.

She is as brash as only a goddess who brings forth new life can be.

The city is primeval, tired, corrupt – occasionally brilliant, true – held hostage by seasons.

Dot does not question why summer has commitment issues.

An Edinburgh summer is usually a skittery, lying, drunk, untrustworthy foe – her legs are always spread – elsewhere. She is elusive and unreliable, a total fucking pisshead. The next day (for months) she pretends she's still far too poorly to make an appearance.

Locals loathe the erratic and often absent entirely – Edinburgh summer.

Talk about her endlessly – will she, or won't she?

Look out windows expectantly each morning.

They buy flower seeds just in case.

Resentfully, they keep out all items of their winter wardrobe.

She loves all the anticipation, doesn't she?

They hate her.

It's an entire country in an abusive relationship with the weather.

She drives many to despair, or drink.

However, if she does arrive!

All is forgiven.

Couples kiss each other on the Meadows, lay down amongst the daisies and rejoice in the plain exultation of

living! Holistic practitioners talk craniosacral therapy —
outside — over multiple shots of coffee. Kids play football, or
rounders, or Grand Theft Auto, or skateboard, or do wheel-
ies on bikes in the middle of the road. People get pierced in
Cockburn Street, or tattooed. Buskers sing their songs a
wee bit louder. Art is made happily on the street. Even the
jakies nod and dance and say fair play tae it. Posh people
cruise out to East Lothian in hatchbacks stashed — for this
one glorious day! Girls with legs rising up to very tight short
shorts — go out fir cocktails — in the early afternoon. Beer
gardens fill with drinkers chatting football, or gossip, or
philosophy, or music, or sex, or death. They all turn up for
summer. Stick by her until she goes. Dot puts the joint out.
She is not going to be here much longer. These ever-present
thoughts of the hustle and motion of her hometown mean
one thing.

Nostalgia is pre-empting her exit from the entire place.
For good!

It's not safe in here — her flat door gives a good impression
of security but in all truth — its screws are loose. Dot can pull
the letter box back with little effort. Stick her arm through.
Turn the latch to let herself in. So can anyone else. Dot can
hear something in the lower levels moving around. Traces
her fingertip over the smooth, cold, metal hammer. That
stairwell is a horror movie whose longest and most dedi-
cated audience are ghosts. She doesn't normally go through
this building on her own at night. She locks herself in here.
There's a clatter below. The sound of a door slamming and
she bolts upright. Heart batters off her chest. Then there is
nothing. It was just . . . it was nothing. Dot tells herself that
again and again until her palpitations begin to ease. Outside

her flat door, and in all the floors below, there are absolutely no human sounds.

The peripheral noise of others has gone.

No boiling kettles; no bare feet in hallways in the middle of the night; no bumping into things while going to the loo with the lights off; no running taps; no brushing teeth; no low moans; no cursing all-of-fate when warm flesh sits on a freezing toilet seat. At sundown, there is no click of lamps going on up and down each floor. No running for the morning bus and slamming the stairwell door. No Sunday mornings in hungover pits. No middle-of-the-night waking, soaked in existential dread. No turning the radio up. No dancing without anyone there. No looking out the window. No drawing the curtains, or the shutters, or doodling in the margins of a diary while blinking at the TV. No diarrhoea after a shock or too much rum, or a wheat binge, or gastric flu. No waiting for death. No texting an ex. No getting ready to go out. No being happy to stay in. There are no ignored phone calls in between bathtime and tears. There are no other tenants, not at dawn or dusk, nor any of the hours in between.

A scratching sound draws near.

Rats.

It is likely rats.

She turns the broken snib on her front door – so quiet!

Dot looks out onto the landing, keeps one foot inside her own hallway.

It is freezing.

What if rats are flocking here from sewers and catacombs? Rats the size of wee dogs. She could wake to find one eating her toes. Dot sleeps with her boots on every night just in case. Something is circling in the building and it's not fucking rats. It's moving in and out of cavities unseen. Dot places both feet out in the cold stone hall. Grips the hammer in a sweaty hand.

Ear cocked.

Blood cold and hot at the same time.

Something *is* in here.

It belongs to the building just like she does.

Each floor is so quiet. The building is listening to her, too. So are the ghosts. They're closing in. Not much time left. The stone steps are so worn, each dips in the middle. The pipes clang. She's not running taps! Faint. Dizzy. Whatever she fears is not real. It isn't real. It is not. She tells herself this just like people tell themselves they will never be the one to go mad on the street one day – to not recognise themselves – to not even know their own name!

Not me.

Not I.

It won't happen.

Until it does.

It will.

Then it will be far too late to do anything about any of it.

What if she tore off her clothes and ran from the building? On Hogmanay!

Nobody would pay attention, probably.

What if it is a human (not a spirit) she can hear wandering this building?

The tourist board might issue a statement on her: 'Homeless woman refused disability benefit or housing is found murdered while squatting in a derelict building.' On Hogmanay! This is really not the look we are going for!

Heartbeat is still too fast.

Felt at .102 above the normal setting for human existence.

Do spirit doctors' hearts beat like other mortals? Maybe a robot stuck a needle in her earth mother in the womb.

– This one comes from the dream world, boys – a pure one – an earth angel – a goddess – born with fangs and a unique pattern to her limbs. Let's curse her to a life of yearning.

Dot knows who it is down there really.

Easier to think it might just be an average murderer than what she really knows.

Dot has seen the sharp tip of horns.

The building croaks and groans and she flies down the stairs.

Pushes open the door at 7F7.

Dot will know what it is when she finds it and she is not living in fear for one minute more, there is something more important than that for her to face right now – she uses the adrenaline to push herself harder and faster – she runs through the sixth floor – there are marks on the walls, old carpets but nothing else, Dot slows down – on the fifth-floor landing and approaches a flat door, it is already ajar.

Pushes it open.

– Is anyone there?

There is no creak but she can tell she is getting closer to something . . .

Dot steps into the long hallway.

There is a bathtub visible through a door on the right.

– Hello?

Into the living room.

An old, empty parrot cage sits on a stand.

Seeds are scattered over a patterned carpet.

She can feel it.

Evil.

It's not the first time Dot has felt that presence.

She hauls her hand back and claws a huge hole into the wall. She kicks the plasterboard and rips chunks of it away – throws them down onto the floor behind her in a gloom of dust – pulls her arm back again – bang, bang, bang – fireworks out on the street – a shudder through the entire building. She has taken off nearly the entire wall before she even looks up. The air turns icy. Blinking she realises her skin has turned as cold as alabaster. A long, low howl rises up from the bowels of the building.

Dot screams.

Steps back – drops the hammer.

– Fucking hell!

She reaches out and then snatches her hand back.

Steadies herself again.

Two skeleton torsos hold hands – and in between them is a child.

The infant is the only one with skull intact.

It looks up at her.

Outside on the street, fireworks crack and there is cheering as bells go off.

Tears in her eyes.

– I'll be back for you, she whispers.

Dot lets tears stream hotly across her dirty face. She knows why those women are in there. In a methodical – pure – rage, she takes apart the walls of every room in the lower floors one after another, until only the basement remains. Its walls come apart easily under her fury – they have been waiting for such a thing. The catacombs are just there and all the undead gather as she walks toward the entrance and lifts up her hammer one last time but she does not go hard, she taps and then uses the claw end of the hammer to clear away what she needs. Dot carefully opens up a shallow altar; two skull heads look at each other. One has fine, long horns.

Queen Bee (21)

*Santa baby, please put a sable
under the tree, for me*

REFLECTED IN the ceiling mirror is a pool of blood. It spreads out on a large, round, purple shaggy rug. Ali lowers his shotgun as Bee wipes her dagger off on the rug. She stands back neatly – to assess her handiwork.

The two young women watch her. One exhales a long curl of smoke from a joint.

– 圣洁的狗屎, one woman says.

– Holy shit indeed, Bee agrees.

The other woman opens a bag of crisps and stuffs a large handful in her mouth and crunches loudly.

– What? I'm hungry!

Davey stands at the window, looking down toward the street.

– There's police coming into the stair!

– You fucking what?

– What do we do with the bodies?

– Bathroom, and we need candles, okay? And you two need to come through here, Bee snaps.

The woman puts her crisp bag down, visibly annoyed.

– Okay!

The shag rug is rolled up and shoved down the back of

the fish tank. Two slim men's bodies are taken down the hall into the bathroom. Both of the women stand at the door looking at Bee as if she's mad while she takes her clothes off.

— I need you — yes, you — the prettier one — take your clothes off.

— You're not my type, Bee.

— I want you to look like you've been in this bath with me — hair wet, towel wrapped around you — come on!

The whirlpool bubbles up on full jets.

— Your friend must pretend she is taking care of the boys through there. If they search us and find these two idiots, we will all go to prison and I don't think you'd like Corn-ton Vale one bit, I fucking hate the place. What are your names?

— Bai.

— Audrey.

Both girls nod.

There is a knock.

Audrey quickly wets her hair and pulls a towel around herself before going to answer the door. She opens it slowly and looks up, half-wearing the towel. Her hair is dripping.

— Oh, we're sorry.

The police officer glances down the hall.

— We heard there was a disturbance.

— Oh, no? Actually, that could have been me and my girl-friend. We were . . . getting carried away, too many drinks at the Christmas office party!

Audrey pulls on the end of a strand of hair.

— Do you live here?

— Yes. I'm a student and I work at the bar in our university. So does my girlfriend.

— What are you studying?

— Terrorism.

— Okay. Well, just want to have a quick look, won't take a minute.

Audrey whispers.

— My girlfriend is in the bath, waiting, we had a little fight you see and I need to go make it up to her . . .

The policeman pulls himself up taller.

— Well, we won't take long.

He steps into the hallway and the bathroom door is wide open and he looks in to see it is barely lit by candles. The whirlpool is full volume. Bee is in the centre of the bubbles. She sits up so they can see her entire upper torso, looking as shocked as she can manage. At that moment, another flat further up in the stairwell blasts out heavy metal music.

— Can I help you, officer?

— There was a disturbance . . .

— Oh, that was upstairs, we heard it too! They are always playing that music — it's not at all festive!

Bee's skin glistens in the candlelight.

— We'll go and see what's going on, sorry to disturb you, ladies.

— Thank you!

Audrey closes the door after the policeman leaves.

Turns to look down the hall.

Ali, Davey and Rab walk silently and look through the bathroom door. Bee drains the bath, still naked she pulls bodies of the two men up from underneath her into a sitting position and looks back at everyone. The corpses are beginning to go stiff and they are still clothed.

– Peter has an erection! You can see it under his trousers, look! Ali says.

Bee towels herself dry, hauls her clothes on and gestures, annoyed.

– Maybe if you are hard when you die, then, you know.

– I think he's going to cum.

– It's becoming one of those days. I've still presents to wrap, you know! Bee hisses and takes out a little glass phial and an even tinier silver spoon.

A wee snort up each nostril.

She can see them all behind her in the mirror. A quiet, ragged breathing sound draws her out of her daydream as they all fall silent.

Peter's corpse blinks.

– La, la, la, la, rip her to shreds . . .

Their ears are all tilted for every sound – the police coming back, or their own blood pumping through their veins – a television downstairs with *Bullseye* on, a familiar whumpf and thud as the darts are thrown – the presenter promising gifts, an audience clapping – a helicopter flying somewhere outside in the city. And this horrible, ragged breathing sound coming from a freshly dead corpse.

– He isn't dead, Ali says.

– He's dead! They can still move and shit fir up to twelve hours.

– Fuck off, Rab!

– I'm telling ye, they piss, shit, blink.

– Get laid?

– Look, it's just what the human body does! It's only gross

if you make it like that, corpses do weird things, it's normal, Bee says.

— The stages of decomposition are just not happening in order, maybe?

Audrey agrees as she starts eating her crisps again; she appears not only unflustered by the events of the last half hour, but actively amused. Ali checks his watch.

— I think by the time you've staked the cunt he should not be breathing like — this prick sounds like he's making a dirty phone call.

— It isnae right, Davey says.

— You stake him, he stops breathing; you drown him, when he's already dead — then what? Three seconds later he's breathing again? Ali asks.

— It's this place — this building's cursed. Every cunt knows it, Davey says.

— It is, Bai agrees.

— We hear things every night. The building has bad energy, Audrey says.

— This isn't fucking *Mastermind*, you're not going to be quizzed on the spunk habits of corpses or the spirit realm of Luckenbooth Close — I've had two men's dead bodies under me in a whirlpool, people — I think I'd know if they weren't dead. Strip the rest of their clothes off, they'll need to be wrapped in the rug to get them out of here.

Ali and Davey undress the men and lay them down as respectfully as they can. Raymond's eyes are closed but just as Ali goes to close Peter's, the corpse blinks very slowly and then ejaculates — just slightly.

Ali crosses himself.

— Fucks sake!

— Can you get pregnant from a Jacuzzi? Audrey asks with wide eyes.

— He's dead, it's just some fucking random dead-person jizz, seriously will you lot grow the fuck up, we've still got a lot to get rid of before Santa can fucking get here the morn!

Ali is shaking and Davey is even jumpier now.

— Fuck you, Bee.

— So — stake him again!

— I'm going to shoot him, just to be sure, Ali says.

— I heard of a woman who gave birth once after she died. She died of a heroin overdose and then a little while later — out pops the baby! The people with her were so high, they thought it was a hallucination.

They all turn to look at Bai.

— You two don't seem that freaked out by any of this. Audrey, Bai?

Bee stares hard at the two women.

— What do you do?

— Nothing.

— Why don't I fucking believe you?

— Perhaps you are a cynical woman, Mrs Fox?

Ali and Davey have pulled the corpses, by their feet, down the hall to roll them in the rug. Rab walks into the living room ahead of his wife. Bai walks barefoot behind them, taking out two gilded daggers in complete silence.

— We need to get home for the kids — lads, can ye take care of the rest of this?

— Aye, Davey says.

— Something doesn't feel . . .

On instinct, Bee turns just as Bai spins down low on the floor and kicks her legs out from under her in one elegant motion, she glides her hand under the sofa and she stabs each of Bee's eyes, killing her instantly. As Ali lunges for his gun, Audrey stabs him in the groin. She turns his own gun up to his chin, puts a cushion on top of it, then fires — feathers fly up into the air. Davey takes off his mask, in shock he lunges forward. Audrey slams her hand hard up into the underside of Davey's nose, sending bone into his brain and killing him instantly.

Rab's roar is savage. Trying to regain his breath, he looks at his wife with profound pain etched over his face. He ages visibly. His hands shake. Audrey gently pulls any weapons out of his reach.

— Do we have to cut their heads off, Bai? What do you think?

Audrey looks at all the corpses.

— Just their ears, or balls for the men — they deserve a rusty knife, those two.

She points at the Triads rolled up in the rug. They're beginning to turn blue.

— Should we make them eat them, Bai? I mean, leave their balls stuffed in their mouths — obviously they can't actually eat them! It would look good, right? It would make a statement? It's — creative!

Rab is in shock. He looks at Audrey and then at Bai, and then his wife and Ali and Davey.

— I don't understand what is . . .

— We could take off their toes. Let the rats deal with the rest, Audrey. If we cut a few toes off, the rats will smell that good steak tartare, huh? Yummy, right? They'll be in here by the dozen. They might eat all the bodies for us. It would be a Christmas feast for them, no?

— That's not a bad idea, Bai.

— Who the fuck are you?

Rab goes to stand up and Audrey points a gun at him.

— Sit down.

Bai gently lifts the fox mask off from Bee. She lays it on the floor so Rab can look at her one last time. Bee's face is angled toward her husband — teardrops tattooed under her eyes, gold dagger in each one. Other than that, she appears untouched. He thinks of their kids. The physical pain of grief floods through every artery and vein; even his feet shake. His teeth begin to clatter.

— I didn't realise who you were, I should have thought . . .

Rab puts his head in his hands.

— We are sorry about your wife. She was quite a woman, but we were sent here to kill Peter and Raymond, cleanly — heads off, symbolic and all that — and you turned up and quite rudely got in our way. We are sorry but . . .

Rab's hands are so shaky, he can't even light a cigarette.

— Could we feed the bodies to the fish, Audrey?

— I don't think so.

— Would a catfish eat them?

— It eats snails and crawfish, not human corpses.

— It's going to get dark, Rab says.

— I think we already got to the dark bit of the evening, Mr Ram, do you not?

— Take your mask off.

— No.

— I don't think you are in a position to negotiate.

Bai has put a large psychedelic mushroom throw over Davey and Ali. Bee's body is sat respectfully up against the wall – they've draped a leather jacket around her shoulders.

Audrey looks sad.

– I didn't want to kill Boadicea, but she had seen our face and worse than that we had seen hers, she wasn't going to let us out of here alive, was she?

– No.

– It is just business, Audrey states firmly.

– I am begging you both to give me tomorrow with my kids.

– Dead men don't go home to their children, Mr Ram, and we have no choice, you know that. Raymond and Peter here were due to die on our contract, and that has been fulfilled. We could have argued with you about who was going to kill them but – that would not have gone any better . . .

– No.

– You were sent here by the faction in Macau, were you not?

Rab nods.

– Yes, I thought so. We were sent from a bigger network in Hong Kong. Many factions wanted these men dead – we could all imagine this job was just double-booked . . . but I don't believe it was, Audrey says.

Bai hops up onto the windowsill and looks down onto the snowy street.

There is a sense of realisation in the way Rab drops his shoulders.

He pulls the mask off.

Both women look at him.

His face is freckled, young, clean-shaven. He has warm eyes.

— Maybe our men in Hong Kong knew you'd come looking for Dora Noyce's cousin — once you realised Raymond and Peter didn't have her. They don't like additional problems, do they, Bai?

— Nope!

Audrey fiddles around at the bar.

She has a quick gin.

Begins to fix up drinks for Rab and Bai.

— None of us like loose ends in this industry, they always come back to get us later. You are very handsome without your mask, Mr Ram. What age are you?

— I'm twenty-six, Rab says.

His eyes are so bright and blue, they glow.

— This is a bad industry for all of us really . . . it never ends well for anyone in it, no? Audrey says.

She hands him the brandy cocktail she has poured for him.

He accepts it.

Bee looks perfectly relaxed.

Rab drinks the brandy down in one go.

— It's not how Audrey and I had planned on spending Christmas Eve, was it? We were going to kill Raymond and Peter nice and clean, go out for dinner, then the theatre — the Traverse has a great production on — then we were going to have drinks at the jazz club — a short stop in London — then fly home. Take presents for all the family. I think we might miss the London flight now.

— Stop chattering, Bai.

— But it is Christmas Eve, and I love this time of year and

317

I have new baubles for Mum – from Jenners! And we could have got more at Harrods. It was meant to be a happy Christmas this year! I told them – it's the wrong time to send us out on this kind of job.

— When would you prefer to do your killing?

Rab places the glass down. He is quiet but full of unbearable rage.

— Easter, I don't celebrate that, Bai says.

Rab's hands grip the cushion on the sofa.

Both women look at him with his broken heart and try not to think about his children getting up tomorrow on Christmas Day and coming down to a tree in an empty room; no mother there and no father there. They look at each other.

— We are sorry, Mr Ram.

— I wish we . . .

He gestures at the two brothers and his wife on the floor.

— What?

— Never had to live this kind of life!

Bai opens the window.

Audrey's monkey carefully climbs down from the top of the curtain pole and goes outside and up the drainpipe.

A smell of city air floods into the flat, clean and cold from the snow, just a faint hint of garlic from a restaurant nearby and woodsmoke from the few chimneys that still use real fires. It has begun to snow outside again – gentle spirals. Audrey aims at the fish tank and shoots. Water gushes into the room – catfish flap at his feet – Rab feels like he is in a tiny snow-globe flat – in a big tall tenement with all its ghosts ready to party for Christmas Eve – in the festive spirit – drinking and arguing – not giving a shit about the living – tiny

318

electric-blue fish swim out the window into snow falling outside – Audrey and Bai pull on expensive leather gloves – a little girl toddles in and picks up his wife's fox mask – giggles – puts it on – the girls are opening the sash window wide now.

– You're leaving me here . . .

– Yes, Mr Ram, we are leaving the bodies with you – the police are going to think that you are insane and that you killed everyone and so they won't ever come looking for us . . . don't worry, you've had so much LSD you won't remember any of this, can you hear that?

Bai looks out the window and down.

– No.

– It's the police.

Audrey pulls up the double-barrel that belonged to his friend – clicks it hard, twice.

She shoots every corpse through the heart again – then the head.

Places the gun next to Rab as if he's just dropped it and he is too doped to move now – he stares into the great kenoma with pupils so wide and black the blue of his eyes is barely visible any more. Bai double-locks the door and puts the bolt on – so it will take the police some time to get in. She climbs up the drainpipe. Audrey climbs out behind her. The two of them are dressed all in black and, unable to be seen from the street, they disappear – just like that – entirely from sight.

Ivor (37)

ain't no sunshine when she's gone

IVOR LIES in the dark with Ray-Ban sunglasses on. He isn't cool enough to be a vampire. But he'll do anything to avoid sunshine. His wife fucked his best friend – in a bed he built for her no less. Ivor doesn't have it in him to care any more. He never thought that at his age he would be homeless – or without his own place, anyway. Esme's room smells of wee and My Little Ponies. It is a plastic, synthetic-haired, ammonia smell.

The city is waking.

Down on the streets cars trail, yellow, blue, green, red.

Street lamps wink out.

Knots in his gut.

It would be better to go blind than to see daylight.

That's a shameful thought.

Why anyone fears darkness, he does not know.

It's a blanket.

It's a solace.

Turn the lights down.

Put a record on.

Walk through a city lit by little moons.

That's what Esme calls the street lights – a whole walkway of little moons. He imagines himself in the Meadows with his niece, her tugging at a kite with the stars behind it, or him taking her out on midnight adventures, or them having a picnic up Arthur's Seat, lit only by candles, or winter when it gets dark early so he can take her out to the ice rink in Princes Street Gardens and run around in the tree maze with her and make her smile. Esme has never asked him why they don't do anything in daylight. She thinks his car has blacked-out windows because he is cool. That's how he drives to the pit. Pulls his cap down. The walk from car to pit entrance has his legs trembling but he does it so he can just get in there, to calm the fuck down and get on with his working day. Without that routine to hide in and with no other way of making money underground . . . he needs to change everything.

In a minute – he'll make breakfast for Esme.

His niece's morning set-up at Blossom's My Little Pony stables is highly elaborate. He knows the score now. First off, Cupcake and Rosedust will bitch about Princess Sparkle. They'll talk about how disappointing she is. That she can't just be cheerful like them. They will cut her pony tail off. Write all over her stable in coloured pencil. They will steal her favourite things. Then they will trot off, very smug and happy with themselves. They'll go look after Baby Half Note and Baby Tic Tac Toe to tell them how awful Princess Sparkle is. Applejack will stay well out of it. She is the plastic-pony version of Switzerland. Very occasionally she will take sides, but only if it furthers her own social status.

There is nothing to admire in that!

A man with shopping bags standing in front of four tanks — that's something to admire. Even more so because he climbed onto one of the tanks when its gun was aimed at him! Stood there so he could talk human to human. Never mind the machine. Or the orders. Sometimes, you have to just look at another person and see they are as human as you are. Unless they are not. Ivor admires the man's dignity and courage and humanity. He has watched the footage four times now. He is trying to learn something. Anyone else would laugh to know that sunlight is a tank to him, but it is no less scary. Ivor admires his workmates for every action they've taken through the strikes. And for the very first time in his entire life — he feels a tiny touch of pride in himself. Not for the thoughts — those, he will never be proud of — but for how he keeps all of it to himself and still tries to do only good.

— Do you sleep with those sunglasses on?

— Fuck off, Jake.

— Uhm just asking!

His pal stretches out beside him, rubs his eyes, reaches for a cigarette.

— I hold ma hand up, you can hate me fir life. I will always be sorry I did it! After I did it . . .

— It?

— Come on, Ivor.

— After you what, Jake?

— Joanne started trying to tell me she only ever got violent in the first place cos ay you. Don't you dare think she's right, Ivor. If it was a man hitting a woman, would it be alright?

— Noh, but everyone would still look the other fucking way.

– I wouldnae.

– Aye, ye fucking would, Jake. And if ye ever saw me, which ye'd try and avoid doing, you'd hope I never brought it up!

Jake kneels over Ivor and takes his head in his hands – one hand on each cheek, gentle as a vet with a newborn lamb.

– It's not your fault, Ivor, not any of it.

– Fuck off!

Ivor hooks him.

It's a solid thud and there's a crack as Jake's jaw slides to the side. He'd like to say it doesn't make him feel really good to see pain on his mate's face but it does.

– I'll take that yin. I deserve it, Jake says.

Snoopy falls over, lit by a toadstool night light. A Girl's World mannequin head looks at them, with her pink hair and blue eyeshadow.

– Mind when I used to go around to Joanne's when she was a wee lassie, Jake. All the council houses were the same but hers had twice as many kids in it. I could see her shadow stand up taller and darker every night when she had to go in. There's just all those scars inside her which nobody else can see. Instead of healing, she just keeps inflicting pain again and again – on herself – on someone, anyone, else – whoever will take it. I feel like the BFG . . . want to get a net and catch her cruel acts and show her them – fizzing with fire! She just dismisses it as soon as she's done something bad.

– It's funny how many total cunts have the ability to do that.

Ivor pulls his cap down over his sunglasses.

– I need tae tell ye something, Jake . . . or maybe I'll just show ye.

His heart races even thinking about it.

Heads over to the window. What if he faints?

Rhona made these curtains.

He has to face this. He has to be able to go to a playground and pick his niece up so she's not the only kid left waiting for a mum who is always late. He needs to be able to earn money. This is ridiculous!

He pulls back the curtains.

The brass hoops sound like knives scraping a blackboard.

Heart pounding fucking hard, skin hot, can't breathe, dizzy, ground feels like it is moving.

Reaches out.

His hand looks like it belongs to someone else.

Watch it like an alien limb just moving toward that shutter clip.

— I am phengophobic, Jake!

Pulls the shutter open. For a minute Ivor feels like he's inside an old Polaroid camera with the flash — bleaching him down through his pores. It feels like the light flows into him — like a burn — rushing through his veins, up into his arteries — scorching his bones.

He is on his knees, crying.

Ivor puts his hand up to try and close the shutter.

He can't reach for it properly because he's beginning to faint — the entire floor is falling away. It feels like he will fall through every floor of this building right down to the basement and only then — in total darkness — will he have a chance for peace. A hand reaches out above him. Closes the shutter firmly. Pulls the curtains shut and tucks them over each other so there is absolutely no light. Very, very gently, she lays her thin wee duvet over his head. Pats him through the soft material.

– There, there, Uncle Ivor, you don't need to do that.

– Did you just wake up, Esme?

– Aye, what are you doing here, Jake?

Esme stands with her hands on her hips, looking angry at him.

– I am here to see Ivor, is that okay with you?

– Noh, it isnae, and it isnae okay with Princess Sparkle – it isnae even okay with Applejack. Uncle Ivor's heart is broken. You know what I think about you, Jake? Yer lips move but you never really say anything so I don't even need to know what you did to him – I can feel it.

Esme pats her chest bone.

– So get out!

– Okay!

Jake scrambles upright.

– Ivor, can ye take that duvet off for just a minute, mate?

– Get out!

Esme screams it.

He can hear her throwing things at Jake, then the front door slams shut and there is a blissful silence.

Ivor's heartbeat slows.

Hot shame.

It is the single emotion he remembers feeling the longest.

His most base and true emotion.

Shame that others would find out, would see him like this – helpless, terrified, childlike, made solely of terror. That shame is toxic. He has seen it in Esme, too. When her mum is always late to come pick her up. Her pals all know. Little

Stardusts and Blossoms with their scathing wee looks and their perfect wee lives – taking all their fucking hidden nastiness out on her. Some of those days before Ivor realised that Rhona had had her benefits stopped – his niece dealt with all of it while hungry. The kid is a fucking angel, as smart and beautiful a soul as anyone could ever possibly know. All of this has to stop. It's never too late. Ever! He reaches one hand out of the duvet, theatrically, as if he were the undead waking – his niece's tiny hand reaches out and squeezes it.

– You can come out now, Uncle Ivor.

– Thanks, Esme. You – are the best protector I've ever had.

– I know.

– Do you know what, Esme?

– What?

– I am going to become that, instead – fir you.

Ivor pulls the duvet off his head and nods at her to open the curtains again, then the shutters a crack. The panic is there – it is there like high-quality hospital speed. He looks at the light and it feels like a giant crocodile is smiling at him through the window – just waiting for him to make one wrong move.

– Do you want breakfast, Esme?

– Aye. Can I have cornflakes, please?

She sings it and he smiles and they walk through to the living room.

– Do you want sugar on them?

– Aye.

He makes a cup of tea for Rhona, leaves it at the side of the sofa and taps her on the shoulder.

— Uncle Ivor — if I got my clothes from Tammy Girl, instead of from What Everyone Wants — d'ye think the lassies at school might stop calling me a scaff and let me play with them?

He gives Esme the biggest hug and tries again not to cry.

It's not good to want to poke the eyes out of eight-year-old girls.

He does though.

Ivor watches Esme sit at the tiny breakfast bar eating her cereal. Big smile at him. Here's a goal he can set for himself: take the tablets his doctor prescribed. Beta whatever-the-fuck-they-are. If it means he is able to do the school run out there in full sunlight then it will be worth it. He will start with that. Make sure his niece never has to wait in that playground on her own with her teacher again.

— What's that, Uncle Ivor?

— Tablets.

— From the doctor?

— Aye.

He takes out the first one. Reads the label: beta blockers first and then an antidepressant. That's what the man says he needs. Maybe he'll make this part of the day: a ritual. Shower — dress — cup of tea — tablets. He swipes tears off his face roughly. He wants to go and stand with his mates on the picket line. So what if he can't tell them about Joanne? Nobody wants to hear that kind ay shite fae a guy. It'll only make it awkward. He'll carry it for all ay them. Keep it to himself. He will not carry her shame any more, though — not even for one more day.

Esme pads back through to her room.

The doctor is a guid cunt, Ivor will give him that.

He'll try it this way, see if it works.

— You are undoubtedly phengophobic, Ivor. I can give you a sick note?

— Thanks, anyway.

Undoubtedly phengophobic!

What if he was — doubtedly phengophobic?

Phengophobic but with a lot of doubt about it?

What if he was timidly phengophobic?

Extravagantly phengophobic?

What if he was just a phengo? No phobic about it.

It does not seem like an adequate word to describe this level of terror. As a boy, he used to beg the moon not to go. Daylight is garish. It has gangrenous tendrils. The sunrays are tentacular. Too loud, cranked up like that. Orbish. Pustulating. Esme goes to her wee plastic table. Holds her hands above her head like a ballerina.

— Time fir the performance, Uncle Ivor.

— Who else is coming?

— They're all here already, silly head . . .

She gestures around the room.

— Okay then.

— They've been stuck in the dark for nearly a hundred years, Uncle Ivor. They can't get out but you can.

— You think so?

— Don't be silly, Uncle Ivor. We know you can. It's why you are here.

— Why have your friends been in the dark so long?

— A bad man put them there.

Esme puts out the teacups and the plastic plates. He'd like to think it's just the tablets . . . he watches as one cup is raised by an invisible hand – then another – and they cheers each other. Esme pushes a tiny cup over to a wee girl he can't see and Ivor gets the most undeniable feeling – that each of these women and girls – would fight the sunlight for him if they had to. He must learn how to do the same now – for them.

1999

Flat 9F9

Dot (27)

i'm going to leave this city one last time

THERE IS a huge roar and clank and groan behind her. Dust billows up the High Street. Dot runs out of the close with the last bits of skeleton in her arms. She has taken some of the temporary railings from Hogmanay and placed them in a square in the middle of the street. Dot has been gathering the bones. Laying them out section by section – on the cobbled High Street for hours.

– The upper floors are falling!

A firewoman runs by and Dot crouches and hides her face a second.

Sirens lilt in from all directions.

A crane comes gliding up from Cockburn Street like some yellow metallic dinosaur.

– It's too late!

Some fire chief shouts it to someone else.

Nobody is paying attention to Dot.

There is a huge crash. The air in the close is thick and black. Firefighters run out. The ground is rumbling. The yellow crane stops. It hangs over a statue next to St Giles'. Dot can see the sea – away down there at the bottom of the High Street where the view lifts out towards Fife. The

Firth of Forth isn't grey today. On this brand-new morning – it is sparkling. Four police cars pull up and park opposite the cathedral. The entire street is being cordoned off. Police are holding their hands out at the crossroads down at the Tron. Nobody can get into this area now. They still don't see Dot working quickly, methodically, with precision behind her square barricade. It's a useful skill. To be unseen. When needs be. To pass without question. All goddesses need it. All girls, all boys, all the devil's children and all of heaven's angels and all the ones who never got in – all of the fallen – in whatever guise they appear on this mortal coil.

The right to pass unseen.

She lays out the bones.

Careful!

Dot is finally glad of her anatomy class at art school. Grateful for her time doing drawings every day for a year.

She takes the first skull and places it above the torso. Whoever treated them did it so well – they are preserved as perfectly as if it were only yesterday. Dot places her hand on the skull cheekbone as she meshes it onto its neck bone. She almost drops the next one – her fingers are blue-cold. Slide it carefully into place. Dot lays the arms out. Places them so the lower arms hold hands with each other. She can tell from the hip bones they were both women. She lays outside arm bones – protectively around their child. She lays their legs out below their torso – placed facing forward so they can walk together – into the future.

Spirits have a future too, if we find it in ourselves to honour them.

The feet are fragile.

331

It takes a held breath and a very steady hand – to place each bone the right way. Carefully, she places the child's arms so they are folded at the hands and she touches lightly where the child's heart used to beat and says a prayer to the primordial matriarch, the first mother, the cosmic light source where all things come from – to guide them home.

Her face is wet with tears.

– The last floors are falling!

No. 10 Luckenbooth Close buries its bricks into the ground, piles and piles of them.

Dot turns both of the women's skull heads.

They look at each other – just like they must have done all those years ago.

– For those who came before us and all who will come after!

Police are busy trying to secure the High Street, to deal with the thick filthy air and the debris. She can barely see the entrance to any of the closes now it is so bad. Dot thinks of the long line of women behind her – all the way back to Lilith – all of them linked in some way – every last one – they have all endured, one way or another. She sobs openly now, her shoulders shake and her eyes blur as her entire being keens toward a pain she was born feeling and has never been able to let go. Dot can picture these skeletons – all three of them – walking right along this street together – laughing – holding hands or going to buy food or first thing in the morning taking in a new day or hurrying back to each other through the rain – how many years ago?

Dot stands.

They emerge from the dust.

First – a woman with long red hair, clear skin, black boots, a hat. She turns – holds her hand out for the woman behind her. She is dark-haired, wearing a fine dress; her horns are as spectacular in life as they are on her skeleton. The child emerges from the smoke and takes her mothers' hands. The two women reach out to place their arms easily around each other. They walk down the High Street toward the cobbled square at the Tron – toward the sea.

The bells of St Giles' call out – a long loud clang and dong echoes across the city.

Edinburgh's daughters – will not stay walled in.

There are blue skies this morning.

Dot gives thanks in silence.

The building is down but she did not fall with it.

Unless – she did?

The afterlife could not be as clear as this.

The crane has been hoisted up. It was meant to pull No. 10 Luckenbooth Close up by the scruff of its neck – what a silly thing to try and do. It was never going to work. She hopes with every one of her own broken bones that every last stone in that building is used for better things. She hopes that every man who profits from a structure built on the murder or poverty of others is held to account or may all his buildings come down. Dot can feel the very devil himself running – through catacombs underneath the city – away from No. 10 Luckenbooth Close.

An officer points to where she is standing over the bones.

She will make sure they are safe until someone else takes responsibility for them.

Dot writes it out as neatly as she can.

Places it below them.

She does it quickly as the police are coming back over.

They still don't see her!

The SKELETONS of LUCKENBOOTH CLOSE – buried in the walls for CENTURIES!

There is a thick layer of stoor over everything: cars, cobbles, lamp posts, street signs. Dot stands right in the middle of the street as two police officers take down the barricade she placed around the skeletons. One raises her hand and calls out. Dot turns as a splitting sound ricochets over the sky – the skeletal wooden beams of Luckenbooth are fractured. She breathes in dusty morning air. Looks up at the David Hume statue with his eternal bloody robes. Statues of men! Like they're the only ones who ever thought about anything. Where are the women? Buried into the bones of the building – that's where the fucking women are! Buried into the building by men who couldn't tame them. The cobbled road of the High Street runs away from her – down the hill – she wants to follow it – walk by all the shops and restaurants and bars, by the church at the crossroads, the Christmas shop with all its different baubles and wee wooden toys and Santas and the smell of cinnamon, the big hotel, her witches shop that she likes for pads and supplies, the Museum of Childhood, the World's End pub, or the one she likes better around the corner from that – the Waverley Bar – where the old owner used to work with a crocodile pinned onto the wall. He was a tough man that landlord, ancient as time and tiny but nobody ever dared fuck with him – you could just imagine the man hunted down that crocodile himself and there was a room full of poets upstairs often reading or drinking. Past the fudge shop, that cafe that does cream teas, Mexican food in the restaurant where she had her first date, coffee outlets, knit-wear, silver and trilobites, the old-fashioned sweetie shop (now gone), the poetry library and graveyards and old clubs sold off for student housing and all the way down to the palace and Scottish Parliament and from up here – a flash of blue – where the Firth of Forth greets the first day of the New Year – past the tat shop with its bagpipes and clay-borns and all the way to the bottom of the Royal Mile, past Holyrood Palace toward Arthur's Seat (perhaps she will go back to look at Mary Queen of Scots' bathhouse – best building in this city) then up the crags to wash her face in the morning dew – cleanse the dirt from her pores and then on up to the raggedy road, or maybe she will turn left at the very top of the cliffs, walk through wet grass until her throat burns and the skies – they are so vast up there! So clear! Step by step, the city entire appears from the slopes of Arthur's Seat. Calton Hill and the top of the pal-ace and the high-rises at Dumbiedykes, all the church spires, the big hunk of rock that makes up Edinburgh Castle – she will go right up to the top and turn around to see the Firth of Forth encircle the city and she will look for the spot back up in town where Luckenbooth Close used to be – know that she is just like all the other residents in this city – or any other – passing through – temporarily – that she is just a Dot who took one building down.

But she is curiously stuck on the cobbles of the High Street right now.

It feels like everyone is walking right through her as a stretcher comes out the close.

– One body found in No. 10, just at the entrance way . . .

The policeman calls it into his boss.

All of the structures are guilty and built on beds of bones. It's time to knock down all the walls. Dot feels wind go right through her – she hears light cloven footsteps, they have come back for her – a hand reaches out to take hers, on the long walk home.

Epilogue

AFTER WE had hosted the waken, after the first lift was carried out, and his body put in the casket and the table cleared and the men had left with his corpse. After I had put the rest of his tobacco in a pouch and got a raw fish from the store. After all of that – I walked down toward the clifftops. I had two small horns growing on my head. The nubs grew longer the minute he died. I poisoned him. It was the least he deserved. I had to take the coffin he built for me down to the shore. No boats would have taken me. On account of my father we were considered an unlucky family and I was the only one left. I found his body rammed into a crevice. The men had dropped him down there the night before. My father was an evil man. He was no fallen angel and even if he was – his acts in this life meant that fact would have made little difference to me anyway. He was the devil himself and he had come back to this earth every other time he'd died before. He put the people around him through hell time and time again. I had to take my part in his history – his sins were not my own but it does not mean I was without obligation. I knew that. My teeth were sharp. His skin no tougher than a goat's.

There was only one way to stop him coming back to these shores.

My name is Jessie MacRae.

I am the devil's daughter.

I committed an act to stop my father from rising back up from his grave.

I ate my father's heart.

Please believe me – it was the least of my duty – it had to happen and it had to be me who did it and no matter what becomes of me after this day – I have no – regrets.